# Old New Land / Altneuland

## Theodor Herzl

Filiquarian Publishing, LLC is publishing this edition of Old New Land / Altneuland, due to its public domain status.

Filiquarian Publishing, LLC

# Contents

## Book One / An Educated Desperate Young Man

## Book Two / Haifa 1923

# Book Three / The Prosperous Land

# Book Four / Passover

# Book Five / Jerusalem

**Theodor Herzl**

# Book One

# An Educated Desperate Young Man

## Chapter I

Sunk in deep melancholy, Dr. Friedrich Loewenberg sat at a round marble table in his cafe on the Alsergrund. It was one of the most charming of Viennese cafes. Ever since his student days he had been coming there, appearing every afternoon at five o'clock with bureaucratic punctuality. The sickly, pale waiter greeted him submissively, and he would bow with formality to the equally pale girl cashier to whom he never spoke.

After that, he would seat himself at the round reading table, drink his coffee, and read the papers with which the waiter plied him. And when he had finished with the dailies and the weeklies, the comic sheets and the professional magazines-this never consumed less than an hour and a half-there were chats with friends or solitary musings.

That is to say, once upon a time, there had been lighthearted talk. Now only dreams were left, for the two good comrades with whom he had been wont to while away the idle, pleasant evening hours at this cafe had died several months previously. Both had been older than he; and it was, as Heinrich had written him just before sending a bullet into his temple,

7

"chronologically reasonable" that they should yield to despair sooner than he. Oswald went to Brazil to help in founding a Jewish labor settlement, and there succumbed to the yellow fever.

So it happened that for several months past Friedrich had been sitting alone at their old table. Now, having worked through to the bottom of the pile of newspapers, he sat staring straight ahead without seeking out someone to talk to. He felt too tired to make new acquaintances, as if he were not a young man of twenty-three, but a graybeard who had all too often parted with cherished friends. His gaze was fixed upon the light cloud of smoke that veiled the comers of the room.

Several young men stood about the billiard table, making bold strokes with their long poles. They were in the same boat as himself, but for all that not too unhappy these budding physicians, newly baked jurists, freshly graduated engineers. They had completed their professional studies, and now they had nothing to do. Most of them were Jews. When they were not too engrossed in cards or billiards, they complained how very hard it was to make one's way "these days." Meanwhile they passed "these days" in endless rounds of cards. Friedrich felt sorry for the thoughtless young fellows, though at the same time he rather envied them.

They were really only a kind of superior proletariat, victims of a viewpoint that had dominated middle-class Jewry twenty or thirty years before: the sons must not be what the fathers had been. They were to be freed from the hardships of trade and commerce. And so the younger generation entered the "liberal" professions en masse. The result was an unfortunate surplus of trained men who could find no work, but were at the same time

spoiled for a modest way of life. They could not, like their
Christian colleagues, slip into pubic posts; and became, so to
say a drug on the market. Nevertheless, they had the
obligations of their "station in life," an arrogant sense of class
distinction, and degrees that they could not back up with a
shilling. Those who had some means gradually used them up,
or else continued to live on the paternal purse. Others were on
the lookout for eligible part is, facing the delicious prospect of
servitude to wealthy fathers-in-law. Still others engaged in
ruthless and not always honorable competition in pursuits
where genteel manners were requisite. They furnished the
curious and lamentable spectacle of men who, because they did
not want to become merchants, dealt at "professionals" in
secret diseases and unlawful legal affairs. Some who in their
need became journalists trafficked in public opinion. Others
ran about to public assemblies and hawked worthless slogans
in order to make themselves known in quarters where they
could make useful party connections.

Friedrich would not resort to any of these shifts. "You are not
fit for life," poor Oswald had said grimly just before going off
to Brazil. "You let too many things disgust you. One must be
able to swallow things. Vermin, for example, or offal. So a
man becomes strong and well-fleshed, and winds up in a good
berth. But you-you are nothing but a noble ass. 'Get thee to a
nunnery, Ophelia!' No one will believe that you are an honest
man, because you are a Jew....What will happen to you? Your
few inherited shillings will melt away long before you can get
a foothold in the law. Then you will be compelled either to do
something disgusting-or to hang yourself. Buy yourself a rope,
I beg you, while you still have a gulden. Don't count on me!
For one thing, I shall not be here. For another, I am your
friend!"

9

Oswald had coaxed him to come along to Brazil, but he had not been able to decide to do so. He did not confide his secret reason to the friend who was going to an early death in a strange land. The "reason" was blond and dreamy, a marvelously sweet creature. Not even to these trusted comrades had he ventured to speak of Ernestine, fearing their jests. And now the two dear fellows were gone. He could not turn to them for sympathy or advice even if he wished. His situation was very difficult. What would they have said if he had told them? Suppose they had never gone away, and all three were now sitting together at the old reading table? Closing his eyes, Friedrich held an imaginary conversation.

"My friends, I am in love. No, I love...."

"Poor fellow!" Heinrich would have said.

Oswald, however: "Such stupidity is quite like you, dear Friedrich!"

"Oh, it's more than stupidity, my friends. It's full-fledged madness. If I were to ask Ernestine Loeffler's father for her hand, he would probably laugh at me. I am a mere lawyer's assistant, with a salary of forty gulden a month. I have nothing left nothing at all. These last few months have been my ruin. I have spent the last few hundred gulden of my inheritance. I know it was madness to strip myself of everything. But I wanted to be near her ...to watch her graceful gestures, to listen to her sweet voice. I had to go to the spa where she was staying for the summer. There were plays, concerts, and all the rest of it. And a man has to dress well in that set. Now I have nothing left, but I love her as much as ever. No, more than ever!"

"And what do you want to do?" Heinrich was asking. "I want to tell her of my love for her, and ask her to wait for me for a few years until I can establish myself."

Oswald's cynical laughter echoed through the reverie. "Yes, yes! To wait! Ernestine Loeffler wait for a starveling until she is passe. Ha! ha! ha!"

Someone actually was laughing close to Friedrich's ear. He opened his eyes with a start. Schiffmann, a young bank clerk whom he had met at the Loefhers, stood before him laughing heartily. "You must have gone to bed very late last night, Dr. Loewenberg, to be sleepy at this hour!"

Friedrich was embarrassed. "I was not asleep," he replied.

"Well, this will be another late night. Of course you're going to the Loeffers'." Schiffmann lounged into a seat beside the reading table.

Friedrich cared little for the young fellow, but tolerated his company because he could speak to him of Ernestine, and often learned from him what plays she was to attend. (Schiffmann had his connections with theatrical box offices, and could secure tickets for the most crowded performances.) "Yes," he replied, "I also am invited there tonight."

Shiffmann, who had picked up a newspaper, exclaimed suddenly, "I say, this is curious!"

"What is it?"

"This advertisement."

"Ah, you read the advertisements, too!" commented Friedrich, with an ironic smile.

"Do I read the advertisements too?" retorted Schiffmann. "I read the advertisements in particular. There's nothing more interesting in the paper except the stock exchange reports."

"Indeed! I never read the stock exchange reports."

"Ah, yes, you... But I! After one glance at the exchange rates, I can sum up the whole European situation...But after that I turn at once to the advertisements. You've no idea of the things one finds there. Heaps of things and people are for sale. That is to say, everything in the world can be bought for a price, but one cannot always pay the price. From the advertising columns I if always find out what opportunities there are. I say: Know everything, need nothing! ...I have noticed a remarkable advertisement for the last few days, but I do not understand it."

"Is it in a foreign language?"

"Well, just look at this." Schiffmann handed the paper to Friedrich, and pointed to a small notice. It read: "Wanted, an educated, desperate young man willing to make a last experiment with his life. Apply N. O. Body, this office."

"You are right," said Friedrich. "That is a remarkable advertisement. 'An educated, desperate young man.' Such a man might be found, of course, but the condition imposed is a very difficult one. A man must be desperate indeed to throwaway his life on a last experiment."

"Well, Mr. Body seems not to have found him. He has been advertising for some time. But I should like to know who this Mr. Body is with his queer tastes."

"It is no one."

"No one?"

"N. O. Body-Nobody. Means no one in English." "Ah, yes. I had not thought of English. Know everything, need nothing. ...But it's time to go if we're not to be late at the Loefflers'. We must be punctual this evening."

"Why this evening particularly?"

"Sorry, but I can't tell! Discretion is a point of honor with me.. ..But be prepared for a surprise...Waiter! Check!"

A surprise? Of a sudden Friedrich felt a vague anxiety.

As he left the cafe with Schiffmann, he noticed a ten year-old boy standing in the outer doorway. The child's shoulders were hunched up in a thin little coat. He held his arms tightly across his body, and stamped on the drifted snow in a sheltered nook. The hopping seemed almost like a pose, but Friedrich realized that with those tom shoes the child must be freezing bitterly. He picked three copper coins out of his pocket by the light of the street lamp. The boy thanked him shiveringly, and ran off.

"What! You encourage street begging!" cried Schiffmann indignantly.

**13**

"I don't imagine the little fellow is running around in this December weather to amuse himself. ...Seemed like a Jewish child too."

"Then let him go to the Jewish Community or to the Israelitsche Allianz, and not loiter about cafes in the evening!"

"Don't get excited, Mr. Schiffmann. You gave him nothing."

"My dear sir," said Schiffmann firmly, "I am a member of the Society against Pauperization and Beggary. Annual dues, one gulden."

# Chapter II

The Loeffler family lived on the second floor of a large house on Gonzaga Street, the ground floor being occupied by the cloth firm of Moritz Loeffier & Co.

When Friedrich and Schiffmann entered the foyer they realized from the number of coats and wraps already hanging there that the evening's gathering was larger than usual.

"Quite a clothing shop," remarked Schiffmann.

Friedrich knew most of the people already assembled in the drawing room. The only stranger was the bald-headed man who stood next to Emestine by the piano smiling at her confidentially.

The girl extended her hand cordially to the newcomer.

"Doctor Loewenberg, come and be introduced to Mr. Leopold Weinberger."

"Member of the firm of Samuel Weinberger and Sons of Bruenn," supplemented Papa Loeffler, not without a touch of solemnity and benevolence.

The gentlemen shook hands politely. Friedrich noted that Mr. Weinberger of Bruenn had a decided squint and very damp palms. He was not sorry, because these characteristics banished the thought that had flashed into his mind as he entered the room. Ernestine and a man like that-simply impossible! She was enchanting as she stood there-slender, graceful, her lovely head a little bent. Friedrich feasted his eyes on her, but had to make room for other guests. Mr. Weinberger of Bruenn, however, kept somewhat obtrusively and persistently by her side.

Friedrich turned inquiringly to Schiffmann. "This Mr. Weinberger is probably an old family friend?"

"Oh, no. They know him only a fortnight, but he is a fine cloth firm."

"What is fine, Mr. Schiffmann-the cloth or the firm?" asked Friedrich, now elated and reassured. Certainly an acquaintance of a fortnight could not be a fiance.

"Both," replied Schiffmann. "Samuel Weinberger and Sons can borrow all the money they want at four per cent. First rate....Things are very elegant here tonight. Look over there. That lean man with the staring eyes is Schlesinger, the confidential representative of Baron Goldstein. He is obnoxious, but very popular."

"Why?"

"Why ask, 'why'? Because he is the agent of Baron Goldstein....Do you know that gray mutton-chop whisker? Not him, either? Where do you come from? That's Laschner, one of the most important men on the stock exchange-a large speculator. He'll stake you a couple of thousand shares as if they were nothing at all. Just now he is very rich. Wish I had his money! Whether he'll have a penny this time next year, I don't know. Just now his wife has larger diamonds than any other woman. ... They all envy her. ..."

Mrs. Laschner sat in a corner with some equally overdressed women passionately discussing millinery. The other groups were still in the reserved ante-prandial mood. Some of the guests, who seemed to be informed as to the nature of the impending surprise, whispered discreetly to one another. Friedrich felt uneasy, without exactly knowing why. Next to Schiffmann, he was the most insignificant guest of the evening. He had never before felt ill at ease in this circle because Ernestine had always kept him by her. But tonight she gave him not a word or glance. This Mr. Weinberger of Bruenn must be a very entertaining companion. Friedrich was suffering from an additional humiliation imposed on him by an unkind Fate. He and Schiffmann were conspicuous by their lack of formal evening costume-a circumstance that marked them as the social pariahs of the gathering. He would have preferred to run away, but lacked courage.

The large drawing room was crowded, but the hosts seemed still to be waiting for someone. Friedrich turned questioningly to his companion in misery. Schiffmann knew the answer, having just overheard a remark by the hostess. "They are waiting for Gruen and Blau."

"Who are they?"

"What! Don't you know Gruen and Blau? The two wittiest men in Vienna. No reception, no wedding, no betrothal party or anything else comes off without them. Some think Gruen the wittier; others prefer Blau. Gruen has more of a tendency toward puns, and Blau pokes fun at people. Blau's had his face

**17**

slapped more than once, but that never upsets him. He has the kind of face that never reddens when it's slapped. Both these men are very popular in the higher circles of Jewish society. Of course, being rivals, they hate each other."

There was a slight rustle in the salon. Mr. Gruen had entered. He was a long, lanky man with a reddish beard and ears that stood off from his head. Blau called his rival's ears "unseamed," because they did not fold inward over the muscle at the upper edge, but lay flat.

Ernestine's mother amiably reproached the famous jester. "Why so late, Mr. Gruen?"

"Because I could come no later," replied he smartly. His hearers smiled in approval. A shadow flitted over Gruen's face. Blau had entered.

Blau was about thirty years old and of medium height. His face was clean shaven, and a pince-nez was set on his sharply curved nose. "I have been at the Wiedener Theater," he reported, "attending a first night performance. I left after the first act."

His announcement aroused interest. Ladies and gentlemen gathered around him, and he proceeded. "The first act, to everyone's surprise, did not fall flat."

"Moriz," called Mrs. Laschner imperiously to her husband, "I want to see that play tomorrow night."

"The librettist's friends also enjoyed themselves immensely," continued Blau.

"Is the operetta so good?" inquired Schlesinger, representative of Baron Goldstein. "No, so bad!" explained Blau. "The playwright's friends enjoy a production only when it is bad."

Dinner was announced. The spacious dining room was overcrowded. There was barely elbow room at the table. Ernestine sat beside Mr. Weinberger. Friedrich and Schiffmann had to take seats at the very foot of the table.

At first there was more clatter of dishes and silver than conversation. Blau called across the table to his competitor, "Don't eat so loudly, Gruen. I can't hear my own fish."

"Fish is no food for you. You ought to eat cutlets made of jealousy." Gruen's adherents laughed; Blau's thought the joke dull.

Attention was diverted from the humorists when an elderly gentleman sitting next to ,Mrs. Loeffler remarked in a slightly raised voice that things were becoming worse in Moravia. "In the provincial towns," he said, "our people are in actual peril. When the Germans are in a bad mood, they break Jewish windows. When the Czechs are out of sorts, they break into Jewish homes. The poor are beginning to emigrate. But they don't know where to go."

Mrs. Laschner chose this moment to scream to her husband, "Moriz! You must take me to the Burg Theatre the day after tomorrow!"

"Don't interrupt!" replied the broker. "Dr. Weiss is telling us about the situation in Moravia. Not pleasant, 'pon my honor."

Samuel Weinberger, father of the bridegroom, broke into the conversation. "Being a rabbi, Doctor, you see things rather black."

"White (Weiss) always sees black," interjected one of the wits, but the pun went unnoticed.

"I feel quite safe in my factory," continued the elder Weinberger. "When they make any trouble for me, I send for the police, or call on the commandant. Just show bayonets to the mob, and it mends its manners."

"But that in itself is a grave situation," countered Dr. Weiss gently.

Dr. Walter, a lawyer whose name had originally been Veiglstock, remarked, "I don't know who it was that said you could do anything with bayonets except sit on them." "I feel it coming," cried Laschner, "We'll all have to wear the yellow badge."

"Or emigrate," said the rabbi.

"I ask you, where to?" asked Walter. "Are things better anywhere else? Even in free France the anti-Semites have the upper hand,"

Dr. Weiss, a simple rabbi from a provincial town in Moravia, did not know exactly in what company he found himself, and ventured a few shy remarks. "A new movement has arisen within the last few years, which is called Zionism. Its aim is to solve the Jewish problem through colonization on a large scale.

All who can no longer bear their present lot will return to our old home, to Palestine."

He spoke very quietly, unaware that the people about him were getting ready for an outburst of laughter. He was therefore dumbfounded at the effect of the word "Palestine." The laughter ran every gamut. The ladies giggled, the gentlemen roared and neighed. Friedrich alone was indignant at the brutal and unseemly merriment at the old man's expense.

Blau took advantage of the first breathing spell to declare that had the new operetta boasted one jest like this, all would have been well with it.

"And I'll be ambassador at Vienna!" shouted Gruen.

The laughter broke out once more. "I too!" "I too!"

Blau assumed a serious tone. "Gentlemen, everyone cannot have that post. I am certain the Austrian Government would not accept so many Jewish ambassadors. You must seek other appointments."

The old rabbi, deeply embarrassed, did not again raise his eyes from his plate while the humorists zealously dissected the new idea. They divided the new empire, they described its customs. The stock exchange would be closed on the Sabbath. Those who served their country or enriched themselves on the stock exchange would receive the "Order of David" or the "meat" sword from the king. But who would be king?

"Baron Goldstein by all means," suggested Blau.

Schlesinger, representative of that renowned banker, was annoyed. "I beg that the person of Baron von Goldstein be left out of this conversation," he said, "at least while I am present."

Almost the whole company nodded approval. The witty Blau did sometimes say very tactless things. Bringing Baron Goldstein into this kind of talk was really going a bit far. But Blau went on. "Dr. Walter will be appointed minister of justice, and will be ennobled under the title of 'von Veiglstock.' 'Walter, count of Veiglstock.' "

Laughter. The lawyer blushed at the sound of his paternal cognomen. "It's a long time since you've had your face slapped!" he cried.

The punster Gruen, more cautious, whispered some word-play on the lawyer's name to the lady next to him. "Will there be theaters in Palestine?" queried Mrs. Laschner. "If not, I shall not go there."

"Certainly, madam," replied Gruen. "All Israel will assemble for the festival performances at the royal theater in Jerusalem."

Rabbi Weiss finally ventured a word. "Whom are you mocking, gentlemen? Yourselves?"

"Oh, no," replied Blau. "We take ourselves seriously."

"I am proud to be a Jew," asserted Laschner. "Because, if I were not proud, I should still be a Jew. I therefore prefer to be proud."

The two serving maids left the room to bring in the next course. "It is better not to discuss Jewish matters in the presence of the servants," remarked the hostess.

"Pardon me, madam,'" retorted Blau quickly. "I thought your servants knew you were Jews." Some of the guests laughed. "Still," declared Schlesinger authoritatively, "there's no need to shout it from the housetops."

Champagne was brought in. Schiffulann nudged Friedrich. "Now it will come out"

"What will come out?"

"You still haven't guessed?'

No, Friedrich still hadn't guessed. But the next moment he knew.

Mr. Loeffler tapped his glass with the point of his knife and rose to his feet. Silence ensued. The ladies leaned back in their chairs. Blau hastily shoved another bit of food into his mouth, and chewed while Papa Loeffler spoke.

"Esteemed friends! I am happy to announce to you that my daughter Ernestine has been betrothed to Mr. Leopold Weinberger of Bruenn, member of the firm of Samuel Weinberger and Sons. Here's to the bridal pair! Hoch!"

"Hochl" "Hoch!" "Hoch!" All were on their feet. Glasses clinked. The guests moved in a procession to the head of the table to congratulate the parents and the new couple. Friedrich walked in the line with a cloud before his eyes. For a second he

**23**

stood before Ernestine, touching his glass to hers with a trembling hand. She looked quickly past him.

Good cheer prevailed. One toast followed another. Schlesinger delivered a dignified address. Gruen and Blau surpassed themselves. Gruen strained more syllables than ever; Blau made all sorts of tactless allusions. The company was in the best of humor.

It all reached Friedrich vaguely, as from a distance. He felt as if he were in a heavy fog, where nothing could be seen and breathing was difficult.

The dinner came to an end. Friedrich's one thought was to get away, far away, from all these people. He thought himself superfluous in the room-in the city, in the whole world. Trying to slip away as the guests thronged out of the dining room, he was intercepted by Ernestine.

"Doctor Loewenberg," she said to him, "you have said nothing to me yet."

"What shall I say to you, Miss Ernestine? ...I wish you happiness. Yes, yes. I wish you much happiness in this betrothal."

But the bridegroom was again at her side. He put his arm around her waist, and drew her away possessively. She smiled.

# Chapter III

As he stepped out into the winter night, Friedrich asked himself
which had been the more disgusting: the possessive gesture of
Mr. Weinberger of Bruenn, or the smile of the young girl
which he had hitherto thought so enchanting. What? The
"partner of the firm" had knows the lovely one only fourteen
days, and yet he was allowed to put his sweaty hand upon her
body. Bile barter! Here went one of his illusions! The
Weinberger firm evidently had much money. He, Friedrich,
had none. In the Loeffler set, where nothing counted except
pleasure and the good things in life, money was all. And yet, he
himself was dependent upon this circle of the Jewish
bourgeoisie. With these people, yet, and upon these people, he
had to live: they were his future clientele. With luck he might
become the legal adviser of a man like Laschner. It would be
altogether too fantastic to dream of a client like Baron
Goldstein. Christian society and a Christian clientele were the
most unattainable things in the world. What was a man to do?
Was he to adapt himself to this Loeffler circle, share their low
ideals, represent the interest of dubious money bags? Such
noble conduct would bring an office of one's own after thus
and so many years, and then he might claim the hand and the
dowry of a maiden ready on a fortnight's acquaintance to marry
the first man who came along. Or, if all this was too revolting,
loneliness and poverty were the alternative.

Lost in these thoughts, he found himself again in front of the
Cafe Birkenreis. Why go home so early to his tiny room? It

was only ten o'clock. To sleep? Yes, if there were so be no awakening...

At the entrance he almost stumbled over a little body. A child was squatting on the steps. Friedrich recognized him as the same boy to whom he had given those coins a few hours earlier. He spoke to him roughly. "What's this? Begging again?"

The child replied shiveringly, in Yiddish, "I'm waiting for my father."

He stood up and began to hop, slapping one arm over the other to warm himself. But Friedrich was so steeped in his own misery that he had no sympathy to spare for the freezing child. He entered the smoke-filled room, and took his usual seat at the reading table. There were few guests in the cafe at that hour, except here and there, in the corners, a few belated card-players who could not bear to part. Over and over again they announced the last, the final, the unalterably final round, "Or my name's mud!" Friedrich sat staring into space until a gossipy acquaintance approached the table. He quickly withdrew behind a paper and pretended to read. His eye was caught by the advertisement that Schiffmann had found so fascinating, Here it was:

"Wanted, An educated, desperate young man willing to make a last experiment with his life. Apply N. O. Body, this office."

How strange! Now the description fitted himself. A last experiment! He was sick of. life. Before flinging it away like his poor friend Heinrich, he might as well try to make somthing of it. He asked the waiter for notepaper, and wrote briefly to N.

26

O. Body. "I am your man. Dr. Friedrich Loewenberg, IX Hahngasse 67."

As he was sealing the letter, someone approached him from behind. "Tooth brushes, suspenders, shirt buttons please!" Gruffy he repulsed the importunate peddler. The man moved off with a tearful glance at the waiter, who might put him out for annoying the guests. Friedrich, conscience-stricken at having frightened the man, called him back and threw a small coin into the basket. The peddler held out his trash.

"I am no beggar. You must buy something. Otherwise, I cannot keep your money."

To get rid of him, Friedrich took a shin button from the basket. The peddler thanked him and went away. Indifferently Friedrich watched as he walked over to the waiter and handed him the recently acquired coin. The waiter pulled out a basket of stale rolls, and gave some to the peddler, who stuffed them hastily into his coat pocket.

Friedrich rose to go. As he passed through the doorway he noticed the freezing boy, who had now joined the peddler. The man gave him the hard rolls. Father and son evidently.

"What are you doing?" asked Friedrich.

"I am giving the boy bread to take home to my wife. This is the first sale I have made today."

"Are you telling the truth?" probed Friedrich.

"I wish it were not the truth," groaned the man. "Wherever I go, they put me out when I try to sell something. If you are a Jew, you might as well throw yourself into the Danube at once."

Though he had so recently resolved to have done with life, Friedrich was interested in this opportunity to be of some service. The affair would divert his thoughts. He posted his letter, and then walked along with the two. He asked the peddler to tell his story.

"We came here from Galicia," said the man. "In Cracow we lived in one room with three other families. We had no source of livelihood. Things can become no worse, I thought, and came here with my wife and children. Here it is no worse; neither is it better:'

"How many children have you?"

The man began to sob. "I had five, but three have died since we came here. Now I have only this boy here and a little girl still at the breast. ..David, don't run so fast!"

The boy turned his head. "Mother was so hungry when I brought her the three heller from this gentleman." "Oh, sir, you were the kind gentleman!"

The peddler tried to kiss Friedrich's hand.

The latter drew back quickly. "What are you thinking of? ...Tell me, my boy, what did your mother do with the few heller?"

"She fetched Miriam some milk."

"Miriam is our other child," explained the father.

"And your mother still went hungry?" asked Friedrich, shaken.

"Yes, sir."

Friedrich still had a few gulden in his pocket. Having done
with life, it did not matter whether he kept them or not. He
could alleviate the need of these people, if only for the
moment.

"Where do you live?" he asked.

"On the Brigittenauer Laende. We have a little room, but have
been told to move."

"Good. I want to see for myself if all this is true. I shall go
home with you:'

"Please do, sir. Though it will afford you no pleasure. We lie
on straw. ..I had intended to go to some other cafes tonight.
But, if you wish, I'll go home now."

They crossed the Augarten Bridge to the Brigittenauer Laende.
David, sidling along beside his father, whispered, "Tateh, may
I eat a piece of bread?"

"Yes, eat," replied the father. Yes, I'll eat some too. There will
be enough for mother."

Father and son pulled the hard crusts out of their pockets and munched audibly.

They paused before a tall building on the Laende that still exhaled a moist, new smell. The peddler rang the bell. All remained quiet. After a bit he pulled again at the brass knob, saying, "The janitor knows who it is. That's why he takes his time. Many a time I have to stand here for an hour. He is a rude man. Often I do not trust myself to come if I haven't five kreutzer to give him for opening the door."

"What do you do then?"

"I walk until the morning, when the house-door is opened:'

Friedrich tugged vigorously at the bell. Once, twice. Behind the gate they heard a rustling, shuffling footsteps, jingling keys. A gleam of light showed through the slits. The gate was opened. The janitor held up the lantern and shouted, "Who was that rang so loudly? What! The Jew baggage?"

The peddler timidly excused himself. "It wasn't I-this gentleman here..."

"Such audacity!" stormed the janitor.

"Hold your tongue, fellow!" ordered Friedrich, throwing down a silver coin.

Hearing the clink of silver on the cobbles, the man became servile. "Oh, I did not mean you, sir. That Jew there!"

"Hold your tongue!" repeated Friedrich, "and light the way upstairs for me."

The janitor stooped to pick up the money. A whole crown! This must be a very great gentleman.

"It's on the fifth floor, sir," said the peddler. "Perhaps the janitor will lend us a bit of candle." "I'll lend nothing to I.ittwak," he shouted. "But if you, sir, want a candle..."

He promptly took the stub out of his lantern and handed it to Friedrich. Then he disappeared, muttering. Friedrich climbed up the five flights. It was well they had the candle; the darkness was impenetrable.

The Littwaks' one-windowed room, too, was in darkness, though the woman was awake and sitting upright on her straw pallet. Friedrich noticed that the narrow room contained no stick of furniture whatever. Not a chair, table, or cupboard. On the window sill were a few small bottles and some broken pots. It was a picture of deepest poverty. A whimpering baby lay at the woman's flabby breast. The mother stared at him anxiously out of her hollow eyes.

"Who is this, Hayim?" she moaned fearfully.

"A kind gentleman," her husband reassured her.

"Mother, here is some bread," said David approaching her.

She broke it with difficulty and slowly put a bit into her mouth. She was emaciated and very weak, but the careworn face still showed traces of beauty.

**31**

"Here we live," said Hayim Littwak with a bitter laugh. "But I don't know whether the day after tomorrow we shall have even this. We have been told to move."

The woman sighed heavily. David cowered in the straw and nestled against her.

"How much do you need in order to remain here?" asked Friedrich.

"Three gulden," replied Littwak. "One gulden twenty for rent, and the rest we owe the janitor's wife. But how shall I get three gulden by the day after tomorrow? We and the children will lie in the street."

The woman wept softly, hopelessly. "Three gulden!"

Friedrich reached into his pocket and found eight gulden. He handed them to the peddler.

"Righteous God! Is it possible?" cried Hayim, as the tears rolled over his face. "Eight gulden! Rebecca! David! God has helped us! Blessed be His Name!"

Rebecca, too, was beside herself with joy. She rose to her knees and crawled toward the benefactor. She held the sleeping baby on her right arm, and reached with her left for Friedrich's hand that she might kiss it.

He cut their thanks short. "Don't make such a fuss about it! The few gulden are nothing to me-it doesn't matter whether I have them or not...David can light me downstairs."

The woman sank back on her pallet, sobbing pitifully in her joy. Littwak murmured a Hebrew prayer. Friedrich left the room, escorted by David. When they reached the second landing, the boy, who had been holding the candle high, stopped short. "God will make me a strong man," he said. "And then I shall repay you."

Friedrich marveled at the little fellow's words and tone. There was something curiously firm and mature about him.

"How old are you?" he asked the boy.

"Ten, I think."

"What do you want to be when you grow up?"

"I want to study. To study very much."

Friedrich sighed involuntarily. "And do you think that is enough?"

"Yes. I have heard that one who studies becomes a free, strong man. I shall study, God helping me. Then I shall go to the Land of Israel with my parents and Miriam."

"To Palestine?" asked Friedrich in amazement. "What will you do there?"

"That is our country. There we can be happy."

The poor Jew boy seemed in no wise ridiculous as he announced his program in a few emphatic words. Friedrich

**33**

recalled those silly jesters, Gruen and Blau, who had made Zionism the butt of their insipid humor. "And when I have something," added David, "I shall repay you."

Friedrich smiled. "I did not give the money to you, but to your father."

"What is given to my father is given to me. I shall repay everything-good and evil." David spoke emphatically and shook his small fist toward the janitor's quarters near which they now stood.

Friedrich placed his hand on the boy's head. "May the God of our ancestors be with you!"

Later he wondered at his own words. He had had nothing to do with the ancestral God since as a child he had gone to temple with his father. This remarkable encounter, however, had stirred old and forgotten things within him. He longed for the strong faith of his youth, when he had communed with the God of his fathers in prayer.

The janitor shuffled forward. Friedrich turned to him. "Hereafter," he said, "you will leave these poor people in peace. Otherwise, you will have to reckon with me. Understand?"

As Friedrich's words were accompanied by a second tip, the fellow murmured meekly, "Kiss your grace's hand!"

Friedrich shook hands with little David, and stepped out on the lonely street.

## Chapter IV

In the reply which Friedrich received to his letter to the N. O. Body of the newspaper advertisement, he was asked to call at a certain fashionable hotel on the Ringstrasse. He came at the hour appointed, and asked for Mr. Kingscourt. He was shown to a salon on the first floor. A tall, broad-shouldered man greeted him there.

"Are you Dr. Loewenberg?" "

I" am."

"Have a chair, Dr. Loewenberg!"

They sat down. Friedrich observed the stranger closely, and waited for him to speak. Mr. Kingscourt was a man in the fifties. His full beard was streaked with gray, his thick brown hair interlaced with silver threads that already shimmered white at the temples. He puffed slowly at a thick cigar.

"Do you smoke, Dr. Loewenberg?" "Not now, thank you."

Mr. Kingscourt carefully blew a smoke ring into the air, and watched it attentively until the cloudy strands were dissipated. Only when the last traces had vanished, he asked, without looking at his visitor, "Why are you disgusted with life?"

"I give no information on that subject," replied Friedrich quietly.

Mr. Kingscourt now looked him full in the face, and nodded approvingly as he flicked the ash from his cigar. "You're right, Devil take it! It's none of my affair. And then, if we put this deal through, you'll tell me of your own accord some time. Meanwhile, I shall tell you who I am. My real name is Koenigshoff. I am a German nobleman. I was an officer in my youth, but the coat-of-mail fitted me too snugly. I can't bear another man's will over mine, be it the best in the world. Obedience was good for a few years. But after that I had to quit. Otherwise, I'd have exploded and caused damage I went to America, called myself Kingscourt, and made a fortune in twenty years of blood-sweating work. When I had come so far, I took a wife. ..What did you say, Dr. Loewenberg?"

"Nothing, Mr. Kingscourt."

"Very well. Are you unmarried?"

"I am. But I thought, Mr. Kingscourt, that you would tell me about this experiment you want to propose to me."

"I'll come to that in a moment. If we should arrange to be together, I shall tell you in detail how I worked my way up and made my millions. For I have millions... What did you say?"

"Nothing, Mr. Kingscourt."

"Energy is everything, Dr. Loewenberg. That's what counts. Want a thing with all your might, and you're dead certain to get it. I never realized until I lived in America what a lazy, weak-kneed lot we Europeans are. Devil take me! In short, I was successful.

"But, by the time I had succeeded, I felt lonely. As it happened, a Koenigshoff, a son of my brother's who was in the guards, made a fool of himself. I had the boy come out to me-just at the time I was courting my wife. Yes, I wanted to establish a family, set up a hearth, seek out a wife upon whom I might hang jewels like any other parvenu. I yearned for children so that they might enjoy the fruits of my drudgery. I wanted to be damned clever, and so I married a poor girl. She was the daughter of one of my employees. I had shown her and her father much kindness. Of course she consented. I thought she loved me, but she was only grateful, or perhaps cowardly. She did not dare to refuse me. So we went housekeeping, and my nephew lived with us.

"You will say that was stupid-an old man between two young people who were bound to attract each other. I called myself an ass when I first found out. But, had it not been he, it would have been someone else. In brief, they betrayed me; from the first moment, I believe. My first move was for a revolver, but then I told myself that really I alone was the guilty one. I let them off. It is human to be base, and every opportunity is a panderer. Avoid human beings if you would not have them ruin you. I collapsed, you see. The thought crept into my mind to end the shabby comedy of my life with a bullet. But on thinking it over, I decided that there was always time to shoot oneself.

"To be sure, there was no point in heaping up more money. I had no more desire for gain, and of the dream of a family I had had enough. Only solitude remained as a last experiment. But it must be a vast, unheard-of solitude, where one would know nothing more of mankind of its wretched struggles, its

uncleanness, its disloyalties. I wanted genuine, deep solitude
without struggle or desire. A full, true return to Nature!
Solitude is the paradise which humanity forfeited by its sins.
But I have found it."

"Truly? Have you found it?" asked Friedrich, who still did not
gather what the American was leading up to.

"Yes, I have found it. I settled my affairs, and ran away from
everything and everyone. No one knew what had become of
me. I built myself a comfortable yacht and vanished with it. I
wandered about the seas for many months. It's a glorious life,
you must know. Wouldn't you .like to try it? Or perhaps you
are already familiar with it?"

"No, I am not familiar with that sort of life," replied Friedrich,
"but I should like to try it."

"Well, then...Life on the yacht is freedom, but not real solitude.
You must have a crew about you, you have to put into a harbor
occasionally for coal. Then you come into contact with people
once more, and that's a dirty business. But I know an island in
the South Seas where one is really alone. It is a rocky little nest
in Cook's Archipelago. I bought it, and had men come over
from Raratonga to build me a comfortable home. It is so well
hidden by the cliffs that it cannot be spied on any side from the
sea. Besides, ships rarely come that way. My island still looks
uninhabited. I live there with two servants, a dumb negro
whom I had in America, and a Tahitan whom I pulled out of
the water at Avarua harbor when he tried to drown himself
over an unhappy love affair. Now I have come to Europe for a
last visit to buy whatever I shall need for the rest of my life
over there-books - apparatus for physics, and weapons. My

Tahitan brings provisions from the nearest inhabited island. He and my negro go over every morning in an electric launch. Whatever else we need can be bought for money in Raratonga, just like anywhere else in the world....Understand?"

"Yes, Mr. Kingscourt... But I do not know why you are telling me all this."

"Why I am telling you all this? Because I want to take a companion back with me-so that I shall not unlearn human speech, and so that there may be someone by me to close my eyes when I die. Do you want to be that someone?"

Friedrich reflected for half a moment. Then he replied firmly, "Yes!"

Kingscourt nodded his satisfaction, but added, "However, I must remind you that you are undertaking a lifelong obligation. At least, it must hold for the rest of my life. If you come with me now, there will be no going back. You must cut all your ties:'

"Nothing binds me," replied Friedrich. "I am all alone in the world, and have had enough of life."

"That's the kind of man I want, sir! You will actually leave this life if you go with me. You will know nothing more of the good or evil of this world. You will be dead to it, and it will have gone under-as far as you are concerned. Does that suit you?"

"It does."

"Then we shall get along very well together. I like your type."
"But there is one thing I must tell you, Mr. Kingscourt.

I am a Jew. Does that make any difference?"

Kingscourt laughed. "I say! That's an amusing question. You
are a man. I can see that. And you seem to be an educated man.
You are disgusted with life. That shows your good taste.
Everything else is frightfully unimportant where we are
going....Well, then, shake hands on it." Friedrich shook the
proffered hand vigorously.

"When can you be ready, Dr. Loewenberg?"

"At any time."

"Good. Say tomorrow. We go from here to Trieste, where my
yacht is anchored....Perhaps you still wish to provide yourself
with some things here?"

"I shouldn't know what to get. This is no pleasure trip, but a
farewell to life:'

"Still, Dr. Loewenberg! You may need money for your
purchases, Draw on me."

"Thank you, I need nothing."

"Have you no debts?"

"I have nothing and owe nothing, my accounts are balanced,"

"Have you no friends or relatives to whom you wish to give something before you go?"

"None."

"So much the better. We're off tomorrow, then. ..But we might begin having our meals together today."

Kingscourt rang for a waiter, and gave his order briefly. An elaborate luncheon was served in Kingscoun's sitting room. The two men soon grew intimate as they talked over the meal. After Kingscourt had so quickly reposed confidence in him, Friedrich felt he ought to tell his own story. He did so briefly and clearly. When he had finished, the American remarked, "Now I believe that you will not leave me once I have you upon my island. Lovesickness, Weltschmerz suffering as a Jew-all that together is enough to make even a young man wish to have done with living. ..."

"With living with people, I mean. Even if you bestow benefits upon them, they deceive you and make you suffer. The philanthropists are the greatest fools of all. Don't you think so, Dr. Loewenberg?"

"I think, Mr. Kingscourt, that there is pleasure in well-doing....That reminds me. You offered me money a moment ago if I cared to leave some behind me before I depart from this world, I know a family in the greatest straits. With your permission, I should like to help them,"

"It's nonsense, Dr. Loewenberg! But I cannot refuse you. I had intended giving you a sum of money to settle your affairs. Will five thousand gulden suffice?"

"Amply!" Friedrich assured him. "J should like to think that my farewell to life was not altogether aimless."

## Chapter V

The Littwak's room by daylight looked even drearier than at night, but Friedrich found the family in an almost happy mood. David was standing near the window-sill with an open book before him, chewing a mighty slice of bread and butter. His father and mother sat on the straw, and little Miriam played with bits of chaff.

Hayim hastily rose to greet his benefactor. The wife too tried to rise, but Friedrich checked her. He knelt beside her quickly and petted the nurseling, who smiled at him sweetly out of her rags.

"Well, and how are things today, Mrs. Littwak?" The poor woman tried vainly to kiss his hand. "Better, sir," she answered. "We have milk for Miriam, and bread for ourselves."

"And we've paid the rent, too," added Hayim proudly.

David had put down his bread and butter, and stood regarding Friedrich steadily with folded arms.

"Why do you look at me so closely, David?" he asked.

"So that I may never forget you, sir. I once read a story about a man who helped a sick lion."

"Androcles," smiled Friedrich.

"My David has already read a great deal," said his mother, in her weak, soft tones.

Friedrich rose, and said jestingly, as he placed his hand on the boy's round head, "And so you are the lion? Judah once had a lion."

"That which Judah once had, he can have again," replied David almost defiantly.

"We cannot even offer you a chair, sir," lamented the housewife.

"It doesn't matter, dear madam. I came only to see how you were feeling today, and to bring something. You are to open this letter only after I have left. It contains a recommendation that will be useful to you. You must eat well, Mrs. Littwak, and bring up this pretty little girl to be as fine a woman as yourself."

"May she have a better fate," sighed the mother.

"And let this chap here study something worth while. Give me your hand, boy! Promise me you will become an upright man."

"Yes, sir, I promise you that."

What remarkable eyes the boy has, thought Friedrich, as he shook the small hand. He laid the bulky envelope on the window-sill and turned to go. "Pardon me, sir," Hayim asked at the door, "but does this letter contain a recommendation to the Community offices?"

"Quite so. It will recommend you there also."

He walked quickly out of the room and ran down the stairs as if he were being pursued. A cab was waiting for him in the street: "Hurry!" he shouted to the driver, and jumped in.

The horses started off at a gallop. It was high time. A moment later David came running breathlessly through the gate, spying in every direction. When he could find no trace of the benefactor, he wept bitterly. Friedrich watched him through the rear cab window, happy to have escaped the flood of thanks. With five thousand gulden the family could probably establish itself.

At the hotel Kingscourt greeted him laughingly. "Well, and have you performed your good works?"

"It would be fairer to say, your good works, Mr. Kingscourt. The money was yours."

"No, no! I object decidedly. I should not have given a penny in order to benefit people. I don't mind your being a fool about loving your neighbor. I'm not any more. The money was an advance to yourself. You were free to use it as you pleased."

"Let it go at that, Mr. Kingscourt."

"If you had told me you wished to do something for dogs or horses or other respectable creatures, you could have had my help. But for humans, no! Don't bring that kind around. They're too vile. Wisdom consists only in recognizing their baseness....There was a story in the papers recently about an old lady who left her fortune to her cats. In her last will she left instructions that her home was to be turned into thus-and-so many fine apartments for the cat tribe, with servants, and all that, to look after them. The writer fellow stupidly said that very likely the old lady was cracked. She wasn't cracked at all, but enormously clever. She wanted to make a demonstration against the human race, and especially against her beastly, fortune-hunting relatives. Help for animals, yes. For humans, no! You see, I feel deeply for that old lady, God rest her soul!"

The vileness of mankind was Kingscourt's favorite topic, and he elaborated it with inexhaustible verve.

Friedrich arranged his few affairs, and was ready to join Kingscourt the following day. He told his landlady that he was making an excursion to the Grossglockner. She tried to dissuade him; one heard so much about mountain accidents in mid-winter.

"It will be all right," he assured her, with a wistful smile. "If I do not return after eight days, you may report me missing to the police. I shall probably be resting peacefully in some mountain cleft. My belongings here I bequeath to you."

"Don't talk sinfully, sir."

"I was only joking!"

That evening Friedrich left Vienna with Kingscourt. He had not gone again to the Cafe Birkenreis, and so did not know that little David Littwak waited for him in the doorway night after night....

Kingscourt's handsome yacht was rolling on the waters of
Trieste harbor. The two men made their final purchases for the
long journey in the town; and then, on a beautiful December
day, the anchor was raised and the yacht steered south and
eastward. In other circumstances, Friedrich would have been
enchanted with the free life of the sea. But, as it was, the sunny
cruise hardly eased his heartache.

Kingscourt was really a delightful person, good-natured despite
the misanthropy he boasted of, charming, and tender-hearted.
When he saw Friedrich depressed, he tried to divert him with
all sorts of pleasantries, treating him like a sick child. Then
Friedrich would say, "If the crew watch us together, they will
get a wrong idea of our relations. They'll take me for the host,
and you for the guest whom I've invited to entertain me. Ah,
Mr.. Kingscourt, you could have found a more cheerful
companion."

"My dear fellow, I had no choice," replied Kingscourt grimly.
"I had to have someone who was disgusted with life, and such
people are not as a rule very good company. But I'll cure you
yet. You'll look at things quite differently when we've left the
human mob behind us altogether. Then you'll become a
cheerful fellow like me. When we're on our blessed island. If
that's not true, may the Devil take me!"

The yacht was very cozy, and equipped with all sorts of
American conveniences. Friedrich's cabin was just as fine as
Kingscourt's. The dining saloon was magnificently decorated.
The hours flew by in congenial talk as they sat together in the
evenings under the friendly, steady light of the ceiling lamp.
There was a small, well-selected library on board, but their
days always seemed too full for books. Kingscourt exerted

himself constantly to distract his companion. As they were crossing the rough waters near Crete, he suddenly came out with a suggestion.

"I say, Dr. Loewenberg, haven't you any desire to see your fatherland before you say farewell to the world?"

"My fatherland! You don't want to turn back to Trieste?"

"God forbid!" roared Kingscourt. "Your fatherland lies ahead of us-Palestine."

"Oh, that's what you meant. You are mistaken. I have no connection with Palestine. I have never been there. It does not interest me. My ancestors left it eighteen hundred years ago. What should I seek there? I think that only anti-Semites can call Palestine our fatherland."

But, even as he spoke, Friedrich remembered David Littwak, and added, "Aside from the anti-Semites, I have heard only one little Jewboy say that Palestine is our land. ...Did you mean to tease me, Mr. Kingscourt?"

"No, may lightning strike me if I did! I meant it seriously. Really, I don't understand you Jews. If I were a Jew, I should be frightfully proud of that sort of thing. And yet you are ashamed of it. You needn't wonder that you are despised. Present company excluded, of course."

"Herr von Koenigshoff, are you perhaps an anti-Semite?" asked Friedrich annoyed. He had called his companion by his German name for the first time, without himself knowing why.

"Now you're excited, my son." Kingscourt was smiling. "I'm a hater of mankind. You know all about that. But you take it amiss if I don't care for the Jews. Comfort yourself, man. I hate the Jews no more and no less than I hate Christians, Moslems, and fire-worshipers. The whole lot aren't worth a charge of powder. I understand good old Nero. One single neck, to be run through at a single stroke. Or, no! Rather let the rascally crew live and worry each other to death."

Friedrich was mollified. "I was stupid," he said. "You took me with you. That's the best proof."

"I'm reminded," continued Kingscourt, "of an affair I once had with one of your fellow-nationals or co-religionists or-Devil take me! In short, with a Jew. It happened in the regiment. We had a volunteer there. Cohn was the creature's name, a low... excuse me! This Cohn was a damned bow-legged fellow, as if created for the cavalry. It happened during the riding lesson. I made the swine jump the barriers. That is, I wanted to make them jump. They didn't want to, or couldn't. It was a bit high, that's true. Well, I cursed them as such God-forsaken swine deserved. I. could still swear in those days, Devil take me! I've forgotten since. ..I gave them to understand in cavalry oaths that they were a cowardly bunch of scamps. I went for Cohn in particular. 'You probably ride notes of exchange better,' I sneered. The blood rushed to the Jew's face. He took the jump, but fell and broke his arm. That worried me for a while. Why must such carrion have a sense of honor into the bargain?"

"Do you think a Jew should have no sense of honor?"

"Oh, I say! How you twist my words....Well, and if the Jews have a sense of honor, why do they put up with all the mischief?"

"What would you have the Jews do, Mr. Kingscourt?"

"What would I have them do? Really, I don't know. Something like that Cohn in the Tiding school. I respected him more after that."

"Because he broke his arm?"

"No, because he showed that he had a will of his own....If I were in your place, I'd do something bold, something big, something that would make my enemies gape. Prejudices, my dear fellow, there will always be. The human pack nourishes itself on prejudices from the cradle to the grave. Well, then. Since prejudices cannot be wiped out, they must be overcome....The more I think of it, the more it seems to me that it must be quite interesting to be a Jew these days. Just because one has the whole world against him."

"Ah, but you don't know how that feels."

"Not pleasant, I can imagine....Now, how about that old Palestine? Shall we have a look at it before we vanish?" "As you please, Mr. Kingscourt."

The prow of the yacht was turned toward Jaffa.

# Chapter VI

Kingscourt and Friedrich spent several days in the old land of the Jews. Jaffa made a very unpleasant impression upon them. Though nobly situated on the blue Mediterranean, the town was in a state of extreme decay. Landing was difficult in the forsaken harbor. The alleys were dirty, neglected, full of vile odors. Everywhere misery in bright Oriental rags. Poor Turks, dirty Arabs, timid Jews lounged about-indolent, beggarly, hopeless. A peculiar, tomblike odor of mold caught one's breath.

They hurried away from Jaffa, and went up to Jerusalem on the miserable railway. The landscape through which they passed was a picture of desolation. The lowlands were mostly sand and swamp, the lean fields looked as if burnt over. The inhabitants of the blackish Arab villages looked like brigands. Naked children played in the dirty alleys. Over the distant horizon loomed the deforested hills of Judaea. The bare slopes and the bleak, rocky valleys showed few traces of present or former cultivation.

"If this is our land," remarked Friedrich sadly, "it has declined like our people."

"Yes, it's pretty bad," agreed Kingscourt. "But much could be done here with afforestation, if half a million young giant cedars were planted-they shoot up like asparagus. This country needs nothing but water and shade to have a very great future."

"And who is to bring water and shade here?"

"The Jews!" And Kingscourt swore a great cavalry oath.

It was night when they reached Jerusalem-a marvelous white moonlit night.

"Donnerwetter!" shouted Kingscourt. "I say, this is beautiful!"

He stopped the cab which was taking them from the station to a hotel, and called to the guide, "You stay here, and tell that camel of a driver to follow us slowly."

"Let's walk a bit, shall we, Dr. Loewenberg?" Again turning to the guide, the old man asked, "What's the name of this region?"

"The Valley of Jehoshaphat, sir," replied the man meekly.

"Then it's a real place, Devil take me! The Valley of Jehoshaphat! I thought it was just something in the Bible. Here our Lord and Savior walked. What do you think of it, Dr. Loewenberg? ...Ah, yes! Still, it must mean something to you also. These ancient walls, this Valley..."

"Jerusalem!" cried Friedrich in a half-whisper, his voice trembling. He did not understand why the sight of this strange city affected him so powerfully. Was it the memory of words heard in early childhood? In passages of prayer murmured by his father? Memories of Seder services of long-forgotten years stirred in him. One of the few Hebrew phrases he still knew rang in his ears: "Leshana Ha-baa be-Yerushalayim,"-"Next Year in Jerusalem!" Suddenly he saw himself a little boy going to synagogue with his father. Ah, but faith was dead now,

**52**

youth was dead, his father was dead. And here before him the walls of Jerusalem towered in the fairy moonlight. His eyes overflowed. He stopped short, and the hot tears coursed slowly down his cheeks.

Kingscourt smothered a few "Devils!" in his windpipe, motioned violently to the coachman behind them to stop, and slipped silently a few paces behind Friedrich.

The latter came out of his trance sighing and embarrassed.

"Forgive me, Mr. Kingscourt," he murmured, "for making you wait here. It was...I feel...so peculiar. I don't know what it is."

But Kingscourt linked arms with the young man, and spoke with unusual gentleness. "You, Friedrich Loewenberg, I like you."

Arm in arm Jew and Christian approached Jerusalem the Holy City by the white light of the moon.

Jerusalem by daylight was less alluring-shouting, odors, a flurry of dirty colors, crowds of ragged people in narrow, musty lanes, beggars, sick. people, hungry children, screeching women, shouting tradesmen.. The once royal city of Jerusalem could have sunk no lower.

The travelers viewed all the famous sites, buildings, and ruins. They walked down the noisome little lane that leads to the Wailing Wall, and were revolted by the appearance of the praying beggars there.

"You see, Mr. Kingscourt," said Friedrich, "we have really died dead. There's nothing left of the Jewish kingdom but this fragment of the Temple wall. And though I fathom my soul to its depths, I find nothing in common with these traffickers in the national misfortune."

He had spoken loudly, without realizing that he might be overheard. Besides the praying beggars and the guides, there was present a gentleman in European clothing who turned and spoke to them. His German accent was foreign but cultured.

"You seem to be a Jew, sir, or of Jewish descent."

"Yes," replied Friedrich, somewhat taken by surprise.

"If that is so, perhaps you will allow me to correct your error," continued the stranger. "More remains of the Jews than the stones of this ancient bit of masonry and these poor wretches here who, I grant you, ply no wholesome trade. The Jewish people nowadays should be judged neither by its beggars nor by its millionaires."

"I am not rich," declared Friedrich.

"I see what you are-a stranger to your people. If you ever come to us in Russia, you will realize that a Jewish nation still exists. We have a living tradition, a love of the past, and faith in the future. The best and most cultured men among us have remained true to Judaism as a nation. We desire to belong to no other. We are what our fathers were."

"Excellent!" cried Kingscourt.

Friedrich shrugged slightly, but exchanged a few civil remarks with the stranger, and then went on. When they turned to .look back from the end of the lane, they saw the Russian Jew sunk in silent prayer beside the Wall.

That evening they saw him again at the English hotel where they were staying. He was dining with a young lady, evidently his daughter. When they met later in the lobby, the conversation of the morning was resumed without any sense of restraint. The Russian introduced himself as Dr. Eichenstamm. "I am an oculist," he explained. "My daughter too."

"What!" cried Kingscourt. "Is this young lady a doctor?"

"Yes. She studied under me at first, and later in Paris. Now she is my assistant. A very learned person, my Sascha."

The young lady doctor blushed at her father's praise. "Oh, papa!" she cried deprecatingly.

Dr. Eichenstamm stroked his long gray beard. "One may say what is true," he said. "We are not here solely for pleasure, gentlemen. We are interested in eye diseases. Unfortunately, there is no lack of them here. Dirt and neglect revenge themselves. Everything is in ruins here. And how beautiful it could be, for it is a golden land!"

"This country?" inquired Friedrich incredulously. "The milk and honey description is no longer true."

"It is always true!" cried Eichenstamm enthusiastically.

"If only we had the people here, all else would follow."

"No," asserted Kingscourt decisively, "there's nothing to be expected from people."

Dr. Sascha turned to her father. "You ought to suggest that the gentlemen see the colonies."

"Which colonies?" asked Friedrich.

"Our Jewish settlements," replied the old gentleman. "Don't you know anything about them either, Dr. Loewenberg? They are the most remarkable phenomenon in modern Jewish life. Societies in Europe and America, the so-called 'Lovers of Zion,' promote the transformation of Jews into farmers in this old land of ours. A number of such Jewish villages already exist. Several rich philanthropists have also contributed funds for the purpose. Our old soil is productive again. You must visit the Jewish villages before you leave Palestine."

"We could if you cared to," shouted Kingscourt to Friedrich, who promptly assented.

The next day they went up to the Mount of Olives with Eichenstamm and Sascha. On the way they passed the elegant residence of an English lady.

"You see," said the Russian, "that new mansions can be erected on our ancient soil. Very good idea to live up here. My own dream too."

"Or at least to have an eye clinic," smiled Dr. Sascha.

From the top of the mountain they admired the view of the hilly city and of the wide circle of mountains that flowed down in stony waves to the Dead Sea.

Friedrich grew thoughtful. "Jerusalem must have been beautiful," he said. "Perhaps that is why our ancestors could never forget it, and always wanted to return."

"It reminds me of Rome," cried Eichenstamm. "A splendid city, a metropolis, could be erected upon these hills once more. What a view from here! Grander than that from the Gianiculo. Ah, if my old eyes might still see it. ..."

"We shall not live to see it," said Sascha wistfully.

Kingscourt marveled silently as he listened to their fantastic notions. When they were alone again, he said to Friedrich, "A remarkable pair, that doctor-father and the doctor-daughter. So practical and yet so foolish. I always imagined the Jews quite different."

The next morning Kingscourt and Friedrich said farewell to the Eichenstamms and drove out to the colonies. They looked at Rishon-le-Zion, Rehobot, and other villages that lay like oases in the desolate countryside. Many industrious hands must have worked here to restore fertility to the soil, they realized, as they gazed upon well-cultivated fields, stately vineyards and luxuriant orange groves.

"All this has come into being during the last ten or fifteen years," explained the head of the village council of Rehobot, to whom Eichenstamm had referred them. "The colonization movement began after the persecutions in Russia in the early

1880's. But, there are villages more remarkable than ours. There's Katrah, for instance, founded by university students who forsook their books for the plow. Such peasants are to be found nowhere else in the world-cultured men working in the fields."

"That's a strong card!" cried Kingscourt. Still greater was their surprise when the village president called on the young men of Rehobot to mount their horses. A sort of Arab fantasy was performed in honor of the visitors. The youngsters galloped far off into the fields, threw their steeds about, and rushed back again shouting, throwing guns and caps into the air mid-career and catching them again. Finally, they rode home in single file singing a Hebrew song.

Kingscourt was beside himself with delight. "May salty lightning strike me! These fellows ride like the devil! That was the sort of thing my great-great-grandfather during the attack at Rossbach-"

But Friedrich was little interested in these manifestations of sound and joyous life, and was glad when they left the villages and returned to Jaffa.

The yacht was under steam. They left the sunny strand of Palestine in December, and steered toward Port Said, where they anchored for two days, and then sailed on through the Suez Canal. On the evening of December 31, 1902, they entered the Red Sea. Friedrich relapsed into deep melancholy. In that mood nothing mattered to him.

After the sun had set Kingscourt called him to the foredeck.

"This evening," said he, "we shall dress for dinner. Here's the menu. Plenty of silvernecks on the ice."

"What's the occasion, Mr. Kingscourt?"

"Don't you know, man! It's the last day of the year. That's no ordinary date, if dates have any meaning at all."

"They have no meaning for us," answered Friedrich listlessly. "Timelessness begins for us now. Isn't that so?"

"Yes, yes, of course. But it's a damned queer day. At midnight we shall sink Time into your Red Sea. Then, with the end of the stupid epoch in which we have been doomed to live, we shall think of something big...I'm having an excellent punch brewed, too. That's the most genuine thing in the universal depravity."

They celebrated. The ship's cook outdid himself. The wines were excellent. Kingscourt, a mighty drinker before the Lord, drank three times as much as Friedrich, and remained quite fresh and clear-headed. But his young companion felt a mist rising before his eyes, and heard Kingscourt's voice as in a dream when the clock struck twelve.

"Midnight!" boomed Kingscourt. "Die, Time! I empty my glass to your death. What were you? Shame, blood, depravity, progress. Put up your glass, man, my isolated contemporary!"

"I can drink no morel" stuttered Friedrich.

"Weak generation!...You ought to be standing on tiptoe here. A classic region! Here your old Moses performed his greatest

**59**

deed....They went through dryshod. Obviously it must have
been just at ebb tide. And that donkey of a Pharoah went right
into the flood! No magic, But it's the very naturalness of the
thing that impresses me. The simplest means! But one must see
those means, be able to make use of them. Just think how poor
a time that was, and yet what your old Moses achieved. If he
were to come back today and see all our marvels-railways,
telegraphs, telephones, machines, this yacht with her screw
propeller, electric searchlights-he would understand nothing at
all. For three whole days" probably, things would have to be
explained to him. But after that he would understand
everything. And what do you think he would do then? He'd
laugh-laugh-grimly-terribly. Because with all this wonderful
progress, humanity doesn't know which way to turn. In private
life one comes to the conclusion that humanity is base. But,
taking it by and large, one discovers that it is merely stupid.
Infinitely stupid, stupid, stupid! Never was the world so rich as
now, and yet never have there been so many poor. People
starve while corn lies moldering. It's all the same to me. The
more perish, the fewer the ingrates, liars, and traitors will be
left in the world!"

Friedrich spoke thickly. "Don't you think, Mr. Kingscourt, that
people would be much better if they were better off?"

"No! If I believed that, I should not be going off to my lonely
island; I should have stayed in the midst of humanity. I should
have told them how to better themselves. They needn't wait to
begin. Not a thousand years, not a hundred, not even fifty.
Today! With the ideas, knowledge, and facilities that humanity
possesses on this 31st day of December, 1902, it could save
itself. No philosopher's stone, no dirigible airship is needed.
Everything needful for the making of a better world exists

already. And do you know, man, who could show the way? You! You Jews! Just because you're so badly off. You've nothing to lose. You could make the experimental land for humanity. Over yonder, where we were, you could create a new commonwealth. On that ancient soil, Old-New-Land!"

Friedrich heard Kingscourt's words only in a dream. He had fallen asleep. And, dreaming, he sailed through the Red Sea to meet the future.

# Theodor Herzl

# Book Two

# Haifa 1923

### Chapter I

The Kingscourt yacht once again appeared in the Red Sea, but this time headed in the opposite direction.

Kingscourt's hair and beard had become snow-white. Friedrich, also as he stood before his cabin mirror, could see the first silver threads on his own temples.

The old man called to him from the foredeck. "Hallo, Fritze! Come up here!"

"What do you want, Kingscourt?" he asked, coming out of his cabin.

"Devil take me if I understand this! I've seen very few passenger ships since we've been in the Red Sea. Freight ships, yes, many. But don't you remember how much traffic there was in these waters twenty years ago, 1902? That was traffic. East Indiamen! Ships bound for China! These wretched hulks we see now are bound only for the African ports and for Madagascar. I've questioned that donkey of a pilot about every ship we've passed. There are no more East Indiamen, Japanese, or Chinese ships here. As I said before, there's nothing but freighters. Perhaps England lost all her Indian possessions while we've been gone. Devil take me! To whom?"

"Why don't you ask the pilot, if you want to know?"

"I'll ask nothing! I'll wait till we get to Europe. I'm not curious. Perhaps you are, Frizchen, eh?"

"No, Kingscourt. It's all one to me. In those twenty years on our beloved island, I lost all interest in the doings of the outside world. I have not a friend or relative left alive. What could I inquire about?"

Kingscourt leaned back in his comfortable easy chair, and puffed at a large Havana. "Well, our island did not disagree with you, Fritz. What a green, hollow-chested Jewboy you were when I took you away. Now you are like an oak. You might still be dangerous to the women."

"You are quite mad, Kingscourt," laughed Friedrich. "I think too much of you to infer that you're dragging me to Europe to marry me off."

Kingscourt was convulsed with laughter. "Carrion! Marry you off! You don't think me that kind of an ass, I hope! What should I do with you then?"

"Well, it might be a delicate way of getting rid of me. Haven't you had enough of my society?"

"Now the carrion's fishing for compliments," shouted the old man, who expressed his good humor best through epithets. "You know very well, Fritzchen, that I can no longer live without you. Indeed, I arranged this whole trip for your sake. So that you would be patient with me a few years longer."

"I say, Kingscourt! You know I can't be vulgar-at least, not so vulgar as you can. But, mildly speaking, that is ..."

"Idiotic?"

"Something of the sort...When was I ever impatient? I was happy on our island, completely happy. The twenty years passed over me like a dream. Wasn't it only yesterday you delivered your farewell address to Time somewhere about here? I should never again have left our blessed island, not I. And now you try to make me think you're going to Europe to please me. Old man, you ought to be ashamed to offer such rotten pretexts! You're curious about things over there. It's you that want to go-not I. The best proof that I care no longer for the inhabited world is that during all those years I never once opened a newspaper."

"Nothing remarkable about that. My first rule of health was: No newspapers!"

"Indeed! A few years ago there was a shipment from Raratonga. All the things in the packing case were wrapped in French and English newspapers. For a moment I was tempted to read them. If they were months-or even years-old, they would still contain news for me. That was in 1917, and I had heard nothing from the world for fifteen years. But I rolled the papers into a bundle and burned them unread. And now you say that I yearn to go back to Europe!"

The old man smirked gleefully. "Now that you've exposed my lies, I'll confess. Yes, I should like to know what's become of the vile world-to see whether the human race is still as stupid and base as it was."

"My dear Kingscourt, I wager we shall be happy to return to our quiet island."

"Your wager finds no takers. I hold the same opinion."

The yacht skimmed through the Suez Canal. At Port Said, they disembarked. There was a lively freight traffic in the harbor, but the shabby bazaars no longer swarmed with the vivid, multicolored, polyglot pageant that had once been typical of the town. This had been the crossways for all who traveled from East to West, and from West to East. The most fashionable globe-trotters had been accustomed to pass through Port Said; but now, except for the natives, only a few half-drunken sailors lounged before the dirty cafes.

The two travelers stepped. into a shop to buy some cigars. When they asked for a better brand than was offered, the Greek shopkeeper replied fretfully, "We don't carry that kind. We no longer have customers for it. No one comes here who wants good cigars-there are only sailors who ask for chewing tobacco and cheap cigarettes."

"How is that possible?" asked Kingscourt. "Where are all the tourists on their way to India and Australia and China?"

"Oh, there have been none here for many years. They now travel by the other route." "Another route?" cried Friedrich. "What other route? Not the Cape of Good Hope?"

The dealer was annoyed. "You choose to laugh at me, sir. Every child knows that people no longer travel to Asia via the Suez Canal!"

Kingscourt and Friedrich looked at each other in amazement. "Of course, every child knows it," shouted Kingscourt, "but you must not think us ignorant if we've not heard of this damned new canal!"

"Just get out, will you!" The Greek pounded furiously on his counter. "First you tease me about expensive cigars, and then you make these stupid jokes. Get out!"

Kingscourt wanted to reach across the counter to whack the Greek over the head. But Friedrich drew the old hotspur away. "Kingscourt, big things that we don't know about have happened while we've been away."

"I believe so myself, Devil take me! Well, we must find out about it at once!"

Returning to the harbor, they learned from the captain of a German trading vessel that traffic between Europe and Asia had taken a new route-via Palestine.

"What?" asked Friedrich. "Are there harbors and railways in Palestine?"

"Are there harbors and railways in Palestine?" The captain laughed heartily. "Where do you come from, sir? Have you never seen a newspaper or a time table?"

"I shouldn't say never, but several years have passed...We know Palestine as a forsaken country."

"A forsaken country... good! If you choose to call it that, I don't mind. Only I must say you're spoiled."

"Listen to me, captain," cried Kingscourt. "We'd like to offer you some good wine. ...We're a pair of damned ignorant wretches. We've thought of nothing but our own pleasure for twenty years. Now, then, what's happened to that old Palestine?"

"You could get to Palestine in less time than it would take to tell you about it. Why not make a slight detour if you've a couple of days to spare? If you wish to leave your yacht, you'll find fast boats to all the European and American ports at Haifa and Jaffa."

"No, we don't leave our yacht. But we could make the detour, Fritze. What do you say? Do you want to take another look at the land of your blessed ancestors?"

"Palestine attracts me as little as Europe. It's all one to me."

They headed for Haifa. The coast of Palestine rose on the horizon on a spring morning following one of the mild, soft nights common in the eastern Mediterranean. They stood together on the bridge of the yacht, and stared steadily through their telescopes for ten whole minutes, looking always in the same direction.

"I could swear that that was the Bay of Acco over there," remarked Friedrich.

"I could also swear to the contrary," asserted Kingscourt. "I still have a picture of that Bay in my mind's eye. It was empty and deserted twenty years ago. Still, that's the Carmel on our rig-ht, and to our left is the town of Acco."

"How changed it all is!" cried Friedrich. "There's been a miracle here."

As they approached the harbor they made out the details with the help of their excellent lenses.

Great ships, such as were already known at the end of the nineteenth century, lay anchored in the roadstead between Acco and the foot of the Carmel. Behind this fleet they discerned the noble curve of the Bay. At its northern end, the gray fortress walls, heavy cupolas and slender minarets of Acco were outlined in their beautiful ancient Oriental architecture against the morning skies. Nothing had changed much in that skyline. To the south, however, below the ancient, much-tried city of Haifa on the curve of the shore, splendid things had grown up. Thousands of white villas gleamed out of luxuriant green gardens. All the way from Acco to Mount Carmel stretched what seemed to be one great park. The mountain itself, also, was crowned with beautiful structures. Since they were approaching from the south, the promontory at first obscured their full view of the city and the harbor. When, at last, the landscape was revealed to them in its entirety, Kingscourt's "Devils!" became legion.

A magnificent city had been built beside the sapphire blue Mediterranean. The magnificent stone dams showed the harbor for what it was: the safest and most convenient port in the eastern Mediterranean. Craft of every shape and size, flying the flags of all the nations, lay sheltered there.

Kingscourt and Friedrich were spellbound. Their twenty-year-old map showed no such port, and here it was as if conjured up by magic. Evidently the world had not stood still in their absence.

They left the yacht and entered a landing boat, in which they were rowed through the swarming ships to the quay. They exchanged impressions in abrupt, broken phrases.

The boat drew in at the stone steps of the dam. As they came up the steps, they noticed a young man who was about to go down to an electric launch that waited for him. He, in turn, catching sight of them, stopped short and stared at Friedrich with wide-open eyes. He seemed thunderstruck.

The old man noticed his behavior and growled, "What does this fellow want? Hasn't he ever seen two civilized people before?"

"That can hardly be the case," smiled Friedrich. "The people on this quay seem more civilized than we do. It's more likely that we look old-fashioned to him. Just look up at that cosmopolitan traffic in the streets. And all the well-dressed people! Seems to me our clothes are a bit out of date."

They instructed their boatman to wait for them at the landing place, and ascended more stone steps leading up to the high-lying street where they had seen the traffic from the water's edge. They thought no more of the stranger who had stared at them so fixedly. However, he followed them and tried to overhear what language they were speaking. Soon he had caught up with them; and the next instant he strode a step in front of them and faced about.

"Sir!" stormed Kingscourt. "What is it you want with us?"

The stranger made no reply, but turned to Friedrich. His pleasant, manly voice trembled with emotion. "Are you Dr. Friedrich Loewenberg?" he asked.

"Yes, that is my name." Friedrich spoke wonderingly.

The stranger impulsively fell upon Friedrich's neck and kissed him upon both cheeks. Then he released him and dried the tears from his face. He was a tall, vigorous man of thirty, whose sunburnt face was framed in a short black beard.

"And who are you, sir?" inquired Friedrich, when he had recovered from the impetuous greeting.

"I? Oh, you won't remember me. My name is David Littwak."

"The little fellow from the Cafe Birkenreis?"

"Yes, sir. He whom you rescued from starvation, with his parents and sister."

"Please don't mention it," parried Friedrich.

"On the contrary, it will be mentioned a great deal. Whatever I am and whatever I have, I owe to you. Now you are my guest. This gentleman as well, if he is a friend of yours."

"This is the best and only friend I have in the world. Mr. Kingscourt'"

# Chapter II

Before they had fully realized what was happening, Kingscourt
and Friedrich had let David lead them up from the dam to street
level. Only then did they receive a full impression of the
wonderful city and its traffic. Before them lay an immense
square bordered by the high-arched arcades of stately
buildings. In the middle of the square was a fenced-in garden
of palm trees. Both sides of the streets running into the square
were also bordered with palms, which seemed to be common in
this region, the rows of trees served a double purpose. They
gave shade by day, and at night shed light from electric lamps
which hung from them like enormous glass fruits. This was the
first detail which Kingscourt pointed out enthusiastically. Then
he proceeded to ask many questions about the great edifices
that surrounded the square. David replied that they housed
colonial banks and the branch offices of European shipping
companies. It was for that reason that the square was called
"The Place of the Nations." The name was apt not only because
the buildings were devoted to international commerce, but
because the "Place of the Nations" was thronged with people
from all parts of the world. Brilliant Oriental robes mingled
with the sober costumes of the Occident, but the latter
predominated. There were many Chinese, Persians and Arabs
in the streets, but the city itself seemed thoroughly European.
One might easily imagine himself in some Italian port. The
brilliant blue of sky and sea was reminiscent of the Riviera, but
the buildings were much cleaner and more modern. The traffic,
though lively, was far less noisy. The quiet was due partly to
the dignified behavior of the many Orientals, but also to the

73

absence of draught animals from the streets. There was no hoof beat of horses, no crackling of whips, no rumbling of wheels. The pavements were as smooth as the footways. Automobiles speeded noiselessly by on rubber tires, with only occasional toots of warning. An overhead rumbling caused the travelers to glance upward.

"All the Devils!" shouted Kingscourt. "What's that?" He pointed to a large iron car running along the tops of the palms, whose passengers were looking down into the street. The wheels of the car were not underneath, but on its roof; it moved along a powerful iron rail.

"An electric overhead train," explained Littwak. "You must have seen them in Europe."

"We have not been in Europe for twenty years."

"Overhead trains are nothing new. There was one running between Barmen and Elberfeld in the 1890's. We installed them as soon as we rebuilt our cities, because they make street traffic safer and easier. Besides, they cost less to build than elevated or surface lines."

"I beg your pardon!" cried Kingscourt. "You speak of cities! Are there more cities like this in Palestine?"

"Don't you know that, gentlemen?"

"No, we don't," replied Friedrich. "We know neither that nor anything else. We know nothing at all. We have been dead for twenty years."

74

"And, indeed, dear Dr. Loewenberg, we thought you dead," said Littwak, pressing his hand.

"Did you inquire about me? And how do you happen to know my name? I don't remember telling it to you at the time."

"We were disconsolate when you withdrew from our thanks. Thinking you might be a regular patron of the Cafe Birkenreis, I waited for you many nights in the doorway. My father too."

"Is your father still alive?"

"Yes, thank heaven, and my mother too. And Miriam, whom you saw as a baby. ...Finally, it occurred to me to describe you to the waiter. He recognized my description, and told me your name. Imagine my grief, however, when the man added that you had been killed in a mountain accident. The newspapers reported your death. I can tell you, Dr. Loewenberg, we grieved much for you. We have always lighted the yahrzeit lamp on the date I found in the papers."

"Jahrzeit?" asked Kingscourt. "What's that?"

"A Jewish custom," explained Friedrich. "Relatives of deceased persons light candles or lamps on the death anniversaries."

"Oh, I have much to tell you, dear Dr. Loewenberg, very much indeed," said Littwak. "But we must not stand here. You will come with me. My house is your home now, gentlemen."

"And our yacht?"

Littwak turned to the liveried negro who had followed him, and instructed him briefly in a low tone. The servant disappeared, and David turned to his guests. "It's all arranged. The boat will go back to your yacht, and your bags will be brought up to Friedrichsheim."

"To-?"

"To Friedrichsheim, my home. You will guess in whose honor it was named. Come, gentlemen, we are driving up."

For all his cordiality, there was something decisive in the young man's tone. "Fritze, he takes over the command," murmured Kingscourt not unappreciatively.

Littwak signaled to an automobile, and asked his guests to be seated. He was about to follow them into the machine when someone called him. "Mr. Littwak! Mr. Littwak!"

He turned. "Ah, it's yours. What do you wish?"

"There was a notice in the morning papers that you were to speak in Acco today. Is that correct?" "I was on my way there, but I shall have to be excused. I have something more important on hand today. Oh, I must telephone at once."

"May I do it for you, Mr. Littwak?"

"If you will be so kind."

"You seem to have distinguished visitors," probed the curious one, pointing backward at the car with his thumb over his left shoulder.

David smiled, but did not reply. He called to the driver at the rear of the car: "Friedrichsheim!"

"That's a familiar face," said Friedrich, as the machine started. "I must have seen it somewhere, but without those gray mutton chop whiskers, and without the eye-glasses."

"Yes, he's from Vienna, too. I've often made him tell me about you. But I did not care to become involved with him just now. Today you belong to me alone. He also was a patron of the Cafe Birkenreis."

Friedrich's memory responded in a flash. "Schiffmann!" he cried laughingly. "So he's here too!" "He and many, many other Jews from all parts of the world," replied Littwak.

Kingscourt, who had been looking curiously in every direction, interposed a question. " Do you mean to say that the Return of the Jews to Palestine is taking place?"

"I certainly do mean to say so."

"Thunder and glory!" shouted the old man. They drove you out of Europe!"

"No," smiled Littwak. "You must not imagine a medieval expulsion. It did not take that form-not, at least, in the more progressive countries. On the whole, it was a bloodless operation. At the end of the nineteenth century and at the beginning of the twentieth, life was made intolerable for us Jews."

"Aha! Spewed you out, did they?"

"The persecutions were social and economic. Jewish merchants were boycotted, Jewish workingmen starved out, Jewish professional men proscribed-not to mention the subtle moral suffering to which a sensitive Jew was exposed at the turn of the century. Jew-hatred employed its newest as well as its oldest devices. The blood myth was revived; and at the same time, the Jews were accused of poisoning the press, as in the Middle Ages they had been accused of poisoning the wells. As workingmen, the Jews were hated by their Christian fellows for undercutting the wage standards. As business men, they were dubbed profiteers. Whether Jews were rich or poor or middle-class, they were hated just the same. They were criticized for enriching themselves, and they were criticized for spending money. They were neither to produce nor to consume. They were forced out of government posts. The law courts were prejudiced against them. They were humiliated everywhere in civil life. It became clear that, in the circumstances, they must either become the deadly enemies of a society that was so unjust to them, or seek out a refuge for themselves. The latter course was taken, and here we are. We have saved ourselves."

"Old-New-Land!" murmured Friedrich.

"Indeed, it is just that," replied Littwak earnestly. He was evidently moved.. "We have set up a New Society on our precious old soil. Our system will be explained to you, gentlemen."

"The Devil! That's all frightfully interesting. There's a tremendous amount to be seen here. ...I didn't want to interrupt your brief against that old Europe, and so didn't ask you about some of the buildings we passed."

"I shall show you everything."

"Now listen to me, esteemed man and Jew, must anticipate with a confession. Otherwise, you may repent your attentions to me. I am not a Jew. Now that you know, will you throw me out, or just disgorge me gently? What?"

"Oh, I say, Kingscourti deprecated Friedrich.

"I guessed from one of your first questions," replied Littwak calmly, "that you were not a Jew. Let me tell you, then, that my associates and I make no distinctions between one man and another. We do not ask to what race or religion a man belongs. If he is a man, that is enough for us."

"Bombs and howitzers! And do all the inhabitants of this region think so?"

"I did not say that," Littwak admitted frankly. "There are other views among us as well." "Aha I thought so at once, esteemed lover of humanity."

"I shall not bore you now with our political controversies. They are the same here as everywhere else in the world. But I can tell you that the fundamental principles of humanitarianism are generally accepted among us. As far as religion goes, you will find Christian, Mohammedan, Buddhist, and Brahmin houses of worship near our own synagogues. To be sure, Buddhists and Brahmins are found only in the port cities. Here in Haifa, for example, in Tyre, Sidon and also in the cities along the railway to the Euphrates-say Damascus and Tadmor."

"Tadmor!" cried Friedrich. "Has Palmyra been restored?"

David nodded. "But only in Jerusalem will you enjoy the universal peace of God."

"My head! My head!" groaned Kingscourt. "How is a person to grasp all this at once?"

They had reached a cross-road where the heavy traffic caused a momentary halt. Their automobile had to wait. Now they realized the advantages of the overhead railway. The great cages went whizzing past on their thick, double' iron rails. They neither interfered with the pedestrian traffic, nor were impeded by it.

From the vantage point of their enforced halt, they looked up several streets, in which the architecture was fascinatingly varied. The dwelling houses for the most part were small and charming, intended for only one family like those in the Belgian cities. The public and commercial buildings, which could easily be recognized, seemed all the more imposing by contrast. Littwak pointed out several as they passed-the Marine Department, the Department of Commerce, the Employment Department, the Department of Education, the Department of Electricity. A large, handsome edifice, with a frescoed loggia in its facade, caught their attention.

"That is the Building Department," explained Littwak. "The headquarters of Steineck, our chief architect. He made the city plans."

"That man had a large task," remarked Friedrich.

"Yes, indeed, but a very grateful one," replied Littwak. "Like
the rest of us, he had abundant material from which to create.
Never in history were cities built so quickly or so well, because
never before were so many technical facilities available. By the
end of the nineteenth century humanity had already achieved a
high degree of technical skill. We merely had to transplant
existing inventions to this country. I shall tell you how it all
happened another time."

They were now in a residential section of the city, upon Mount
Carmel, where there were many elegant mansions surrounded
by fragrant gardens. Several houses of Moorish design had
close wooden lattices over some of their windows. David
anticipated their question, saying that these were the homes of
prominent Moslems. "There's my friend Reschid Bey," he
added.

A handsome man of thirty-five was standing beside a wrought
iron gate as they drove by. He wore dark European clothing
and a red fez. His salute to them was the Oriental gesture
which signifies lifting and kissing the dust. David called to him
in Arabic, and Reschid replied in German-with a slight
northern accent. "Wish you much joy of your guests!"

Kingscourt stared. "Who's the little Muslim?" he asked. "He
studied in Berlin," replied David laughingly. "His father was
among the first to understand the beneficent character of the
Jewish immigration, and enriched himself, because he kept
pace with our economic progress. Reschid himself is a member
of our New Society."

"The New Society?" repeated Friedrich. "What's that?"

"Dearly beloved," added Kingscourt, turning to David. "You must instruct us like newborn calves in all that's worth knowing. We know neither the old nor the new society."

"Oh, but," replied Littwak, "you know the old order, or you did know it. I shall explain our New Society to you at our leisure. Now there is no more time. In a moment we shall arrive at the house which is henceforth to be your home."

The serpentine road opened wider and wider prospects. Now the city and harbor of Haifa lay before the entranced eyes of the travelers. On the near side the broad bay with its zone of gardens; beyond, Acco with its background of mountains. They were on the summit of the northern ridge of the Carmel. To the right and to the left, to the north and to the south, a magnificent expanse lay spread out before them. The sea glittered blue and gold into an infinite horizon. White-capped waves fluttered over it like gulls toward the light brown strand. David ordered the driver to stop the car so that they might enjoy the unique view. As they alighted, he turned to Freidrich. "See, Dr. Loewenberg, this is the land of our fathers."

Friedrich did not know why his eyes grew warm with tears at the young man's simple words. This was an altogether different mood from that of the night in Jerusalem twenty years before. He had looked then upon moonlit Death; now, Life sparkled joyously in the sun. He looked at David. So this was the Jewboy beggar! A free, healthy, cultured man who gazed steadfastly upon the world and seemed to stand firmly in his shoes. David had barely referred to his own circumstances in

**82**

life; he could hardly be poor, though, if he lived in this district of villas and mansions. He seemed to be a prominent citizen, too. On the drive many people had greeted him in the streets. Even elderly men had been the first to bow. Here he stood on the heights of the Carmel, an expression of profound joy upon his features as he gazed out over land and sea. Only now did it seem to Friedrich that he could recognize in the upstanding man before him the remarkable boy of the Brigittenauer Laende in Vienna, who once upon a time had said that he would return to the Land of Israel.

# Theodor Herzl

## Chapter III

Friedrichsheim was a large, pleasant mansion in the Moorish style, set in gardens. Before the entrance lay a stone lion. The cry of the little son of the peddler echoed back to Friedrich through the years. "What Judah once had, that he can have again! Our old God still lives!" And the dream had been fulfilled.

The gatekeeper rang a bell to announce David's arrival. Two footmen awaited them on the steps.

"Have Mrs. Littwak and Miss Miriam meet me downstairs in the drawing room, please," said David to one of the servants. The man hurried up the carpeted stairway of the great hall. The second servant opened the door of the drawing room for them. They entered a high-vaulted room containing magnificent works of art. Rose-colored silk covered the walls. The furniture was of the delicate English style. From the ceiling hung a shimmering electric chandelier of crystal and gold. Plate glass panes let in full daylight through a French door and four windows. The room overlooked a flower-covered parterre with a marble parapet, behind which one caught glimpses of the sapphire blue sea. At either side of the main doorway of the drawing room stood silver candelabra of a man's height. A large portrait of an elderly man and wife in simple, dark clothing hung in a narrow panel.

"My parents!" said David, seeing Friedrich glance at the portrait. "I should certainly not have recognized them," smiled

**85**

Friedrich. "And who is this?" He pointed to a painting over the great chimney place which portrayed a slender, black-haired young woman of great beauty.

"My sister Miriam. You will judge for yourself in a moment whether it is a good likeness of her." Miriam entered with David's wife, a blooming young matron.

"Sarah! Miriam!" cried David, his voice breaking. "We have most welcome, most unexpected visitors. This day has brought me the greatest happiness of my life. You will never guess, never imagine whom we have the good fortune to entertain. Him we thought dead: our benefactor, our savior!'"

The young women looked bewildered. "But not Friedrich Loewenberg?" questioned the girl. "Even he, Miriam., even he! Here he stands before you!"

She hurried toward Friedrich with outstretched hands, greeting him joyously like an old friend.

He felt strangely moved at hearing his name pronounced in her charming voice. These delightful new people, the magnificent surroundings, threw a spell over him.

"And this gentleman is Mr. Kingscourt, Dr. Loewenberg's friend; therefore our own friend and guest." David told them briefly how he had spied the gentlemen at the quay, and at once recognized Friedrich. As a little boy he had deeply impressed the features of the friend in need upon his mind. Moreover, Friedrich had really changed but little. Of course he could not permit these gentlemen to go to a hotel. They must be his guests.

**86**

Sarah wished to have the visitors shown to their rooms immediately, but David undertook to escort them himself. "Let us go upstairs," he said. "I want to present to you a young man who bears the not uncommon name (in our home) of Friedrich."

The whole party went up to the first landing, David leading the way. He stopped before a door at the end of the corridor. "This is where the individual makes his habitat," he said with a happy smile as he opened the door.

In the center of a white room, a round-faced baby sat enthroned on a high chair. He had worked off his shoes with his feet, and was now ridding himself of his socks by patiently rubbing his toes against his fat little calves. An elderly nurse stood before him with a bowl of milk porridge. The child beat the mixture merrily with his Spoon. Playing with the food seemed to him much more important than eating it.

"This blockhead is my son Friedrich," cried David. For the first time something like pride rang in his voice.

Young Friedrich let his spoon drop. Kingscourt's white beard had fascinated him. He crowed loudly, and reached out his little arms to the old man. Kingscourt held out his index finger, and the little fellow gripped it.

The others started to leave the room, but Kingscourt stood as if rooted. Friedrich turned at the door and called, "Aren't you coming, Kingscourt?"

"This fellow won't let me go," replied the flattered Kingscourt. And he remained in the nursery for a whole hour.

From that moment dated the friendship between the old misanthrope and the youngest Littwak. What they talked about no one knew, because little Friedrich had not yet learned to speak, and Kingscourt, with the most violent oaths, denied any love whatever for the child. But it leaked out through the servants that Kingscourt often sidled into the nursery when he knew no one would be there, and played the silliest pranks. He would set the child astride on his shoulder, or lie flat on the floor so that he might crawl over him safely. When the baby cried, Kingscourt performed the most amazing dances to entertain him, and sang antiquated German songs in a hoarse voice that he tried to soften. On the very first day of his acquaintance with the little one, Kingscourt seemed rather distraught. at the luncheon table; but with so much to ask and to tell about, his sudden weakness for Fritzchen went unnoticed for the moment.

A delicious luncheon was served in the paneled dining room. Kingscourt was especially taken with the wines. They were all Palestinian, he was told, some of them from David's own vineyards. The first Jewish villages, established in the early 1880's, had, as a matter of fact, begun with viniculture. The best .varieties of grape had been introduced into Palestine, and flourished.

Miriam excused herself before the end of the meal. She had to go to her class. After she had left the room, David replied to a question which Friedrich asked about her. "Yes, Miriam is a teacher at the girls' high school. Her subjects are French and English."

"So the poor girl has to drudge at giving lessons," growled Kingscourt.

David laughingly took up the implied reproach. "She does not do it for a livelihood. I don't have to let my sister starve, thank Heaven. But she has duties and performs them, because she also has rights. In our New Society the women have equal rights with the men."

"All the Devils!"

"They have active and passive suffrage as a matter of course. They worked faithfully beside us during the reconstruction period. Their enthusiasm lent wings to the men's courage. It would have been the blackest ingratitude if we had relegated them to the servants' hall or to a harem."

"You told us on our way here," interrupted Friedrich, "that Reschid Bey is also a member of your Society. Your mention of harems reminds me of a question."

"Which I can guess. No one is obliged to join the New Society. And those who do join are not compelled to exercise their rights. They do as they please. In your own day you must have known men in Europe who were not interested in elections, who never took the trouble to vote, and who could not by any means have been persuaded to take office. So it is with our women and their rights. Don't imagine that our women are not devoted to their homes. My wife, for instance, never goes to meetings."

Sarah smiled. "But that's only because of Fritzchen."

Kingscourt, losing himself for a moment in a vision of the nursery, murmured absently, "I can understand that."

"Yes," continued David, "she nursed our little boy, and so forgot a bit about her inalienable rights. She used to belong to the radical opposition. That is how I met her, as an opponent. Now she opposes me only at home, as loyally as you can imagine, however."

"That's a damned good way of overcoming an opposition," boomed Kingscourt approvingly. "It simplifies politics tremendously."

David proceeded with his explanations. "I must make it clear to you, gentlemen, that our women are too sensible to let public affairs interfere with their personal well-being. It is a common human trait-not only a feminine one-not to concern ourselves with things we already possess. The way was paved for our women during the last century. In some countries women had been granted the suffrage, both active and passive, in representative local bodies and professional organizations. They showed themselves clever and able. They wasted no more time than the men, and talked no more foolishly. There was-really no point at all in letting all this valuable experience go to waste.... For the rest, politics here is neither a business nor a profession, for either men or women. We have kept ourselves unsullied by that plague. People who try to live by spouting their opinions instead of by work are soon recognized for what they are. They are despised, and get no chance to do mischief. Our courts have repeatedly ruled in slander suits that the term 'professional politician' is an insult. That fact speaks for itself."

"But how do you fill your public offices?" asked Friedrich. "Judging by the public buildings you pointed out to us, we must infer that there are officials here."

"Certainly. We have both salaried and honorary positions. But the salaried positions are allotted for skill and merit only. There is a healthy prejudice against partisans of any kind whatever. Paid officials are not allowed to take part in public discussion. But it is quite different with the honorary officials. For filling the honorary positions we have one simple principle: Those who try to push themselves are gently ignored; while, on the other hand we take great pains to discover real merit in the most obscure nooks. We thus make certain that our precious commonwealth will not become the prey of careerists. Our president, for example, is a venerable Russian oculist. He accepted office most unwillingly, because he was obliged to give up his practice."

"Was it so lucrative?" asked Kingscourt.

"Not at all. He worked mostly among the poor. He turned his practice over to his daughter, who is also a prominent physician. She now heads their great eye clinic. A fine woman, who has never married, and devotes her skill to the sick poor. She is a good example of how a sensible society uses the old maids, the single women who used to be sneered at or looked upon as a burden. Here they find their own salvation and that of others. Our whole department of public charities is conducted by ladies of that type.

"In philanthropy, too, we have created nothing new. We have merely systematized the old facilities, centralized them properly. Hospitals, infirmaries, orphan asylums, vacation

**91**

camps, public kitchens-in short, all the types of benevolent institutions with which you were familiar have been merged here and placed under a unified administration. We are thus able to care for every sick and needy applicant. There are fewer demands on public charity here because conditions-I have the right to say so-are better on the whole. But there are poor among us, because we have not been able to change human nature. Here, too, people are brought low by their own vices or lack of responsibility or misfortune-deserved or undeserved. We give medical aid to the sick, and find work for the well...As I said before, we have discovered no new devices in philanthropy. Merely used and developed what already existed. You must have been familiar with the old institutions for aiding people through work and with employment exchanges. Here, everyone has the right to work and therefore to bread. This also implies the duty to work. Beggary is not tolerated. Healthy persons caught begging are sentenced to hard labor. The needy sick have only to apply to the public charities. No one is turned away: The various hospitals are connected with the charity headquarters by telephone. By taking thought in due season, we obviate any lack of beds. We should be ashamed to send a patient from one hospital to the other as used to be done in the old days. If one hospital is full, an ambulance in its courtyard will at once take an applicant to another where beds are available."

"But all that must be very expensive," remarked Friedrich.

"No. You must keep in mind the fact that systematic planning makes everything more economical. The old society was rich enough at the beginning of this century, but it suffered from ineffable confusion. It was like a crowded treasure-house where you could not find a spoon when you needed one. Those

**92**

people were no worse and no more stupid than we. Or, if you like, we are neither better nor cleverer than they. Our success in social experiment is due to another cause. We established our Society without inherited drawbacks. We did indeed bind ourselves to the past, as we were bound to do-there was the old soil, the ancient people; but we rejuvenated the institutions. Nations with unbroken histories have to carry burdens assumed by their ancestors. Not we. The administration of any state you may have been familiar with will be an example of what I mean. Interest and amortization charges on very old debts were an enormous item. There were but two alternatives: either to go into dishonorable bankruptcy or to drag along with the heavy old burdens. The New Society was better off to begin with. I shall prove this to you in detail later on.

"For the moment, I wish merely to answer your question about the cost of our public charities. Even though they are adequate to all the demands for efficient service to the sick and the needy, our institutions are far cheaper than those of the old order. Buildings and equipment are paid for, now as then, out of public funds-in so far as synagogue offerings and bequests do not suffice. Personnel is provided for through a system of membership service. All members of the New Society, men and women alike, are obligated to give two years to the service of the community. The usual thing is to give the two years between eighteen and twenty-after completing their studies. (I want to add, by the way, that education is free to the children of our members from the kindergarten through the university.) In this two-year-service period we have an exhaustless reservoir of assistants for those institutions whose social usefulness is generally acknowledged. Such institutions are directed by paid officials."

"I understand," said Friedrich. "Your army consists of professional officers and volunteers."

"I accept the analogy," replied David, "but it is merely an analogy. There is no army in the New Society."

"Woe's me!" jeered Kingscourt.

David smiled. "What would you have, Mr. Kingscourt? Nothing on earth is perfect, not even our New Society. We have no state, like the Europeans of your time. We are merely a society of citizens seeking to enjoy life through work and culture. We content ourselves with making our young people physically fit. We develop their bodies as well as their minds. We find athletic and rifle clubs sufficient for this purpose, even as they were thought sufficient in Switzerland. We also have competitive games -cricket, football, rowing-like the English. We took tried and tested things, and tested them allover again. Jewish children used to be pale, weak, timid. Now look at them! The explanation of this miracle is the simplest in the world. We took our children out of damp cellars and hovels, and brought them into the sunlight. Plants cannot thrive without sun. No more can human beings. Plants can be saved by transplantation into congenial soil. Human beings as well. That is how it happened!"

"When I listen to you," remarked Friedrich meditatively -"and what we have already seen and expect to see confirms what you say-I might be ready to believe this thing real, and not a Utopia. And yet there's something missing.

"I begin to grasp the meaning and scope of your New Society," he continued. "That does not puzzle me. It is something else. I admit that what you have shown us ought not to seem strange, since we saw all these things in Europe-even though in sporadic and unharmonious forms. But though I see, hear and touch your social order, I still cannot understand how it came into being...How shall I put it? I understand the new order perfectly as far as I am acquainted with it. But I do not understand how it was born. The transition from the old order to the new is what escapes me. Had I been born into the world today, I should have accepted it just as I accepted the world I was actually born into. Granted that even then I should have thought much of it wonderful if I had suddenly looked at it with the eyes of a twenty years' absentee. Had we, for instance, been away from the world from 1880 to 1900, electric light, the telephone, transmission of electric power by wire would have been even more overwhelming. You show us nothing new in the technical sense, and yet I seem to be dreaming. The point of transition is lacking."

"I shall show you that as well," replied David. "I shall tell you my own story, in which you yourself played so large a role. But not now. You must be tired from the trip. First of all you must rest, and this evening, should you be so inclined, we shall go to the opera. Or to the theater to the German, English, French, Italian or Spanish theater."

"Schwerenot!" shouted Kingscourt. "Is all that here? Just as it was in America in my time. They used to have theatrical companies from everywhere. But that you should have it here..."

"Is certainly not surprising," completed David. "The distance from Europe to Palestine is much less than to America. And the journey is more convenient for people who are afraid of

**95**

seasickness, since they can come all the way by rail. The network of railways begun in the nineteenth century in Asia Minor was completed long ago. Trains run now to Damascus, Jerusalem and Bagdad. Since the railroad bridge over the Bosphorus was finished, it is possible to travel directly, without change of cars, from Saint Petersburg or Odessa, from Berlin or Vienna, from Amsterdam, Calais, Paris, Madrid or Lisbon to Jerusalem. The great European express lines all connect with the Jerusalem line, just as the Palestinian railways in turn link up with Egypt and Northern Africa. The north-to south African railway (in which the German emperor was interested as long ago as the 1890's) and the Siberian railway to the Chinese border, complete the railway system of the Old World. We are at an excellent junction in that system."

"Devil take it, that's funny!"

"Railways are certainly not new to you, Mr. Kingscourt. There was nothing experimental about it. The Russian Chinese railway was already complete twenty years ago, the Bagdad line was under construction, and the Cape-to Cairo line projected. Palestine, lying at the exact geographical center of traffic between Europe, Asia, and Africa, could hardly have been left out any longer."

"My dear host, that is not what surprises me. But-may I say so-I am surprised that you Jews should have done it. You don't mind?"

"Only we Jews could have done it," replied David calmly. "We only....We only were in a position to create this New Society, this new center of civilization here. One thing dovetailed into another. It could have come only through us, through our destiny. Our moral sufferings were as much a necessary element as our commercial experience and our cosmopolitanism. But enough of this for today. Rest now, and we shall see about entertainment later. Tomorrow, in Tiberias, I shall tell you more.

# Theodor Herzl

## Chapter IV

They could not think now of rushing off to Europe immediately. However, Friedrich felt in duty bound to suggest to Kingscourt that they leave Palestine: The old man could hardly be expected to concern himself with the Jewish destiny. But Kingscourt swore he would stay as long as they would have him. All this was damned interesting; and if Dr. Friedrich Loewenberg no longer cared for his own nation, he, Kingscourt, wasn't that kind of a monster.

When the captain of the yacht presented himself for instructions, he was therefore told to send up a supply of clothing to Friedrichsheim, and to give the crew a holiday.

The guest rooms to which they' had been assisted adjoined one another. Kingscourt in his shirt-sleeves, stood in the connecting doorway, commenting with vigorous gestures on everything they had heard and seen. Friedrich reclined in an easy chair and gazed dreamily out through the open balcony door over the Mediterranean. No more delightful place of sojourn than this could he imagine. What splendid people his hosts were. And how easily they moved in all this high, free affluence. David-cheerful, energetic, self-confident, and yet modest. His wife a picture of happy young motherhood. This splendid girl Miriam, who was devoting herself to much more serious duties than the daughters of wealthy Jewish comes in his day would have dreamed of. For the first time in many years Ernestine Loeffler came into his mind. How madly he had loved her, and how easy she had made it for him to say good-by to the world.

Would Miriam be capable of making a marriage like Ernestine's? Amusing thought. Queer it should have occurred to him. No, this girl was a different sort. These people were different from that odious Loeffier set. Who knows would it not have been better, more manly, more dignified, to have striven and struggled than to have run away?

"Kingscourt," he sighed out loud, "I am asking myself whether we did not sheer a false course when we made for our blessed isle yonder? How did we spend twenty beautiful years? Hunting and fishing, eating, drinking and sleeping, playing chess. "

"And with an old donkey, what?" growled Kingscourt, whose feelings were hurt.

"Drop the 'old donkey' stuff," laughed Friedrich. "I could not and would not live without you any more. But, for all that, it's a pity not to have been more useful. Here's the world come along a big stretch, without one's having had any part or achievement in it all."

"Oh, that! Here the man went to my school for twenty years, and still entertains such thoughts! Say right out that you want to join this New Society!"

"I don't say that because I still do not know it well enough. It does, however, seem less repulsive than the old order."

"Less repulsive! Less repulsive!" jeered the old man. "Go right ahead and join this pure society. I can go on alone under my own steam. You'll see how well I'll get along by myself."

"Oh, I say, Kingscourt, don't get excited. I shall remain here as long and no longer than you do yourself.'"

"Is that a promise?"

"My word of honor....and I shall not join David's society unless..."

"Unless what?"

Friedrich smiled at his own thought. "Unless you also join it."

It was long since Kingscourt had laughed so uproariously. "Ha! Ha! Ha! Fritze, what silly-billy notions you have. Oh, hot ha ha ha! Don't you see me a member of a Jewish society? Me, Adalbert von Koenighoff, a royal Prussian officer and Christian German nobleman! No, Fritze, that's too good, too good!"

"The junker speaks!"

"Now he's piqued. You're an exception in my eyes. One's none."

"And what is your objection to David Littwak?"

"None so far. Seems a strapping fine fellow."

They were interrupted by the host himself, who came to inquire their wishes for the evening. Did they prefer a play or a concert? He placed a newspaper with amusement notices before them.

Kingscourt pointed to the paper without looking at it. "Do so many lies still grow in the world?"

"Only as many as the readers want," retorted David. "A vast number, then," grinned Kingscourt.

"It depends. On the whole, the co-operative papers are truthful and decent."

"What kind of papers?"

"The co-operative ones. The press naturally had to be co-operative in our mutualistic economic order."

"Halt! Halt!" cried Kingscourt. "Not so fast, please! Under what kind of economic order do you live?"

"A mutualistic order. But please don't imagine a system of cast-iron rules, rigid principles, or anything stiff or hard or doctrinaire. It is only a simple, flexible modus operandi.

It too already existed in your day like everything else you see here. All kinds of industrial and commercial co-operative societies were then in existence; and you will find all kinds operating effectively here. The whole merit of our New Society is merely that it fostered the creation and development of the co-operatives by providing credits, and-what was even more important-by educating the masses to make use of them. Economic science had long ago recognized the significance of the co-operatives. But, in practical life, they succeeded-when they did succeed by accident and with much difficulty. Their members were usually too poor to hold out until the inevitable success could be achieved. And all the while they had to be

fighting the covert or open opposition of the threatened
interests. Provision merchants were not of course happy over
the advent of the consumers' co-operatives. The cabinetmakers'
co-operatives were no joy to the furniture manufacturers, and
so on. The combined power of habit, friction, and the
inhibitions imposed by old customs worked against the
formation of the co-operatives. And yet their method provides
the mean between individualism and collectivism. The
individual is not deprived of the stimulus and pleasures of
private property, while, at the same time, he is able, through
union with his fellows, to resist capitalist domination. The
plague, yes, the curse of the poor has been removed-they no
longer earn less as producers and pay more as consumers than
the rich. Here the bread of the poor is as cheap as the bread of
the rich. There are no speculators in the necessaries of life. You
know how in the co-operative method has, indeed, become one
of the strongest motives in the new Palestinian colonization,
due chiefly to the efforts of the organized labor movement. It is
much more developed in agriculture, however, than in industry
or commerce the old days they used to ruin hundreds of
thousands of people through their practices. Nor did we allow
the old type of small tradesman to come into existence, but
established consumers' co-operatives at the very beginning of
our enterprise. There you have another example of the
advantages of our freedom from inherited burdens. We did not
have to ruin anyone in order to ease the lot of our masses."

"But what about the newspapers?" asked Friedrich. "We were
speaking of them. How can they be organized cooperatively?
Do they belong to the editors-or how else is it done?"

"Very simply. The co-operative newspaper belongs to its
subscribers. Their investment is limited to the amount of their

**103**

subscription; and they are not liable beyond that. The larger the circulation of a paper, the greater, of course, its income from advertisements, announcements, etc. These profits belong to the readers-to the subscribers, rather. They are reimbursed for the cost of their subscription from the annual profits. When business is very good they receive one hundred per cent on their investment. Sometimes even more."

"Incredible! Marvelous!" shouted Kingscourt. "They actually pay you a bonus for reading the papers!"

"Did you never hear what incomes the great newspapers used to have? Though their salary lists and cable tolls were very heavy and always growing, they constantly reduced their subscription price. The largest papers were sold at less than the cost of production, and yet the profits of the publishers were always on the increase. The principle of reimbursement to the subscribers out of profits was already implied in that situation. You will find the same thing here, except that the lion's share of the owners is divided among the members of the co-operative newspaper enterprise.

"The editorial staff of the newspaper is also its business department, and you may be assured that these highly trained workers-whose labors alone make the printed page worth the reading-are better off now than formerly. It is they who earn the money for the subscribers, and even the man in the street realizes that. Our papers work Unceasingly to broaden the education of the public. They instruct, but they also entertain. And they serve the practical needs of business no less than the ideal ones of art and science. Our journalists nowadays work in a very different spirit, knowing that their services to the public are recognized and appreciated. And how very seriously they

**104**

take their duties-since the responsibility for the policy of the paper rests now directly upon themselves."

"That sounds alluring," interjected Friedrich, "but it seems to me that the co-operative newspapers must be slavishly subject to the moods of the public. Being entirely dependent for their livelihood upon their readers, the editors must try to be complaisant, to flatter the public, to pander to its passions."

"And if that were the case," replied David, "would it be anything new? Didn't just those things happen in the old days? Were there not editors who kept their ears close to the ground, who suppressed this and exaggerated that in accordance with what they thought their readers wanted? And, at that, they could never be sure of hitting the mark. It is different here. At their annual meetings, the newspaper co-operatives not only render reports, but the organized reading public lays down the lines of the policy for the following year."

"Horrible'" cried Kingscourt. "Meetings with a hundred thousand subscribers!"

"What are you thinking of, Mr. Kingscourt? The subscribers elect one or two hundred representatives. The procedure is simple. Candidates announce their desire to stand for election in the newspapers themselves. Each subscription slip has a coupon attached which serves as a ballot. Five hundred or a thousand votes are cast for one delegate to the annual meeting. Candidates announce themselves in some such formula as this: 'I desire to advocate this or that policy at the general meeting. Those who favor it are asked to vote for me.' "

"Very good," replied Friedrich. "The public receives ample accounting, then. But I still do not see that this serves the public good on the whole. New ideas and new movements are rarely understood at first. You might as well ask children whether they wish to study as inquire of the public whether it desires to have its views broadened or improved your public opinion co-operative must necessarily debase the popular intelligence to the extreme. I mean to say that it is bound to turn the thoughts of the people either toward reaction or toward revolution. They will be deaf to the value of new things or blind to the value of old ones. The benefits of spiritual leadership, which can come only from gifted individuals, are lost to you."

"You did not allow me to finish, Dr. Loewenberg. I did not say that the co-operative newspaper is the only form known here. The co-operative society merely succeeded the old newspaper enterprises which, when you consider the amount of their invested capital, their expensive technical equipment, and the high cost of news-getting, were really very large industrial undertakings.

"But we also have newspapers founded and conducted by private individuals. I myself have such a newspaper, which I need in a struggle I am carrying on in the New Society. My chief Opponent, Rabbi Dr. Geyer, has a paper of his own also. I shall not keep my paper going after the campaign is over, but he will probably do otherwise, since he lives by these bickerings. There are several other privately owned newspapers, recognized as such, which serve various purposes. If a new tendency or a creative spirit appears among us, every opportunity exists for influencing public opinion. Men have to fight hard for their convictions here just as they used to do

**106**

elsewhere. They must be steadfast, courageous, persevering in defending them. And that is not bad. Believe me, gentlemen, our mutualism has not made us the poorer in strong personalities; the richer, if anything. Here the individual is neither ground between the millstones of capitalism, nor decapitated by socialistic leveling. We recognize and respect the importance of the individual, just as we respect and protect the private progeny which is his economic foundation."

"Thank Heaven for that," commented Kingscourt. "I thought you had abolished the difference between mine and thine."

"If we had, nothing of what you have seen and are to see here would have come into being," returned David. "No, we were not so mad as all that. We did not abolish the spur to work and effort, discovery and invention. Talent must have its due reward; effort as well. We need wealth so that we may tempt the ambitious and nurture unusual talent.

"I myself am a member of the well-to-do class. I am a ship-owner. My business is the type which, now as formerly, can be conducted successfully either by individuals or by stock corporations. It is the great merit of mutualism that it does not exclude either the creation or the continuance of new economic forms.

"In my firm, for instance, you will see an interesting example of a mixed form. I am the owner. My employees have a co-operative society which, with my approval and encouragement, is becoming more and more independent of me. At first they had only a consumers' co-operative society, but later they expanded it to include a savings fund. You must remember that our workingmen, as members of the New Society, are

**107**

automatically insured against accidents, illness, old age, and death. Their savings-capacity is therefore not split up by provision for these contingencies.

"I have voluntarily made over a share of the firm's profits to the savings fund of my employees. I did not do this out of magnanimity, but for selfish reasons. By this method of profit-sharing, I not only ensured their continued devotion to the firm, but created for myself a favorable opportunity for selling the enterprise when I should get ready to retire. I shall then turn the business into a stock company, having already granted a purchasing option upon it to my employees' savings fund at a moderate rate of interest. We have no differences over wages or anything else. It is, if you choose to call it so, a patriarchal relation, but one expressed in ultra-modern forms. If a demagogue were to try to incite my men, I should not need to have him thrown out-they'd simply laugh him out of court, so that he'd be glad to run away. They know what they are about, and there's an end to all vague socialistic notions." "You're still a young man," boomed Kingscourt cordially, "but you've come a damned long way."

"I began early. We were among the first immigrants. Personal merit had nothing to do with it, or very little. I was swept along with the general tide of prosperity. But I want to tell you about that only when we get to Tiberias."

"Why Tiberias?"

"You will understand when we reach there. You evidently don't know what festival we are to celebrate tomorrow. ...But, now, gentlemen, please make your choice. Or perhaps you'd rather hear the program from an oral newspaper."

**108**

David lifted two receivers from the wall, and handed them to his guests.

Kingscount laughed. "Your Excellencey cannot impress me with .that thing. I know the trick. They had a spoken newspaper like that in Budapest twenty-five years ago."

"I did not intend to show you anything new. By the way, this oral newspaper is also co-operative." "But this one doesn't yield any profits, since it carries no advertisements."

"On the contrary. Its advertisements command the highest rates. The reader of a printed newspaper is not obliged to look at the advertising columns. But he is defenseless against advertisements that come through the receiver. Listen in. You may happen to hear one." They put the receivers to their ears. They were informed about a dock fire in Yokohama, a theatrical premiere in Paris, and the latest quotations on the New York cotton exchange. Then, very clearly enunciated, they heard:

"At Samuel Kohn's...Best grades of diamonds, genuine and artificial Lowest prices guaranteed. At Sa-muel Kohn's, Great Gallery, 47."

They laughed heartily.

"Sometimes," said David, "the wording is so clever that the listener does not suspect that he is listening to an advertisement. This paper yields enormous profits. The subscribers pay one shekel a month for the service, and get back far more than that in profits. There are no expenditures for

**109**

paper, printing, or mailing. However, the municipality of Haifa and the New Society make this enterprise pay them tribute. And representatives of the New Society supervise the 'paper' at its headquarters so that no false or alarmist reports or obscenities may be dictated into the apparatus."

Friedrich was struck by a word which David had used.

"Tribute?" he asked. "How can the Haifa municipality or the New Society (you still have to explain the latter to us) simply make a private enterprise pay them tribute when it is profitable?"

"This is a very special instance. A telephonic newspaper must lay its cables somewhere. Now, under our streets, tunnels have been provided for the reception of all kinds of pipes and cables (present and future) for gas, water, sewage, and so on. This tunnel runs under the pavement, and a section of it branches off into every house. All the houses are fitted with subterranean connections for these cables. We do not have to tear up our pavements every time we wish to installa new utility. You may, if you like, regard this as symbolic of our whole system. Large cities, as you knew them, used to grow up without aim or plan. When illuminating gas, water supply, sewer pipes or electricity were to be installed, the streets had to be eviscerated time after time. No one knew the exact condition of the various services until there was an explosion. When we, however, drew up our plans, we knew just what utilities a modern city required, and therefore laid tunnels under our streets to accommodate them. The original cost of these tunnels was quite high, but they have more than justified themselves. Compare the budget of the Haifa municipality with that of Paris or Vienna, and you will realize how much revenue we derive from our tunnels. Since

**110**

this telephonic newspaper also runs its wires through the street tunnel, it must pay a rental in proportion to its income. This rental accrues to the public treasury."

"The first remarkable thing I've found here," declared Kingscourt, "is that you pave your streets with Samuel Kohn's best diamonds. You're a damned clever lot. I never should have thought of it."

"There's a sting to your compliments, Mr. Kingscourt," replied David in a friendly tone. "But perhaps you'll reverse your judgment when you've been with us for a while."

"Fine! You'll find me quite ready to admit that I'm an old ass. But I do require evidence! ...And now, in the Devil's name, take us to the theater."

"To whichever you choose, dear Littwak."

"Well, gentlemen, since you won't decide, I suggest we leave it to the ladies."

They agreed.

# Theodor Herzl

## Chapter V

The ladies were already in evening dress.

"These gentlemen," said Sarah, "will probably not care to go to plays which they can see as well in London or Berlin or Paris, though, as it happens, there are excellent French and Italian companies in Haifa just now. I should think they would find the Jewish plays more interesting."

"Are there Jewish plays?" queried Friedrich in surprise.

"Haven't you already heard," teased Kingscourt, "that the theater is completely judaized?"

Sarah glanced at the paper. "At the national theater tonight there is a biblical drama called 'Moses.' "

"A noble theme," remarked David.

"But too serious. There's 'Shabbatai levi' at the opera. And at some of the popular theaters there are Yiddish farces. They are amusing, but not in very good taste. I should recommend the opera." Miriam supported her sister-in-law's suggestion, saying that "Sabbatai Levi'" was the best composition of recent years, rich though the period had been in musical creation. But they must hurry. The opera house was half an hour's ride distant.

"Won't it be too late to get tickets?" asked Kingscourt.

**113**

"The box office will probably be sold out by this time," replied David, "because most of the co-operators must have used their subscription tickets. But I have had a box ever since the opera house was built."

"Is the opera also a co-operative society?" cried Friedrich.

"Subscriptions, Fritze. They call it co-operative here. Something like the newspapers."

"Quite the same thing, Mr. Kingscourt," laughed David. "Don't let them bluff you. There's nothing new here. It only seems so." He began to draw on a pair of white gloves.

Gloves! White gloves! Neither Kingscourt nor Friedrich had any. In all the twenty years on their quiet Pacific is land, they had had no use for such fripperies. But now they were back in civilized society, and in the desperate predicament of accompanying ladies to the theater. One must behave like a civilized human being. Kingscourt asked whether they would pass a glove shop on their way to the opera? No, there were no such shops. The old gentleman became peevish.

"Are you teasing me? You're wearing some on your own thumbs. Did you make them yourself? Are you a member of the glovers' co-operative too?"

David cleared up the misunderstanding while the others laughed. There were no special shops for gloves because, like all other articles of clothing, they were sold only in large department stores.

Two autos waited for them before the entrance to the house. Sarah, Miriam and Friedrich entered the first, Kingscourt and David the second. It was a mild southern evening like the soft nights on the Riviera at this season. Below them lay Haifa like a sea of light. In the harbor and the roadstead as far as Acco the lights of the numerous ships were reflected like stars in the mirroring waters.

As they drove past Reschid's house they heard singing in a magnificent female voice.

"She's a friend of ours," said Miriam, "Reschid's wife. She is well bred and well educated. We often see her, but only in her own house. Reschid adheres strictly to the Moslem customs, and that makes it difficult for her to come to us."

"But," added Sarah, "you must not think that that makes Fatma unhappy. Theirs is a very happy marriage. They have charming children. But the wife never leaves her home. Surely, peaceful seclusion is also a form of happiness. I can understand that very well, though I am a full-fledged member of the New Society. If my husband wished it, I should live just as Fatma does and think no more about it."

"I can confirm that," said Miriam, caressing the speaker's hand.

"I understand," said Friedrich thoughtfully. "In your New Society every man may live and be happy in his own way."

"Every man and every woman," said Sarah.

**115**

The travelers found themselves once more in the brightly lighted streets. The autos stopped before a large building with all its windows lighted up.

Was this the opera? No, it was a large bazaar like those in Paris.

"The Bon Marche," cried Kingscourt.

David smiled. "Something of the sort. We have only such bazaars. No small shops at all."

"What" cried Kingscourt. "Have you put all the small tradesmen out of business? Have you killed the poor devils dead?"

"No, indeed. We did not have to kill them, because we simply did not let them be born."

Friedrich, who had been admiring the window displays with the ladies, now asked, "How's that? You prohibited petty trade. Is that your freedom?"

"Everyone is free here, and may do as he chooses," replied David. "We punish only those crimes and misdemeanors which were penalized in enlightened European states. Nothing is forbidden here that was not forbidden there. We do not consider petty trade a misdemeanor, but poor business. That was one of the problems our Society had to solve. It was very important to do so, especially at the beginning, because such large numbers of our people were petty tradesmen. My good father himself-you probably remember, Dr. Loewenberg-earned his poor crust as a peddler. And peddling is certainly the

**116**

most wretched form of petty trade. He used to carry his basket from one cafe to the other."

"One moment, Mr. Littwak!" roared Kingscourt. "I say, you don't seem to be ashamed of it." "I? Far from it. My father suffered torments for my sake.

I should be the last person-" "I like that! Shake hands!'" Kingscourt caught the young

man's hand, and pumped it vigorously. On their way to the glove department, Friedrich probed further. "How did you get around petty trading," he asked, "if you did not forbid it by law?"

"Quite simply. Through this thing here-the large bazaar. Such large emporiums and mail order houses with branches everywhere were inevitable in an era of steam engines and railways. They did not happen by accident. No clever merchant conceived them in a flash of insight. It was a development forced by iron necessity.

"Mass production had made this type of distribution imperative. Naturally, the small tradesmen became discouraged and bewildered, and were forced out of business, like the stagecoach drivers when the steam engine appeared. But the drivers realized their plight sooner than the tradesmen with their short-sighted shrewdness. The tradesmen were the more helpless because their business consisted chiefly of their bit of capital, and that had usually vanished by the time they realized the impending peril. They, poor souls, were not to blame for their own ruin. The new epoch attacked them without so much as a causus belli.

"But-and this is one of the keys to our prosperity-the obsolete forms of commerce never got a foothold here. We started off with the new era. No man was stupid enough to set up a little shop beside a great bazaar. No man any longer went from house to house or from town to town with a pack on his back when he knew that the price lists, samples, and newspaper advertisements of the mail order houses had preceded him. Petty trade and peddling no longer promised the least profit. Therefore, when our people entered the new conditions, they did not try to adopt those means of earning a livelihood.

"In old Europe, where so many rights had been won at different periods, and had to be protected none the less, this was a trying problem. The lower strata of the commercial middle-class were seriously endangered by the department stores. Yet, if the large shops were to be closed by law, a legal question would arise: at what point did they become 'large?' Were they to be weakened through high taxes? That course would profit the public' treasury little, while the small tradesmen would not be much the gamer.

"Moreover, the public wanted and in fact needed these large bazaars where, without loss of time, one can purchase all sorts of things at the low prices made possible by mass distribution. (Manufacturers are of course able to allow lower prices to large firms than to small ones.) In brief, both production and consumption required the large bazaar. No one was ruined here because, as I have said commerce was then in its beginnings. We had a social-political motive: that is to say, we wanted to cure our small tradesmen of certain outworn, uneconomic, and injurious forms of trade."

The ladies were showing slight signs of impatience at David's detailed explanations. They would be late for the opera. But Kingscourt wished to ask still more questions as he held up his great red hands to the saleswoman who was trying to force them into the white gloves.

"Your story, excellency, does not quite hold water. Today I see that you have much commerce here. But it could not have been like that to begin with. These great structures could not have been set down on the bare ground, nor could there have been crowds of customers waiting to rush into them. Tell that to your little Fritzchen, not to an old hand like me."

"Nor, Mr. Kingscourt, did it happen that way. Things developed naturally. When the Jewish immigration to Palestine began on a large scale, there was a sudden and enormous demand for merchandise. We had not yet produced anything, and needed everything. This was known to the whole world, because the Jewish immigration took place in the full light of day. Large firms hastened to establish branches in the important Palestinian towns. It was not only Jewish firms which took advantage of the opportunity to sell their shopworn goods. German, French, English and American department stores went up in a twinkling. At first they were housed in iron barracks. Later, however, as the stream of immigrants grew, and people wanted more and better merchandise (because in the meantime they had settled down and begun to prosper), the barracks gradually gave way to stone structures.

"The New Society carefully refrained from hampering these large undertakings. On the contrary, we encouraged them because they offered us a double advantage. For one thing, they provided the common necessaries promptly and cheaply; and,

**119**

for another, their presence restrained our small tradesmen from engaging in unproductive business. We did not want to be a nation of shopkeepers."

"Indeed?" asked Friedrich. "Are there no small traders at all here?"

"Oh, there are, indeed!" was the reply. "No one is subject to rules and regulations here. We live under no despotism, whether monarchistic or socialistic. Every one does as he sees fit. The cheapest and the most expensive goods -let us say, second-hand clothing and jewelry-are handled mainly by individual traders. These are by no means all Jews. Greeks, Levantines, Armenians, and Persians engage in this sort of business much more than the Jews-especially than the Jews affiliated with the New Society."

"How's that? Are there Jews who do not belong to the New Society?" "Yes, of course there are...But now we really must be going." David turned to the saleswoman. "How much for both pairs of gloves?"

"Six shekels."

"All the devils!" marveled Kingscourt. "What's that?"

David smiled. "Our currency. We have renewed the ancient Hebrew coinage. A shekel is equal to a French franc. Since you are not provided with Palestinian currency, allow me to pay for you."

He threw a gold coin on the counter, and received some silver in exchange. As they turned to go, Kingscourt pinched David's arm and growled at him banteringly. "So you didn't abolish money in your New Society. Should have been surprised if you had."

David, who by this time understood the old man's manner, retorted in the same vein. "No, Mr. Kingscourt, we could not bear to part with money. For one thing, we are damned greedy Jews. And for another, money is an excellent expedient. If there hadn't been any, it would have had to be invented, you know."

"Boy, you talk after my own heart. I have always said so. Money is a good thing-a fine thing. It's only that it has been spoiled by people."

Theodor Herzl

## Chapter VI

When they entered their box at the opera, the overture was almost finished. Many people were staring up at them from the auditorium, and the ladies hastened to seat themselves. Friedrich and Kingscourt were surprised at the magnificence of the building. Yes, said David, it had been under construction for five years, and was subsidized by the New Society. An ordinary theater was usually completed within a year once the co-operative had been established.

In the next box sat two bejeweled and overdressed women, one elderly and the other young, on either side of an elderly man. They saluted the Littwak party with a striking show of respect. To Friedrich it seemed that the Littwaks rejected rather than acknowledged the greeting. The older woman and the man he seemed to have met somewhere or other in the dim past.

"Who are those people?" he whispered to David.

The latter shrugged. "A Mr. Laschner, his wife and daughter."

Laschner! The rich Viennese stock broker. Suddenly Ernestine's betrothal party flashed before his mind's eye. The recollection was both amusing and painful.

"I must say, I should never have expected to see them here."

"They did not come until our house was finished," said David. "Palestine now has the same comforts as in the European large

**123**

cities. But a Laschner meets with the same contempt here as elsewhere. ...We did not indeed abolish money, my dear Mr. Kingscourt; but it is not everything here. The members of our New Society have become so free in the economic sense that the old, disgusting kowtowing to wealth has naturally disappeared. Mr. Laschner may have money, he may spend as much of it as he pleases; but no one takes off his hat to him for that reason. Of course, if he were a decent sort, we should gladly accept him. We expect everyone to show a sense of solidarity. This man, however, has not even troubled to join the New Society. He did not care to assume the duties of our commonwealth. He therefore lives here as a stranger. He may move about freely like any other stranger, but no one respects him. You will understand that."

"Do I understand it!" murmured Kingscourt, looking contemptuously toward the upstarts' box....

The curtain went up, showing a public square in Smyrna; the rising prophet surrounded by his first disciples. Kingscourt asked Miriam to explain the theme of the opera.

"This Sabbatai Zevi," whispered the girl, "was a false messiah who appeared in Turkey in the seventeenth century. He succeeded in creating a large movement among the Oriental Jews, but in the end he himself became a renegade from Judaism and ended ignominiously."

Kingscourt nodded his understanding of the story. "I see. A wretched fellow. Of course that would make a good theme for an opera."

A group of opposition rabbis stood near the synagogue in the
public square, singing angry choruses after the pseudo-messiah
and his friends had left the stage. A young girl devoted to the
prophet rebuked the belligerent mob in a long aria. The anger
of the people then turned against this rash defender; and, had
not Sabbatai opportunely returned, it would have gone ill with
her. Even his enemies were overawed by the personality of the
leader of the masses. They withdrew before him timidly. The
maiden threw herself at his feet. He lifted her gently and sang a
duet with her after the operatic custom. The act was brought to
an effective close by the proclamation of a rabbinical ban
against Sabbatai, who declared that he and his friends would
leave Smyrna the girl implored him to take her with him. She
would follow and serve him wherever he went...The curtain
fell...

During the entr'ante they discussed the florid hero of the opera.
"That swindler will go far," commented Kingscourt. "I can
imagine that."

"He seems to have been a dreamer originally," said Sarah. "He
became dishonest only after he had a following."

Miriam smilingly quoted Goethe's saying: "Crucify every
visionary in his thirtieth year. For, once he knows the world,
the deceived will turn deceiver."

"But it is strange," said Friedrich, "how such adventurers are
always able to win the people's confidence."

"There seems to be a profound reason for that," remarked
David. "It was not that the people believed what they said, but
rather that they said what the people believed. They soothed a

**125**

yearning. Or, perhaps it would be more correct to say, they sprang from the yearning. That's it. The longing creates the Messiah.

"You must remember what dark days those were when a Sabbatai and his like appeared. Our people was not yet able to take account of its own situation, and therefore yielded to the spell of such persons. It was only at the end of the nineteenth century, when the other civilized nations had already attained to self-consciousness and given evidence thereof, that our own people-the pariah-realized that its salvation lay within itself, that nothing was to be expected from fantastic miracle-workers. They realized then that the way of deliverance must be paved not by a single individual, but by a conscious and alert folk-personality. The Orthodox, too, realized that there was nothing blasphemous in such a view. Gesta Dei per Franco the French used to say. 'God works through the Jews,' said our truly pious ones who did not permit intriguing rabbis to stir them up. God Himself, in His inscrutable wisdom, decides what instruments will serve His ends. Such was the sensible reasoning of our pious Jews when they threw themselves enthusiastically into the national enterprise of restoration. And so the Jewish nation once more raised itself to nationhood."

"Bravo!" roared Kingscourt.

Someone knocked at the door of the box. In response to David's summons, a gray-bearded man (he whom Friedrich had noticed at the embankment) sidled in with a servile smile. Schiffmann of the Cafe Birkenreis!

"I have ventured to come," he said, excusing himself to David, "because I recognized someone I used to know. I doubt whether Dr. Loewenberg still remembers me."

"Of course, Mr. Schiffmann," smiled Friedrich, extending his hand.

"Strange, as I live! So you did not die!"

"Apparently not!.. And did you recognize me at once?"

"Upon my honor, no. Someone came to my rescue. A lady you once knew very well. Can't you guess?" He smiled significantly.

Friedrich was terror-stricken. He guessed suddenly who it was, but dared not pronounce the name.

"Well, Dr. Loewenberg, can't you really guess? Have you forgotten all your old friends?"

"I know of no friends in this country, except these here," replied Friedrich a bit dryly, glancing around the box. "Her first name is Ernestine," smirked Schiffmann.

"What! Miss Loeffler!"

"No, Mrs. Weinberger. You must know about her marriage. You were at the betrothal party. Indeed, it was there I saw you last. You disappeared immediately afterwards."

"Yes, yes! I recall! And is Miss-Mrs. Weinberger living here?"'

"To be sure! There she is, in the seat next to mine. I shall point her out to you:' He leaned close to Friedrich, so that the others, who were looking down into the auditorium, could not hear him. "Entre nous.. she is not too well off. Her husband, that Weinberger, is a Schlemihl. He went bankrupt in Bruenn, began over again in Vienna as a commission merchant, and finally landed here. But he's the same Schlemihl as ever. They'd have a tough time of it if I didn't look after them. And you know how accustomed she was to silk gowns and opera boxes and balls. Nowadays, if I didn't send her theater tickets occasionally, she'd have to mope at home. Times change:'

Friedrich tried to shut off Schiffmann's flow of confidences. "I should be interested by all means to meet Madam Ernestine again. Where is she sitting?"

"Aisle seat, next to the last row. You can see her if you bend over the rail. I am going do now. When you see me in my seat. Her daughter is sitting next to me, and she is next to her daughter. ..It was a very great pleasure indeed to see you again. You are remaining with us, I hope. For some time at least?"

"I don't know. It depends upon circumstances, Mr. Schiffmann!" "Very good. If you want me, you need only send a telephone message. ...My respects, ladies and gentlemen."

He sidled out of the half-open door as he had come in.

"I don't care for that one at all," muttered Kingscourt to Friedrich. The latter shrugged.

The opening of the second act showed Sabbatai holding court in Egypt. There was a great feast, with singing and dancing.

**128**

But Friedrich saw and heard very little of it all. He was absorbed in old dreams. There she sat, next to Schiffmann. At first he was under an odd illusion. Ernestine Loeffier had not changed in the least in twenty years. Was it possible? There were the same delicate young features, the same tender young form. But he realized his error after a moment. This young girl was not Ernestine, but Ernestine's daughter. Mrs. Weinberger was the fat, faded, gaudily dressed woman in the next seat. She was looking up to him, smiling an invitation, and nodded vigorously in response to his bow.

In that instant something crumbled to dust that had endured through twenty years. His first keen resentment had mellowed in the solitude of Kingscourt's island, and he had recalled her with a certain wistfulness. In the end, his love dissolved in a rosy twilight. But in his dreams he had always seen her in her youthful form. His sudden glimpse of the result of the natural process of aging was a shock. He felt a sense of shame, but also of relief. That he should have been heartsick over this woman! Was it possible!

He was awakened from his reverie by a gentle voice. "How did you like it?" Miriam was asking.

"Thank God it's over!" he replied absentmindedly.

"Did you think the second act as bad as all that?"

He was embarrassed. "No, Miss Miriam. I did not mean the second act. I was thinking of an old thing I had imagined to be still alive. But it is dead."

She gave him a surprised glance, but asked no more questions.

**129**

A gentleman entered the box, and was introduced to the newcomers as Dr. Werkin, secretary to the President. He was a slender man, with a short, brownish-gray beard. His keen eyes looked out from behind a pair of gleaming spectacles. He presented the President's compliments, with an invitation to Mr. Kingscourt and Dr. Loewenberg to visit him in his box.

Kingscourt was dumbfounded. "Us! What kind of a president is he? And what does he want of us poor desert pilgrims?"

"The President of our New Society," explained David, smiling. "The old gentleman with the white beard. In the first box."

They glanced in that direction. "Confound it!" cried Kingscourt. "I seem to remember meeting him. But where?"

"The oculist at Jerusalem," Friedrich reminded him.

"Dr. ..."

"Eichenstamm," prompted David. "He is our President."

"And did he recognize us after all these years?" asked Kingscourt, still amazed.

"The gentlemen were recognized, by Dr. Eichenstamm' s daughter," said Dr. Werkin, "and she pointed them out to him,"

"May I come too, Dr. Werkin?" asked David.

"Certainly, Mr. Littwak. The President would like to hear how your campaign against Geyer is going."

Dr. Werkin led them to the aged president, who awaited them standing in an elegant little salon curtained off at the back of the box. He was leaning heavily upon a cane.

"What a reunion, gentlemen, eh?" The old man's voice quavered as he shook hands with each in turn.

"Yes, Devil take me, Mr. President, if I expected to find all this!"

"Let us be seated, gentlemen. I am not very robust any more, as you see," smiled Eichenstamm, sinking into the easy chair an attendant placed for him. "Yes, yes! Our people has come upon happier days. But, for me, those were the better days. You know the saying, 'Senectus ipsa morbus. ..' Well, we must take things as they come."

He pointed to the lady who stood beside him, wearing a simple black silk gown. "My daughter Sascha recognized you, and reminded me of that day at the Wailing Wall. Ah, that was a long time ago, my friends... Yes, yes, the erstwhile Wailing Wall."

"Erstwhile?" repeated Friedrich. "Is it gone? Has not even that last fragment remained?"

The President looked at him and shook his head. "You could not have been in Jerusalem if you speak like that," he said.

David modestly drew nearer. "No, Mr. President. These gentlemen have just arrived. They have seen very little."

**131**

The President placed his hand on the speaker's arm. "I am glad to see you, dear Littwak. You are always a joy to me-and especially now. You must be steadfast in your fight. You are right. Geyer is wrong. My last word to the Jews will be: The stranger must be made to feel at home in our midst. God keep you as you are, Littwak. ...You have seen little of our country, gentlemen, but you already know one of our best men. I am proud of Littwak hereas proud as if I had had some share in making him so able and so upright."

David flushed deeply. He cast down his eyes like a little boy, and stammered, "But-Mr. President!"

"You mustn't mind my praising you to your face, dear Littwak. I am an old man, with nothing to gain from your favor. ...You see, my friends from afar, I am the outgoing, he the incoming wave. ...Give me a glass of tea, Sascha!" The tea was served him Russian fashion.

When, in the course of the conversation, the newcomers mentioned that they had been absent for twenty years from the civilized world, Sascha asked, "But don't you regret the time you lost? You could have benefited so many people."

"No, madam, we're not sorry at all. We are two seasoned misanthropes. We want to do good to no one but ourselves. That's our program. Eh, Fritze?"

"You're jesting," returned Sascha. "You must be. Good deeds bring more happiness than anything else."

"Miss Sascha speaks from experience," said David. "She herself knows that kind of happiness very well, since she is at the head of the greatest eye clinic in the world. May I bring these gentlemen to your clinic, Doctor, when we come to Jerusalem? ...Large numbers of people, gentlemen, have had their eyesight saved or restored there. You can imagine what a benefaction that clinic is for the Orient. People come to it from all over Northern Africa and Asia. The blessings bestowed by our medical institutions have won us more friends in Palestine and the neighboring countries than all our industrial and technical progress."

Sascha parried the praise. "Mr. Littwak overestimates my slight accomplishments. I have done nothing new. But there's a very big man in this country-a bacteriologist named Steineck. You must see the Steineck Institute. You will find it awe-inspiring."

"Have you made any plans for seeing the country, gentlemen?" inquired the President.

"I am taking my guests to Tiberias first, Mr. President. We go up tomorrow to visit my parents."

"To celebrate the Passover, eh?" asked the old gentleman. "Remember me to your parents, Littwak. And you must bring your friends to call on me in Jerusalem. I shall count on it."

He shook hands with them once more, and they parted as the orchestra began the overture to the third act.

As they walked back through the empty foyer, Kingscourt remarked, "That president of yours seems to be a fine chap. A bit old and infirm though. Why did you choose him especially?"

"I can tell you that in a word, Mr. Kingscourt. Because he did not want to accept office."

"Oho! That's better still."

"Yes. We follow a principle laid down by the sages of Israel. 'Bestow honors upon him who seeks none!'"

# Book Three

# The Prosperous Land

## Chapter I

An enormous touring car stood before the Littwak home. It was a divine spring morning.

"Donnerwetter!" shouted Kingscourt, in high spirits. "That's a real Noah's ark, with room for every sinful man and beast!"

"There will be only eleven of us in all!" said David.

"Eleven? I see only nine," counted Kingscourt. "Unless you count little Fritzchen for three. It wouldn't be a bad idea to take him along."

The baby, on his nurse's arm, seemed to realize that he was the topic of conversation. "O-oh!" he crowed, and reached out for Kingscourt's white beard.

"We shall pick up two friends on the way to Tiberias," said Sarah. "Reschid Bey and the architect Steineck.

"In the meantime, the servants had stowed a mass of hand luggage under the seats. Only one basket, containing milk

**135**

bottles and other provisions for the baby, was placed on top of a seat. The driver and a negro footman climbed up to their places at the rear of the car. On the upholstered seats in front sat Miriam, Sarah, and Friedrich. Kingscourt chose a place behind the glass shield, ostensibly to be sheltered from the wind, but really because he had overheard that Fritzchen was to be put there. He climbed in first, and let them hand the baby to him. Once, however, Fritzchen was in Kingscourt's arms, he refused absolutely to go back to his nurse. David, entering the car last, tried to exert his paternal authority. In vain.

Kingscourt was very angry-or said he was. "Such a naughty rascal! Leave me at once!"

"Please give him to me," begged David. "Even if he yells."

Kingscourt, however, had not the faintest idea of surrendering Fritzchen. He set the baby on his lap, and tickled his chin and chest until he laughed out loud. "Such a fellow! Doesn't care if he makes old Kingscourt the laughing stock of all Haifa! Lucky no one knows me here!"

As the car drove out through the gateway of Friedrichsheim, the negro played a jolly tune on his horn. Fritzchen clapped his hands delightedly.

"I say!" cried Kingscourt. "It's almost like the good old days. The position with his horn!"

"He's calling Reschid," explained David. "We don't want to lose any time." Reschid was already waiting in front of his house. They greeted him cordially. From behind an upper-story lattice a lovely feminine hand waved a handkerchief.

"Good-by, Fatma!" called Sarah smilingly to the invisible one. "We shall bring your husband back safely. Don't worry!"

"Kiss the children for me, Fatma" cried Miriam.

Reschid's bags were stowed in the car, and he took a seat beside David. The white hand waved a last farewell, and the motor ark wheezed forward.

Friedrich turned to Miriam. "So that poor lady must remain at home alone."

"She is a happy and contented woman," replied Miriam. "She wants her husband to enjoy this little trip, I'm sure. He would not have thought of coming with us if it had annoyed her. They are both very fine people."

"Nevertheless, I admire a woman who remains obediently behind her lattice. On a morning like this, ladies."

"Isn't it delightful?" beamed Sarah. "Spring days like these come nowhere but in Palestine. Life has a better savor here than anywhere else."

Friedrich was happy, inexplicably happy. He was young again, exuberant. He teased his charming companion. "How about your school, Miss Miriam? Have you hung your duties on a hook for a while?"

"He knows nothing!" laughed Miriam. "Absolutely nothing at all about Jewish things. Allow me to inform you sir, that our Passover vacation began today. We are going to visit my

**137**

parents at Tiberias because we shall celebrate the Seder there. Didn't David tell you anything about it?"

"Your brother hinted to me several times that we should hear more about the Jewish exodus in Tiberias. So that was what he meant....Well, I still remember the Egyptian exodus from my childhood."

"He may have meant something else, too," said Mariam thoughtfully.

When the car reached the bottom of the road that ran down the side of the Carmel, it turned not toward the town, but to the right, heading for the suburb watered by the Kishon river. They made a halt in front of a charming little home on the tree-planted quay, where a gentleman with a gray mustache stood gesticulating violently. With head thrown back, he looked at them over the rims of his glasses, and shouted, "If I'd been you, I'd not have come at all. Here I've been standing for half an hour! Never again shall I be prompt!"

David held out his watch silently.

"That proves nothing!" cried Steineck. "Your watch is slow. I don't believe in watches, anyway. Here, take my plans. Don't crush them, please. So! Now we're ready!' He shoved three enormous rolls of carton which he had under his arm at David and Reschid, and climbed into the car panting. But hardly had the car started when he shouted anxiously, "Stop! Stop! I've forgotten my traveling bag."

"They'll send it along with your other luggage," replied David soothingly. "I've sent the large pieces to Tiberias by train, you know, because we're making a detour."

"Impossible!" lamented the architect. "My speech is in that traveling bag. We must go back for it."

And they had to turn back. The traveling bag was fetched and stowed in the car. Steineck heaved a sigh of relief, and suddenly became very cheerful. The touring car, with its comparatively limited space, now harbored two famous bawlers-Kingscourt and Steineck. Like the old misanthrope, Steineck made a frightful uproar in delivering himself of the most commonplace remarks. Hardly had they been introduced when they began to shout into each other's ears. David and Reschid were hugely amused. Suddenly Kingscourt stopped shouting and placed his forefinger on his lips.

"Mr. Steineck," he whispered, "you spoke very loudly, but Fritzchen fell asleep in spite of the noise." He carefully lifted the sleeping child from his lap and handed him to the nurse, while the others smiled broadly.

Steineck's feelings were hurt. "I don't believe, Mr.-'" Kingscourt," he whispered, "that I spoke any more loudly than you did."

The road along which they were traveling constantly gave the strangers occasion for surprised questioning. There was of course less traffic here than in the town, but numerous bicycles and motor cars speeded past them, and horseback riders appeared and disappeared on the soft bridle path which ran parallel with the road. Some of the riders wore the picturesque

**139**

Arab costume, others the conventional European clothing. Occasionally, too, camels filed past, singly and in cavalcades-picturesque and primitive relics of an obsolete era. The car rolled along comfortably on the smooth roadway. To the left and to the right they saw small houses with garden plots, and behind them well-cultivated fields that now were freshly green. Kingscourt noticed that wires strung on poles along the road had extensions into the houses.

"Are those telephone wires?" he asked. "And what kind of people live here?"

Reschid enlightened him. "Most of them are artisans. This is a shoemakers' village. The wires carry power into their homes for their machines. Is that new to you?"

"Oh, no. The principle of power transmission was already well known in my time, but it had very little practical application. And where does the power come from, if I may ask?"

"There are several electric companies. The people here draw most of their power from the brooks of the Hermon and the Lebanon, or from the Dead Sea Canal."

"No!" roared Kingscourt, overwhelmed.

"Yes!" bellowed Steineck.

"These artisans are half-peasants," interposed David. "They are organized co-operatively in both capacities. They sell their products to large department stores, mail order houses, and export firms. Near the larger towns, industrial activities predominate and the farming is more or less incidental, the

**140**

artisans raising little more than they need for their own households... just some fruits and vegetables for the city markets. In the coastal zone, which is very much like the Riviera, they grow (as in the vicinity of Nice) tomatoes, artichokes, melons, petits pois-, haricot vers, etc. Our early vegetables are shipped to all parts of Europe-to Paris, Berlin, Moscow, and St. Petersburg-by rail.

"In other districts, again, farming predominates, and there are only modest home industries...though these, too, are well equipped with modem technical facilities.

"Villages like this one are scattered all over our prosperous land. Up yonder, in the Valley of Jezreel, for example, you must not expect to see the filthy nests that used to be called villages in Palestine. Today you will see a new village which is typical of innumerable settlements both to the east and the west of the Jordan."

After crossing the Kishon Bridge, the car glided past luxuriant orange and lemon groves whose red and yellow fruit gleamed through the foliage.

"Devil take me!" cried Kingscourt. "But this is Italy!"

"Cultivation is everything!" roared Steineck aggressively, as if he were being contradicted. "We Jews introduced .cultivation here."

"Pardon me, sir!" cried Reschid Bey with a friendly smile. "But this sort of thing was here before you came-at least there were signs of it. My father planted oranges extensively." He turned to Kingscourt and pointed to a grove at the right of the road. "I know more about it than our friend Steineck, because this used to be my father's plantation. It's mine now."

The well-tended grove was a beautiful sight. The ever-blooming trees bore flowers, green and ripe fruit, simultaneously.

"I don't deny that you had orange groves before we came," thundered Steineck, "but you could never get full value out of them."

Reschid nodded. "That is correct. Our profits have grown considerably. Our orange transport has multiplied tenfold since we have had good transportation facilities to connect us with the whole world. Everything here has increased in value since your immigration."

"One question, Reschid Bey," interrupted Kingscourt. "These gentlemen will pardon me, but you are much too modest. Were not the older inhabitants of Palestine ruined by the Jewish immigration? And didn't they have to leave the country? I mean, generally speaking. That individuals here and there were the gainers proves nothing."

"What a question! It was a great blessing for all of us," returned Reschid. "Naturally, the land-owners gained most because they were able to sell to the Jewish society at high prices, or to wait for still higher ones. I, for my part, sold my land to our New Society because it was to my advantage to sell."

"Didn't you say a moment ago that those groves we passed were yours?':

"To be sure! After I had sold them to the New Society, I took them back on lease."

"Then you shouldn't have sold them in the first place."

"But it was more advantageous for me. Since I wished to join the New Society, I had to submit to its land regulations. Its members have no private property in land."

"Then Friedrichsheim does not belong to you, Mr. Littwak.'

"Not the plot. I leased it only till the next jubilee year, as my friend Reschid did his groves."

"Jubilee year? Please explain that. I really seem to have overslept myself on that island."

"The jubilee year," explained David, "is not a new but an ancient institution set up by our Teacher Moses. After seven times seven years, that is to say, in the fiftieth year, land which had been sold reverted back to its original owner without compensation. We, indeed, arrange it a bit differently. The land now reverts back to the New Society. Moses, in his day, wished to distribute the land so as to ensure the ends of social justice. You will see that our methods serve the purpose none the less. The increases in land values accrue not to the individual owner, but to the public."

Steineck anticipated a possible objection from Kingscourt. "You may perhaps say that no one will care to improve a plot that does not belong to him, or to erect fine buildings upon it."

"No, sir, I should not say that. I know that in London people build houses on other people's land on ninety-nine year leases. This is quite the same thing....But .I wanted to ask you, my dear Bey, how the former inhabitants fared -those who had nothing, the numerous Moslem Arabs."

"Your question answers itself, Mr. Kingscourt," replied Reschid. "Those who had nothing stood to lose nothing, and could only gain. And they did gain: Opportunities to work, means of livelihood, prosperity. Nothing could have been more wretched than an Arab village at the end of the nineteenth century. The peasants' clay hovels were unfit for stables. The children lay naked and neglected in the streets, and grew up like dumb beasts. Now everything is different. They benefited from the progressive measures of the New Society whether they wanted to or not, whether they joined it or not. When the swamps were drained, the canals built, and the eucalyptus trees planted to drain, and 'cure' the marshy soil, the natives (who, naturally, were well acclimatized) were the first to be employed, and were paid well for their work!

"Just look at that field! It was a swamp in my boyhood. The New Society bought up this tract rather cheaply, and turned it into the best soil in the country. It belongs to that tidy settlement up there on the hill. It is a Moslem village-you can tell by the mosque. These people are better off than at any time in the past. They support themselves decently, their children are healthier and are being taught something. Their religion and ancient customs have in no wise been interfered with. They have become more prosperous-that is all."

"You're queer fellows, you Moslems. Don't you regard these Jews as intruders?"

"You speak strangely, Christian," responded the friendly
Reschid. "Would you call a man a robber who takes nothing
from you, but brings you something instead? The Jews have
enriched us. Why should we be angry with them? They dwell
among us like brothers. Why should we not love them? I have
never had a better friend among my co-religionists than David
Littwak here. He may come to me, by day or night, and ask
what he pleases. I shall give it him. And I know that I, too, may
count upon him as upon a brother. He prays in a different
house to the God who is above us all. But our houses of
worship stand side by side, and I always believe that our
prayers, when they rise, mingle somewhere up above, and then
continue on their way together until they appear before Our
Father."

Rechid's gentle words had moved everyone, Kingscourt
included. That gentleman cleared his throat. "Hm-hm! Quite
right. Very fine. Sounds reasonable. But you're an educated
man, you've studied in Europe. I hardly think the simple
country or town folk will be likely to think as you do."

"They more than anyone else, Mr. Kingscourt. You must
excuse my saying so, but I did not learn tolerance in the
Occident. We Moslems have always had better relations with
the Jews than you Christians. When the first Jewish colonists
settled here half a century ago, Arabs went to the Jews to judge
between them, and often asked the Jewish village councils for
help and advice. There was no difficulty in that respect. So
long as the Geyer policy does not win the upper hand, all will
be well with our common fatherland."

"Yes! Who's this Geyer I'm always hearing about?"

**145**

Steineck went purple as he shouted, "He's a cursed pope, a provocateur, a blasphemer who rolls up his eyes. He wants to bring intolerance into our country, the scamp! I am certainly a peaceful person, but I could cheerfully murder an intolerant fellow like that!"

"Oh, so you are a peaceful person," laughed Kingscourt. "Now I can imagine what your others are like."

"Of course they're much gentler," jested David.

The car had left the plain and was gliding eastward into rolling country. It took the upgrades as easily as the down. The hillsides everywhere were cultivated up to the very summits; every bit of soil was exploited. The steep slopes were terraced with vines, pomegranate and fig trees as in the ancient days of Solomon. Numerous tree nurseries bore witness to the intelligent efforts at forestation of the once barren tracts. Pines and cypresses on the ridges of the hills towered against the blue skies.

They drove through a lovely valley with an amazing profusion of flowers. It was covered with a brilliant carpet of white, red, yellow, blue and green. As the breeze carried the fragrance toward them, the travelers felt as if they had been plunged into a sea of perfume. This valley was the property of a great perfume industry they were told! Jasmine, tuberoses, geraniums, narcissus, violets and roses were grown there in immense quantities.

Men working by the roadside saluted Littwak, Reschid and Steineck as they drove past. All three seemed to know many of the obviously contented farmers.

At Sepphoris, the car stopped for the first time in front of the Greek church. David excused himself for a moment. He was going in to pay a brief call to the priest in his handsome parsonage.

The others also left the car and went a little way around the foot of the hill to see the ruins of an old church, from which there was a wide view over the fertile plain extending to the base of Mount Carmel. The ruins, explained Miriam, were those of a church dedicated to Joachim and Anne, parents of Mary, the mother of Jesus, who had lived in the vicinity. The new Greek church was used by the colony of Russian Christians near Sepphoris. David was a friend of the priest's, and was inviting him to the Seder at Tiberias. Just then he appeared with the dignified clergyman, who regretted that he could not join them immediately. He would take the electric train that passed through Nazareth in the afternoon, and would probably reach the elder Littwaks' villa before the motor party.

They made their farewells to the priest, and the car continued northward toward the plain.

# Theodor Herzl

# Chapter II

Outside of Sepphoris, they had to halt at a railway crossing because a train was due. It appeared presently, rushing southward at great speed. When the visitors remarked that the locomotive had no smokestack, they were told that this line, like most of the Palestinian railways, was operated by electric power. There was one of the great advantages of having begun from the beginning. Just because everything here had been in a primitive, neglected state, it had been possible to install the most up-to-date technical appliances at once. So it had been with the city planning, as they already knew; and so it had been with the construction of railways, the digging of canals, the establishment of agriculture and industry in the land. The Jewish settlers who streamed into the country had brought with them the experience of the whole civilized world. The trained men graduated from universities, technical, agricultural and commercial colleges had brought with them every type of skill required for building up the country. The penniless young intelligentsia, for whom there were no opportunities in the anti-Semitic countries and who there sank to the level of a hopeless, revolutionary-minded proletariat, these desperate, educated young men had become a great blessing for Palestine, for they had brought the latest methods of applied science into the country. So David related.

Friedrich pricked up his ears at a phrase which had played so decisive a role in his own life. He turned to his friend with a question that was incomprehensible to the others. "An 'educated, desperate young man.' Remember that, Kingscourt?

**149**

No wonder a Jew applied. There were many of us like that in the old days. Most of us, in fact,"

But Kingscourt was too much engrossed in David's narrative to pay heed to Friedrich's sentimental recollections.

"You're a damned shrewd nation. Left us with the old scrap iron, while you travel about in the latest machines!"

"Were we to take obsolete stuff when we could have new things just as cheaply?" cried Steineck. "Moreover, everything you see here already existed in Europe and America a quarter of a century ago-especially in America. The latter had gone far ahead of the stick-in-the-mud Old World. Naturally we learned from America how to build electric railways and similar things."

"For us," added David, "the transition to the most up-to-date transportation facilities was not expensive, because we had no old stuff to amortize. We did not have to drag along worn out rolling stock until it was totally useless. Our railway coaches are very comfortable-well lighted and well ventilated, free from smoke and dust. There is practically no jolting despite the high speed. Workingmen no longer have to travel in cars like cattle pens. Of course, every precaution is taken on our railways for safeguarding the public health.

"You will also be interested to know that railway fares are very low here. We have adopted the system of fares in vogue in Baden during the reign of the kindly, wise Grand Duke Friedrich! From the viewpoint of the public interest, we have tried to make it as easy as possible for the workers to find employment. It does not happen here that railway coaches are shunted back and forth empty from a place where there is an acute shortage of labor to another where there is acute unemployment merely because railway fares are prohibitive. Our network of railways stretches from Mount Lebanon to the Dead Sea, and from the Mediterranean to the Hauran like a system of sluices for fertilizing the country with man power.

"Our freight traffic, both inland and transit, has grown very extensive because we have harbors and grain elevators, and our railways link up with the trunk lines of Asia Minor and Northern Africa. ...

"However, I don't want to go into the social and economic features of our railway system just now. You know all about these things, gentlemen, even though you were away from the world so long. They were commonplaces long ago.

"'But what was not recognized in those days," said David, turning aside from the railways, "was the beauty of our beloved land. The improvements we have made count for a great deal, of course. But the natural, God-given charm of Palestine lay unseen and forgotten for long centuries. Where in the world will you find a country where the springtime is so accessible at all times of the year? Palestine has warm, temperate and cool zones which lie not far apart from each other. In the southern part of the Jordan Valley, for instance, the country is almost tropical. The mild seacoast provides all the pleasures of the French and Italian Rivieras, while the 'majestic ranges of the Lebanon and the Anti-Lebanon, the snow-covered Hermon are not far away. All these places can be reached by rail within a few hours. God has blessed our land."

"Yes," confirmed Reschid, "travel is really a great pleasure here. Sometimes I board an observation car without intending to go anywhere in particular. I do it just to enjoy the views."

"Honored host," said Kingscourt, "we ought to have been introduced to all that immediately, with all due respect to this very comfortable ark."

"I had two reasons, gentlemen," said David, justifying himself, "for not letting you travel by rail today. First, you see more of the country and of the people from an auto; second, the tourist traffic is very heavy just now on the Haifa-Nazareth- Tiberias line S (during the Easter season). It is true that the cosmopolitan pilgrimages to the holy places of Christendom are very fascinating, but I wanted first to show you the organized life of our commonwealth."

Ah, that reminds me," said Friedrich. "How did you solve the question of the Holy Places?"

"It was no great feat," replied David. "When, with the advent of Zionism at the end of the nineteenth century, the problem of the Holy Places came up, there were many Jews who, like yourself, thought it insoluble. Having been away so long, you still entertain this obsolete view. As a matter of fact, it soon became clear through public discussion and from the declarations of statesmen and princes of the church that the obstacle existed only in the imagination of over-timid Jews. The Christian Holy Places have been held by non-Christians from time immemorial. Centuries having passed since the crusades, a more enlightened view concerning these hallowed sites has gradually found acceptance. Geoffrey of Bouillon and his knights grieved because Palestine was held by the

Moslems. But did the fin de siecle knights and noblemen harbor the same emotions? And their Governments? Would any Great Power have dared to ask its parliament for an extraordinary grant for the re-conquest of the Holy Land? The point was that such a war would have been waged less against the Turkish Empire than against other Christian powers; it would have been a crusade against the Cross rather than against the Crescent. The conclusion was thus reached that the status quo was the best possible status, for all concerned. However, that was what might be termed a utilitarian-political view. But parallel with it there is a higher and if I may use the term-an ideal-political point of view. The actual possession of the Holy Sites was not in question: religious susceptibilities were more at ease when the sites were not held by anyone temporal power. The Roman legal concept of res sacrae, extra commercium was applied to them. That was the safest and in fact the only means of retaining them permanently as the common possession of Christendom. When you visit Nazareth or Jerusalem or Bethlehem you will see peaceful processions of pilgrims of all the nations. Steadfast Jew though I am, these scenes of devotion stir me profoundly."

"At Nazareth or Bethlehem," added Steineck, "one is reminded of Lourdes in the Pyrenees. There is the same vast tourist traffic-the hotels, hospices, convents."

They had reached the extensive plain, which was thickly sown with wheat and oats, maize and hops, poppies and tobacco. There were trim villages and farmsteads in the valley and on the hillsides. Cows and sheep grazed ruminating in succulent meadows. Here and there great iron farm machines B gleamed in the sunshine. The whole landscape was peaceful and joyous.

They drove through several villages where men and women were at work in well-ordered farmyards, children played, and old men sunned themselves in front of the houses. The further they drove, the larger the number of pedestrians they saw on the roads. All were evidently bound for a common destination, which seemed to be a large village on an elevation to the south. As they overtook the pedestrians, some called after them. Others, however, removed their hats with ill grace or even glanced sullenly aside. The procession continued to swell in their wake. Hardly had the Littwak car passed when people jumped out of every farmyard in order to follow it. Some ran, others jumped into the saddle. Still others tried to overtake the auto on bicycles. The strangers gathered that their party was being expected.

So it turned out. A group of villagers was ready to receive them in front of the spacious community house. This settlement, with its fine farm buildings, cattle and fields, was known as "Neudorf" ("New Village").

A hundred-throated "Hedad!" greeted them as the car stopped.

"'Hedad!' means 'Hurrah' in Hebrew," explained Reschid to Kingscourt.

"Thought at once it must mean either 'Hurrah' or 'Down with them'!" chuckled the old man.

Before entering the community house, they listened to a Hebrew song of welcome sung by a moir of neat school children under the direction of their teacher. Fritzchen awoke, and crooned an inarticulate accompaniment from his nurse's arm.

Friedmann, the head of the community, was a sturdy farmer of
about forty. He came forward and delivered a short speech of
welcome to the visitors in the Russian-Yiddish dialect,
addressing himself particularly to Littwak and Steineck as
party leaders.

"Donnerwetter!" growled Kingscourt into David's ear. "I did
not know you were a party leader."

"Only for the time being, Mr. Kingscourt. For a few weeks. It
is not my vocation,"

A second farmer now stepped forward-a robust, sunburned
man. He twisted his hat between his calloused palms, and
spoke with some embarrassment. "Mr. Littwak, Mr. Steineck,
you will permit me also to say something."

Arms were stretched out to restrain the unauthorized speaker.
"Mendel must not speak!" "Mendel's not allowed to speak!"
they cried.

Mendel, however, defiantly stood his ground, his determination
growing as he was hindered. "I shall speak!"

Tumult. "No!" "No!" came cries from the majority of those
present, but Mendel's supporters were angrily demanding a
hearing for him.

David quieted them with a gesture. "Of course he must speak."

"You see...Mr. Littwak is cleverer than you donkeys," sneered Mendel at his opponents. "Well, then...What I want to say is that Friedman did not speak for the whole community."

More confusion. "Yes, yes! He did. He is our spokesman."

Mendel went on unperturbed. "He may greet our guests. Yes, he must do that....He spoke for the whole of Neudorf when he did that. We are not rude to our guests. But he has no right to welcome them as party leaders. There is a party here in Neudorf which does not follow Mr. Littwak. That is what I wanted to tell you, Mr. Littwak and Mr. Steineck."

"Indeed?" Kingscourt quizzed Steineck. "We seem to have come into the enemy's territory."

"They won't devour us," replied the architect. "We have come here to convert them. I shall soon set their peasant skulls to rights. But, for heaven's sake, where is my speech?" He searched through the traveling bag which the footman handed him. "It's not here."

"Didn't you have it in your suitcase?" asked Sarah, laughing.

"I remember now! I stuck it into my trunk!"

"Oh, speak ex tempore," suggested Miriam.

Steineck gave her a despairing glance. He was usually unlucky with improvised speeches.

The crowd of farmers opened passageway in their midst for a visitor. "Here comes Reb Shmuel!"

Reb Shmuel was an aged, bent man of most gentle demeanor. He took David's hand in both of his and greeted him cordially. Obviously, he did hot side with Mendel and the opposition.

Miriam told the strangers in an undertone that the white-bearded rabbi had come with the earliest group of immigrants. When he came this fertile plain was still waste land; the plain of Asochis over there-behind the mountain range to the north-was covered with swamps, and the broad Valley of Jezreel to the south still showed the effects of age-long neglect. Rabbi Shmuel was the comforter of the people of Neudorf, most of whom had come from Russia to take up the struggle with the ancient soil. He had been and remained a simple country rabbi, staying with his village congregation, though he had often been called by large urban communities. He was universally honored for his wise and God-fearing life. The eastern part of the village called the Garden of Samuel, where he had his little home, had been named in his honor. When he preached in Neudorf on festival days, people came long distances to hear him.

The guests were served with the drink of welcome and light refreshments. On the grounds behind the community center an airy assembly hall had been improvised by stretching long strips of sail cloth over poles and the tops of trees. Thither the crowd now made its way. A temporary platform had been put up, and a row of chairs arranged for the visitors. The villagers sat on long benches or stood.

Friedman was the first speaker. He enjoined the audience not to interrupt the visiting speakers even when they might not agree with all that was said. Neudorf's reputation for courtesy was at

**157**

stake. He then called upon Steineck. That gentleman stepped up to the platform, cleared his throat several times and began to speak. He was rather halting in his manner at first, but warmed up as he developed his argument.

"Dear friends! I have had-hm-an accident-hm-hm-on my trip. That is-I have-hm-lost the prepared address I had intended to deliver here. It was a good speech-a fine one, in fact. You must take my word for it, since you will not hear it." A ripple of laughter passed through the audience. Steineck proceeded.

"In our New Society, we-hm-have come to a turning point-hm-I say to you only this-a turning point." Speaker paused to wipe the perspiration from his brow. "What does this turning point consist of, my dear friends? ...But before I turn to this-hm-turning point, I should like-hm-to touch on the past. What was that past-your past, our past? Hm? The Ghetto!"

"Very true!" came cries from the audience.

"Who brought you out of the Ghetto? Hm? Who?"

"We ourselves," called Mendel in a loud voice. The crowd hushed him to silence.

Steineck grew heated. "Who is that, we ourselves? Him? Is it Mendel, or someone else?"

"The people'" shouted Mendel.

"Please do not interrupt me! I accept Mendel's word. The people. Yes! Certainly, the people. Hm-but by itself-the people could not have done it. Hm. Our people were scattered allover the world, in small, helpless groups. They had to be gathered together before they could help themselves."

"Yes, yes!" bawled Mendel. "The leaders! We know all that!"

"Be silent, Mendel! At once!" thundered Friedman from the platform. "Mr. Steineck, please continue."

"Hm, yes. I continue. The leaders, says Mendel. I believe, hm-he means to be sarcastic. But it is true. Hm! Where was your Geyer, who now incites you, in those days? I shall tell you! He was an anti-Zionist rabbi! I knew him myself. He opposed us violently then also. But he gave other reasons. Oh, quite other reasons. But in one way he has remained the same. Hm. I shall tell you what he was, what he is, what he will remain. He is a rabbi of the immediate advantage. When we early Zionists began to seek out our land and our people, this Dr. Geyer abused us. Yes, he called us fools and swindlers."

A young farmer of about twenty-five came forward and spoke up respectfully. "Pardon me, Mr. Steineck. That is not possible. It was always known that we Jews are a people, and that Palestine is the land of our ancestors. Dr. Geyer could hardly have asserted the exact contrary in those days."

"But that is just what he did do," frothed Steineck. "He denied our people and our land. He read Zion out of the prayer book, and dared to tell the sheep who listened to him that it meant something else. Zion was everywhere but in Zion!"

"No, no!" cried several in the audience. "Geyer did not say that! Impossible!"

Rabbi Shmuel had arisen, supporting himself on his cane. He raised a hand for silence.

"It is true," said he. "There were such rabbis. Geyer may have been one of them. That I do not know. I have to take Steineck's word for it. But indeed there were such rabbis, there were such...." He sat down trembling.

Steineck, whose words had begun to overflow once he had got under steam, proceeded. "These rabbis who sought the immediate advantage made our lives a burden to us. Geyer is doing the same thing now. In those early, difficult days, he did not so much as want to hear the name of Palestine mentioned. Now he is more Palestinian than any of us. Now he is the patriot, the nationalist Jew. And we-we are the friends of the alien. If we listened to him, he would make us out to be bad Jews or even strangers in his Palestine. Yes, that's it. He wants to turn the public against us, to sow suspicion between you and I. This pious man rolls his eyes to heaven and all the time seeks his immediate advantage." In the old Ghetto days, when the rich men had all the influence, he talked to suit their notions. The nationalist-Palestinian idea made the rich men uncomfortable, and so he interpreted Judaism to suit them. He used to say then that the Jews ought not to return to their homeland, because it would upset the captains of industry and the great bankers. He and his ilk invented the myth of the Jewish mission. The function of the Jewish people was asserted to be to instruct the other peoples. Therefore, they alleged, we must live in the dispersion. Had not the other nations already hated and despised us, they would have ridiculed us for such arrogance. And Zion was not Zion! The fact was, of course, that we not only did not teach the other nations, but that they taught us-day by day and year by year-bloody, painful lessons.

Finally, we roused ourselves and sought we way out of Egypt. And we found it. Then, to be sure, Dr. Geyer also came here, and brought with him all his old arrogance and hypocrisy.

"Nowadays, thank God, the Jews conduct their public affairs differently. It is not the rich alone who make the decisions, but the whole community. Communal leadership is no longer a reward for success in business. Leaders are chosen not for their wealth, but for their talent and their ability to command respect in the eyes of the public. Therefore, the instincts of the masses must be flattered. A theory for the immediate advantage of the masses must be found, or at least for what the masses imagine to be to their immediate advantage. Therefore, an anti-alien slogan is proclaimed. A non-Jew must not be accepted by the New Society. The fewer get a place near the platter, the larger the portion of each. Perhaps you believe that that is to your immediate advantage. But it is not. If you adopt that stupid, narrow-minded policy, the land will go to wrack and ruin. We stand and fall by the principle that whoever has given two years' service to the New Society as prescribed by our rules, and has conducted himself properly, are eligible to membership no matter what his race or creed.

"I say to you, therefore, that you must hold fast to the things that have made us great: to liberality, tolerance, love of mankind. Only then is Zion truly Zion! You will elect your delegate to the Congress. Choose one who thinks not of the immediate advantage, but of the lasting good. But if you choose a Geyer man, you will not deserve to have the sun of our Holy Land shine upon you. So! I have spoken."

The applause was slight. The speaker had scored several times with his audience, but his conclusion was obviously unfortunate. Only one person present was particularly pleased with the last words, and he said as much to the architect when the latter sat down beside him in a bath of perspiration. The pleased individual was Mr. Kingscourt, but he had no vote in Neudorf.

# Chapter III

"Does anyone else wish to speak?" asked the chairman.

"I do!" shouted Mendel, and leaped up to the platform. "Mr. Steineck," he began, "has just delivered an address to us. You might say that it was good, and again you might say that it was insulting. I say it was insulting."

Friedmann interrupted him. "You, Mendel! I won't allow you to be insulting."

"Who's insulting?" retorted Mendel. " I say he is! He said we were not worthy to have the sun shine upon us. Because we don't want to let everyone in. Who toiled and moiled over the soil? We! Who pulled out the stones? We! Who drained the marshes! We! Who dug the canals, who planted the trees, who sweated and froze until all this was finished? We! We! We! And now, suddenly, it's not to belong to us. No...that's no way to talk. When we came here, there was nothing, nothing at all. Now Palestine is a model country. We've sunk our blood and sweat and toil into it!

"I don't understand that about the immediate and the permanent advantage. Perhaps you do. As for Dr. Geyer, he doesn't appeal to me much. I don't like what he said in the old days. But I do know that now he is right. What we made with our own hands must remain ours. We shall let no one take it away from us. So! .I have no more to say!"

**163**

Subdued applause greeted Mendel's words, but people were obviously restraining themselves out of respect to the visitors.

Mendel stepped down, and David ascended the platform. He was very grave as he began to speak in a clear, carrying voice.

"My friends! You will listen to me. You know I am one of yourselves. I worked in the fields just as you did, by my father's side. I have risen a bit in the world, but I know the joys and the pains of the farmer. I know how you feel. Nevertheless, I must say that Mendel is wrong.

"To begin with, no one wants to take away anything that belongs to you. I should fight beside you to the last breath against any such attempt. But there is no question of infringing upon your hard-earned rights. The fruits of your labors will remain your own, and be multiplied. The issue is quite different from what has been told you.

"Mendel means well, but he is mistaken. He is mistaken chiefly because he thinks that all we see here is the work of your hands. Your hands made it indeed, but your brains did not conceive it. You are not so ignorant, thank Heaven, as the peasants of other times and countries; but you do not know the origin of your own happier circumstances. What is Neudorf? A person who looks at the settlement for the first time without knowing its history will wonder-or rejoice-that so prosperous a village has been founded in the Vaadi Rumani, on the old Roman road to Tiberias. I have brought two strange gentlemen with me today, and I was proud to be able to show them many fine things on the way here-our fields with the ripening barley, our meadows, our tree nurseries, our well-built houses and blooded cattle and up-to-date machinery; our irrigation system

**164**

and our reclaimed moors. I say 'our,' though I own no acre of land here nor a single head of cattle. Everything is yours, but I feel so much at home here that I venture to speak in this fashion. And if these gentlemen ask me who conjured up all this within twenty short years, I shall reply in Mendel's own words: 'We! We! We!'

"Yes, we. But how? Did we simply come here and work with our hands as Mendel says we did? With our unskilled hands that were so unaccustomed to work on the soil? How could we have achieved results that no one else had achieved here before? No one, I mean to say, except the German Protestant farmers who founded several colonies in this country toward the end of the last century. We not only kept pace with those highly efficient Germans, but outstripped them! How did that happen?

"True, you worked with all the fervor of Jewish love for the sacred soil. That soil was unproductive for others, but for us it was a good soil. Because we fertilized it with our love. Our first settlers had proven thirty years earlier what could be done here. Yet their settlements were worth little from the economic viewpoint because they were based on a false principle. With all their modern machinery, those settlers were able to create only the old type of village. But you have the New Village. And that, my friends, is not the work of your hands only.

"Don't imagine I am jesting when I say that Neudorf was built not in Palestine, but elsewhere. It was built in England, in America, in France and in Germany. It was evolved out of experiments, books, and dreams. The unsuccessful experiments of both practical men and dreamers were to serve you as object lessons, though you did not know it.

**165**

"In the old days there were peasants just as hardworking as yourselves, and yet they could make no headway. These old-time peasants did not know their own soil. They did not know what was in it, because they were too narrow-minded to have it chemically analyzed. They merely sweated over their land, and worked much harder than was necessary. They either worked the wrong fields or used wrong methods. They could not operate their farms economically because they were too befogged to see three feet in front of their noses. When they borrowed money for improvements, they became so deeply involved in usurious debts that the best crops could not extricate them. They had no insurance against hail or cattle plagues. No individual farmer could afford to have his land drained or irrigated. A bad crop ruined him; but good crops did not enrich him because he did not know how to reach the world markets. Of hired labor he had either too little or too much. He could not afford to educate his hungry children, and they grew up as ignorant as he himself and his ancestors. The new transportation facilities seemed to have been invented for his ruin. In virgin countries, agriculture was conducted as a large-scale industry. Machinery enriched the large landowners and still further impoverished the small ones. A new order of slavery was created. The free farmer became a serf, and his children drifted into the industrial wage slavery of the factory.

"The foundations of the old order were undermined through its peasantry. Many a noble soul sighed over the situation, studied and experimented in the hope of improvement. All the aids of science and experience were invoked. Everyone realized, however, that in an age of machinery the basic conditions of human life had to be adapted to our new knowledge of natural forces. The nineteenth century, however, was a curiously backward era.

"At the beginning of that era, muddle-headed visionaries were taken seriously, while sober, practical men were branded as lunatics. Napoleon the Great did not believe that Fulton's steamboat was practical. On the other hand, the absurd Fourier easily won adherents for his phalansteries, which were intended to provide homes and workshops for several hundred families. Stephenson, the inventor of the railway, and Cabet, the dreamer of Icaria, were contemporaries. I could mention many other names with which you may not be familiar."

David's words were listened to attentively, though he was delivering what was an academic lecture rather than a popular oration. As he stopped for breath, Mendel rose and said civilly, but loudly, "Come to the point! What has all that to do with our Neudorf?"

"Very much, my friends," responded David calmly. "A socialistic dream rose to answer every new machine invented during that peculiar nineteenth century, which has always seemed to me like a great factory where ingenious machinery was served by wretched human beings. Clouds of smoke ascended from the chimneys of that factory, and darkened the blue heavens. Those beautifully formed, dissolving smoke clouds, however, symbolized the socialistic promises for the society of the future. When the wishful human beings looked up, they no longer saw the heavens, but the factory-born clouds of a Utopia.

"But there were rosy clouds as well. Take the famous one of the American, Edward Bellamy, who outlined a noble

**167**

communistic society in his Looking Backward. In that Utopia, all may eat as much as they please from the common platter. The lamb and the wolf feed in the same pasture. Fine. Very fine. Only then, the wolves are no longer wolves, and human beings no longer human. After Bellamy's book came Freiland, a utopian romance by the publicist Hertzka. Freiland is a brilliant bit of magic, which may well be compared with the juggler's inexhaustible hat. Beautiful dreams, indeed, or airships if you care to call them that-but not dirigible. Because these noble lovers of humanity based their ingenious schemes on a false premise. The scholars among you-and I know that in Neudorf today as in Katrah thirty years ago, there are educated peasants-will understand me when I say that they were guilty of a petitio princpii. They used as evidence something that still had to be proven, namely, that humanity had already achieved that degree of maturity and freedom of judgment which is necessary for the establishment of a new social order. Or, perhaps they were clear enough about it in their own minds, and lacked only the bit of solid ground that Archimedes needed for his lever. They believed that the most important factor in creating a new order of things was machinery. Machinery was their sine qua non. But that is not correct. No ...it is power that counts. Now and always, power is the thing. For, having power, I can exploit the newest inventions to the utmost. But we-we had the power that was needed. Whence did we have it? From the terrible pressure to which we were subjected on all sides, from poverty and persecution. That was the centripetal force that drew all our scattered forces to a focus, and strengthened a union that included not only the downtrodden, but the powerful; not only the young, but the wise; not only thoughtless enthusiasts, but cultured men and women. Not only hands, but heads...all together. A people, a whole people, found itself together-nay, found itself again.

"We made the New Society not because we were better than others, but simply because we were ordinary men with the ordinary human needs for air and light, health and honor, for the right to acquire property and security of possession. And since we were about to build ourselves a home, we chose a 1900 model, and not one of the year 1600 or 1800 or any other date. All this is certainly clear and obvious. We did nothing very meritorious. We achieved nothing extraordinary. We did only that which, under the given circumstances and at the given moment, was an historical necessity."

Mendel shouted an interruption again. "To the point! Get to the point!"

"I have almost finished," said David pleasantly. "I wish only to recall your beginnings to you. Without the gigantic social-economic labors of the nineteenth century, your beginnings would have been impossible. Individual Jews participated in those labors, but by no means Jews alone. What resulted from the common endeavors ought to be claimed by no one nation for itself. It belongs to all men. Anyone who is grateful to those old pathfinders, or even merely curious about them, will find it worth while to look into the subject. And in this connection, my friends, the Anglo-Saxon race deserves the highest praise. For it is among the English that we find the first traces of the co-operative social order, which we have taken over and adapted. German science, too, has added its profound word here. If anyone here cares to know more about this subject, I shall be glad to refer you to books on the co-operative movement in England, Germany, and France:'

**169**

A young peasant raised his hand. "What do you wish, Jacob?" inquired the chairman.

The youngster flushed, and spoke up modestly. "I merely wanted to tell Mr. Littwak that we have the history of the pioneers of Rochdale in our village library."

"Give it to Mr. Mendel to read," replied David. "It is a very beautiful, instructive story. The honest pioneers of Rochdale, as they are called, did much for you. That is to say, they achieved a great deal for the whole of humanity -though they were thinking of themselves alone.

"When you go to your consumers" co-operative societies and buy goods of the best quality and at the lowest prices, you have the pioneers of Rochdale to thank for it. And if your Neudorf is a prosperous producers' co-operative you owe it to the poor martyrs of Rahaline in Ireland. The peasants of Rahaline themselves did not know that they were performing an act of historic significance when, in 1831, they founded the first New Village in the world with the help of their landlord, Mr. Vandaleur. Yes, many decades were to pass before the most learned and cleverest of men grasped the idea of Rahaline. The consumers' co-operative society of Rochdale was understood much sooner than the Rahaline idea of the New Village based on cooperation in production. But, when we founded our New Society, we naturally began with the new type of village rather than with the wretched old one. There is nothing here in Neudorf that was not implied in Rahaline. The one difference is, that instead of a Mr. Vandaleur, we have a large association to which everyone belongs; that is, the New Society."

The young peasant once more raised his hand. The speaker came to a surprised halt. "Will you not tell us the story of Mr. Vandaleur and Rahaline, Mr. Littwak?" he asked shyly.

"Gladly, my friends. Ireland at that time was a poor country with a most wretched population. The agricultural tenants were a demoralized proletariat who had even become thieves and murderers. A squire named Vandaleur had a particularly violent set of tenants on his estates. At the beginning of 1831, the distress in Ireland was very great. The peasants, in their desperation, committed shocking crimes. Mr. Vandaleur had a steward whom the laborers hated for his severity; and in their desperation, they murdered him. What did Vandaleur do then? Something magnanimous. Instead of inflicting additional severities upon these people, he conceived the superhuman idea of being kind to them. He called the defiant, miserable men together, united them in a laborers' co-operative, and leased his estate of Rahaline to the new association. The aims of this co-operative were; to work with a common capital, to extend mutual aid to the members, to improve the standard of living, and to educate the children. The machinery and farm equipment were to belong to Mr. Vandaleur as landlord until the co-operative society had paid for them. It was to put its profits into a reserve fund for this purpose. The society managed its business without interference. A committee of nine was chosen from among the men themselves. Each member of this committee was responsible for a definite branch of the work-for the labor on the estate, home industries, the administrative business of the society, and so on. The daily tasks were assigned by the committee. Everyone had to do his share. The association paid its members at the prevailing scale of wages. The members were taxed with a small amount for a sick fund and similar purposes. The men of Rahaline were

**171**

apparently laborers working for a landlord, but actually they were working for themselves, since Mr. Vandaleur reserved the right of supervision only. The enterprise was remarkably successful, and Mr. Vandaleur derived a larger income-in rent and in interest-from Rahaline than previously. And the laborers, who had been living in the deepest poverty, began to prosper suddenly, without any transition period at all, as if they had been touched by a magic wand. They worked well and vigorously. They knew that they were working for themselves; and the knowledge lent them more than human endurance. The men who had murdered their steward now carried out the most important tasks without supervision except from each other. A record was kept of the hours each man worked and of the amount of work accomplished; and at the end of the week, he received as much as he had actually earned. There was no parity of wages! The diligent worker received more, the slacker less."

"Bravo!" cried a voice in the crowd. (Laughter.)

"It was soon seen that the laborers of Rahaline worked twice as hard as any others in that district," continued David. "Yet it was the same soil; the people were the same. It was merely that they had discovered a saving principle: that of the agricultural producers' co-operative. They were paid not in cash, but in labor tickets, which were valid only at the general store of Rahaline. But at that store, which also belonged to the co-operative society, they could obtain everything they needed. The store carried goods of the best quality only, and sold them at wholesale prices. Historians estimate that the people of Rahaline saved fifty per cent on their purchases.

172

"Every member of that co-operative society, moreover, was
certain of steady employment (and, in case of illness, of an
equal allowance from the sick fund) for every day in the year.
Sick and incapacitated members received medical attention and
maintenance. When a father died, the children were
supported....But I don't want to go on telling you about things
that you can find better told in books. I should prefer to send
you the works of Webb-potter, Oppenheimer, Seifert, Huber
and others for your library."

The modest young peasant interrupted again. "How did it
finally work out in Rahaline, Mr. Littwak?"

"After only two years of this system, Rahaline became very
prosperous. Homes and furnishings, food and clothing,
improved methods of education, and a general rise in the
standard of living-all these attested to the well-being of the
peasants. The net annual profits (exclusive of the rent on the
leasehold) increased, and the co-operators would probably have
taken over the estate after a few more years had not Mr.
Vandaleur left his own project in the lurch. He gambled away
his fortune in Dublin, and fled to America. His creditors sold
Rahaline, the tenant co-operators were driven off the estate,
and the blessed isle once more sank in a sea of misery...."

"But the lesson of Rahaline was not lost. It was treasured by
economists; and when we led our people back to the beloved
soil of Palestine, we founded thousands of Rahalines. A
Vandaleur would have been neither strong nor reliable enough
for us. A powerful collective body was essential. That body is
our New Society. It is the landlord which provided you with
land and farm equipment, and to it you owe your present
prosperity.

"The New Society, however, did not evolve all this by itself. It did not derive it either from the brains of its leaders or from the pockets of its founders alone. The New Society rests, rather, squarely on ideas which are the common stock of the whole civilized world. Now, my dear friends, do you understand what I mean? It would be unethical for us to deny a share in our commonwealth to any man, wherever he might come from, whatever his race or creed. For we stand on the shoulders of other civilized peoples. If a man joins us-if he accepts our institutions and assumes the duties of our commonwealth-he should be entitled to enjoy all our rights. We ought therefore to pay our debts. And that can be done in only one way-by the exercise of the utmost tolerance. Our slogan must be, now and always- 'Man, thou art my brother!' "

The aged rabbi arose and applauded with his trembling hands. The audience followed his example, and hailed David vociferously as he was about to step down from the platform. But Mendel roared in a mighty voice, "Then the aliens will take the bread out of our mouths!"

Whereupon David turned back and motioned that he had something more to say.

"No, Mendel," he replied. "That is an error. Those who come later will not make you poorer, but richer. The wealth of a land is in its workers. Your own experience has taught you that. The more workers come, the more bread there is in a just society like ours. Naturally, you are not being asked to give up your good fields, the rights you have won, to others. But, just as it is good for Neudorf when new settlements are founded on its outskirts, so it is good for the New Society as a whole to

**174**

expand. Everyone must earn for himself the values he wishes
to enjoy. And the more values are created in the country, the
richer our commonwealth becomes. Your parents, who had an
active share in creating the history of Neudorf, know that from
their own experience. At first there were only twenty families
here. I ask you: Did they become worse off when, gradually,
thirty, fifty, a hundred families joined them? I ask you: Did the
early settlers become poorer or richer?"

The audience now, for the first time, caught his full meaning,
and applauded impetuously: "Littwak is right!" "We are all
more prosperous now!" "Yes, yes!"

"There is your answer," concluded David. "What has held good
hitherto will be equally true in the future. The more people
come here to work, the better off everyone will be. It is not
altruism alone that prompts me to proclaim: 'Man, thou art my
brother!' Sheer self-interest, also, urges that we declare:
'Brother, thou art welcome here!'

"The elders among you remember this place twenty years ago-
how desolate and deserted it was. The first settlers took the best
land. Those who came after them took the next best, and
improved that. Later comers found ever poorer soil, but they
made it fruitful. Stony soil became fertile, swamps were
thoroughly drained. Because land in the vicinity of a village,
even when of poor quality, always attracts new settlers.

"Today Neudorf is a garden-an immense, splendid garden,
where life is good. But all your cultivation is worthless and
your fields will revert to barrenness unless you foster liberal
ideas, magnanimity, and a love of mankind. These are the

**175**

things you must cherish and nurture. And because I know that you will do as: I say, 'Hedad! Hedad! Hedad! for Neudorf!'"

"Hedad for Littwakl Hedad for Neudorfl" shouted men and women together. Despite his laughing protests, the speaker was lifted to their shoulders and carried in a procession.

That day Dr. Geyer lost the votes of Neudorf.

# Chapter IV

After the meeting the visitors observed the model agricultural equipment of Neudorf. Kingscourt was particularly interested in the chemical experiment station and the up-to-date engine house. Friedrich lingered for a while in the elementary school and the public library. The latter contained many popular scientific works. Miriam, as a teacher, answered all his questions. At first he was pleasantly surprised by the things she told him; but the more he heard about the physical and spiritual development of the growing generation, the more depressed he became. At last he sighed heavily.

"What's the matter?" Miriam asked sympathetically.

"My heart is heavy, Miss Miriam. I see now that I neglected a duty. I could have had, would have been obliged to have a share in all this wonderful work of national restoration. I was an educated man, and ought to have foreseen what was coming. But, no. I was absorbed in my own petty troubles. I ran away, and stupidly wasted twenty years. I can hardly tell you how all this I see affects me. I-I am ashamed of myself."

She tried to comfort him.

"No, Miss Miriam, you mustn't try to console me. Your own life is so useful that you can contradict me only out of the kindness of your heart, and not out of conviction. I am ashamed of my passivity, of my egotism. It was my duty as an educated man to have taken the part of my unfortunate people.

**177**

I neglected that duty shamefully. Pity me if you can, Miss Miriam, but do not despise me!"

"Despise you! How could I do that?" she returned softly. "You, the benefactor of our house!"

"Please don't mention that again," he begged. "Your praise merely humiliates me. I know only too well that I do not deserve praise. The intellectuals of my time had the duty, similar to the noblesse oblige of earlier days, of working for the improvement of mankind. Each ought to have helped according to his ability and insight. Not all your kindness, Miss Miriam, can make me believe that I have no cause for self-reproach."

"Is it too late, then?" she asked. "You could still join the ranks of the New Society. You would be shown where you might be most useful. You have heard my brother say that we welcome all forces. And how glad we should be to have you!"

"You really think it is not too late, Miss Miriam?" He was overjoyed. "Could I still become a useful human being?"

"Of course!" she smiled.

Hope stirred within him. He felt suddenly rejuvenated. New perspectives opened before him. But after a moment he recalled his situation, and sighed once more.

"Ah, no, Miss Miriam. It would have been too beautiful, I cannot do as I choose. I cannot remain here. I am not free." She paled slightly as she repeated in a voice that trembled, "Not free?"

"No, I am tied to someone for life."

"To whom, if I may ask?" She spoke tonelessly.

"To Mr. Kingscount." He explained his relation to the old man. He had given his word of honor never to leave him. He could therefore remain in Palestine only as long as his friend chose to stay-and that would probably not be overlong.

Miriam's face brightened. "And if Mr. Kingscourt were to release you from your promise?" she asked.

"He would not if I did not ask him to. But the very request for release would be disloyal and ungrateful to the splendid old chap. He is the best friend I have in the world, and he has only me. What would become of him if I left him?"

"He would have to remain here too," she suggested.

Friedrich thought this quite out of the question, knowing the old man as he did. At best Kingscourt would travel about the country for a few days or weeks, and then there would be no holding him back. He would go on to Europe.

The others had finished their rounds by this time. A simple luncheon was served at Friedmann's house. They sat at table for a while after the end of the meal, talking of Neudorfs past and future. Most of the villagers had returned to their farms on the outskirts after the morning's meeting. There were therefore only a few-those who lived in the village proper-to see them off, which they did with much waving of caps and handkerchiefs.

On either side of the high road were well-tilled fields, vineyards, tobacco plantations, tree nurseries. Nowhere a rod of barren ground. A little way beyond the road a machine was mowing a field of clover. Wagons piled high with dried alfalfa for cattle fodder passed them in both directions.

Miriam explained the natural and agricultural features of the country to Friedrich, who knew little of such things. The summer crops were already peeping out of the ground -maize, sesame, lentils, vetches. Electric plows were being guided over fields still damp from the winter rains in preparation for the next sowing. Workers were carefully transplanting tobacco stalks from the seed beds, throwing away the weaker of the two plants set at each interval. The hop stalks were full grown, and the farmers were propping them up with eucalyptus branches or with wire netting. The branches were not pruned, so as to leave the blossoms protected against the rays of the sun.

Steineck suddenly broke into the conversation with praises of the eucalyptus, a splendid Australian tree of which hundreds of varieties had been brought to Palestine at the beginning of the systematic large-scale colonization. Nothing could have been begun without the eucalyptus, which grew rapidly, drained swamps as if by magic, and served many purposes of use and of ornament. Or, at least, the success achieved could not have come so quickly. Steineck's praises of the tree were unceasing.

"Yes," assented Sarah jestingly. "Mr. Steineck has expressed his gratitude to the eucalyptus by immortalizing it in stone. It is his favorite decoration for his buildings."

The joyousness of the landscape reflected itself in the mood of the party. The springtide was burgeoning on every side. Every meadow and every ditch was covered with a vivid tapestry of tiny blue iris, upstretching, rosy sword-lilies, sun-eyed tulips, gorgeous orchids. Here and there were orchards of apricot and mulberry trees.

The road ran through a romantic defile with weird, rocky caves where the defenders of the Jewish land had hidden from their enemies in the bitter days of the last struggle for independence. David spoke of those days feelingly.

A short distance beyond Neudorf, the roadway made a sudden turn-and the lovely plain and lake of Kinneret were revealed in the noon sunlight. Friedrich gave an involuntary cry of delight at catching his first glimpse of the unexpected, magnificent landscape.

Boats, large and small, furrowed the broad, gleaming surface of the lake. Sails shimmered, brass fittings glittered in the sunlight. On the farther shore numerous white villas nestled on green wooded heights. Here was Magdala, a sparkling, pretty new townlet with beautiful houses and gardens. But the car sped on to Tiberias without stopping, taking a southerly direction along the lake shore. The vivid pageant reminded them of the Riviera between Cannes and Nice at the height of the season. Fashionable folk were driving in elegant little equipages of all kinds-mostly motor cars with seats for two, three, or four passengers. But old-fashioned wagons, drawn by horses or mules, were not missing. Along the lake shore the travelers saw cyclists, horseback riders and gay strollers in the cosmopolitan mob that is so typical of fashionable bathing resorts. They were told that the medicinal hot springs and the beautiful situation of Tiberias attracted visitors from Europe and America who had always sought perennial spring in Sicily or Egypt. As soon as first-class hotel accommodations were available in Tiberias, the tourists had streamed thither. Experienced Swiss hotel-keepers had been the first to recognize the climatic advantages and scenic beauty of the spot, and prospered accordingly.

The car now passed some of these hotels. Men and women on the balconies were watching the kaleidoscopic traffic on the lake and the highroad. White-clad young men and girls played tennis in courts behind the hotels. Hungarian, Roumanian and Italian bands in national costume performed on several large terraces. All of which the travelers noted on the wing, their destination being somewhat beyond this point. They drove through Tiberias from north to south, glancing down neat little side streets which branched off from the main thoroughfare. There were vast, silent mansions in beautiful open squares, stately mosques, churches with Latin and Greek crosses, magnificent stone synagogues. The little Oriental harbor teemed with traffic. At the southern end of the town were more hotels and villas on a beautiful thoroughfare stretching along for a distance of half an hour's walk. Everywhere there were gardens. At the end of the thoroughfare at the hot springs came the bathing establishments.

Half-way between the town and the baths, the auto stopped before the trellised gate of a villa half-hidden in foliage.

"Here we are!" cried David, alighting.

The gate was opened, and an old gentleman appeared on the threshold. He raised his skull cap with a happy smile. "Where is he, David, my child?"

Friedrich was overcome, realizing that here, too, in the home of the elder Littwak, his arrival had been eagerly awaited. Nothing strange about it, of course. They had telephoned ahead to announce his coming.

This dignified old man who carried himself so well could he be the wretched peddler to whom he had once tried to give alms in a Viennese cafe! What a remarkable transformation! And yet it had all happened in the most natural way in the world. The Littwaks had been among the first to hasten to Palestine at the beginning of the great new national enterprise, and reaped the rewards of the prosperity they helped so faithfully to create.

Yet the house had its sorrow: Friedrich was immediately taken to an upper veranda overlooking the lake, where the invalid mother lay back in a wheel chair. She reached out her waxen, emaciated hand to Friedrich as he approached, and looked infinite gratitude at him out of her painstricken eyes.

"Yes," she said quavering after the greetings had been exchanged, "yes, dear Dr. Loewenberg, Tiberias is beautiful, and the baths are excellent. But one must come here while there is still time. I came too late. Too late."

Miriam stroked her mother's face. "You are looking better since you came here, Mother. The cure has done you good. You will realize it only after you come home."

Mrs. Littwak smiled wistfully. "Dear child, I am content. I am already at the gates of Paradise. Look at this view of mine, Dr. Loewenberg. The Garden of Eden, is it not?"

**183**

Friedrich stepped to the balustrade and looked out over the landscape. The shimmering blue waters of Lake Kinneret. The shores and distant heights softly outlined in the spring air. The steep declivities of the Jaulan hills on the farther side of the lake, mirrored in its depths. The Jordan flowing into the northern end of the lake. In the distance, the majestic, snow-crowned Hermon, a venerable giant overlooking the smaller ranges and the rejuvenated land. To the left, nearer the town, gentle inlets, lovely beaches, the plain of Kinneret, Magdala, Tiberias itself-a new gem set among the dark ruins of the fortress on the hillside. Verdure and bloom everywhere. A young world, and fragrant.

"The Garden of Eden, indeed!" murmured Friedrich to himself. As he felt Miriam standing beside him, he caught her hand and pressed it softly, as if to thank her that life could still be so beautiful.

The invalid saw from her chair, and her heart beat faster for joy.

"Children!" she murmured inaudibly, and sank into reverie.

# Chapter V

The little villa which the Littwaks had rented for the period of the cure was too small to house all the guests. Miriam remained with her parents, while David reserved rooms for the rest of the party at a hotel near the baths. The baggage had been sent on ahead. After greeting the elder Littwaks, they drove to the hotel, where they found everything arranged for their convenience and comfort.

Entering the lobby, they were cordially greeted by an elderly lady and two gentlemen. David made the necessary introductions. The lady was Mrs. Gothland, an American Jewess, whose manner was so winning that people always took to her at once. Under its frame of gray hair, her face was still fascinating. The gentleman in the black Anglican clerical frock was the Reverend William H. Hopkins of the English church in Jerusalem. He had a long, patriarchal white beard, and dreamy blue eyes. To Kingscourt's astonishment, he felt complimented when the former took him for a Jew. The second gentleman was Professor Steineck, a bacteriologist, and brother of the architect of that name. The professor was a jolly, quick-tempered, absentminded scholar, who always spoke as if lecturing to an audience of partially deaf people. He and his brother idolized each other, but usually quarreled within five minutes after they met. So it was on this occasion. The architect had suggested that the strangers visit the Steineck Institute, his brother's famous laboratory.

**185**

The professor frowned. "I don't mind, understand," he shouted, "but there's nothing to see when you get there. Not worth the trouble. A house with some rooms and some hutches for guinea pigs. In each room, a worker making experiments. That's all. Understand? My brother always gets me into these dilemmas!"

Mrs. Gothland smiled. "The gentlemen don't believe you. Everyone knows that your Institute is one of the sights of this country."

Professor Steineck roared until the room re-echoed. "Nothing of the sort! Is it microbes you want to see? It's characteristic of microbes that they can't be seen. Not with the naked eye, at any rate. They're fine sights. Everyone knows I don't believe in microbes. I breed them with one hand and fight them with the other. Understand?"

"No!" roared Kingscourt, delighted. "Not a word. Seems to be some kind of chemical kitchen. What do you cook there, Professor?"

"Pest, cholera, diphtheria, childbed fever, tuberculosis, hydrophobia, malaria, smirked the Professor.

"Pfui, Deibel!"

Mrs. Gothland explained. "The Professor refers to cures for all those enemies of mankind. Very well, then, we'll go without him. We'll not even ask him along. Admission is not denied to distinguished strangers, and someone will be there to show us around."

"Stop!" cried the Professor. "Then, in Heaven's name, I'll go with you. Otherwise, you'll jump into my stupidest assistant, who'll show you the streptococcus for the cholera bacillus. Understand?"

"Not one word," confessed Kingscourt.

The party dispersed for the moment. The architect had plans for a new English hospital near Jerusalem which he was to submit to the Reverend Mr. Hopkins. Sarah went off to provide for the baby's needs. David excused himself to fetch Father Ignaz, another Seder guest, from the Franciscan convent. They arranged to meet at the Littwak villa before dinner. Mrs. Gothland promised to bring the gentlemen on time, and drove off to the Steineck Institute with Kingscourt, Friedrich, Reschid Bey and the Professor. After a fifteen minute drive they reached an unpretentious building of moderate size on the south shore behind a promontory.

"We don't need a large building for our purpose," explained the Professor. "Microbes don't take up much room. My stables are in those annexes over there. I use many horses and other creatures. Understand?"

"Ah! You ride a great deal," said Kingscourt. "I can understand that-in this magnificent country."

"Country nothing! I use horses and donkeys and dogs in brief, the whole menagerie-for serum. I produce great quantities of it. My stables reach all the way down there, where you see the air factory."

"Wha-at!" shouted Kingscourt. "Most esteemed horse-poisoner, you're not trying to tell me that you manufacture air here, I hope! There's plenty. The air here is capital in fact!"

"I meant liquid air, of course. Understand?"

"Ah, yes! To be sure I understand. They had it in America in my time. So you have the liquid air industry in Palestine also?"

"Yes, and many other industries. All of them, as a matter of fact! We are quite famous for our refrigerating devices. This is a warm country. From here down along the Jordan, at any rate, the country is pretty well heated the year round. We have therefore developed the refrigerating industries. Understand? On the principle that the best stoves are to be found in the cold countries, while one freezes bitterly in an Italian winter. We, for our part, have provided ourselves with plenty of ice for the warm weather. In the heat of the summer, for instance, you will find blocks of ice even in the most modest homes. And anyone who wishes may buy wreaths of flowers in ice for the dinner table for a trifling sum."

"Oh, I know that stunt!" cried Kingscourt. "I saw a wreath of fresh flowers in ice at the world's fair in Paris in 1900."

"I was not trying to tell you anything new. We have merely used the existing devices. Cooling apparatus is a common necessity here, and is produced cheaply, since competition keeps the prices low. "People of moderate means cannot, of course, go off to the Lebanon in the summer any more than the same class in Europe can afford expensive vacations. However, through science we have learned how to make ourselves more comfortable and more healthy. Understand?

**188**

"Our enterprising business men and technically trained youth have transplanted all known industries to this country. The cosmopolitan drift of industry was already evident in your day. Why should we not have secured all these things, since it was to our advantage to do so? There were latent treasures in our land, if only we knew how to draw them forth. The chemical industries were the first to be developed here, being, so to speak, the most easily transportable. Did you ever happen to study chemistry, Mr. Kingscourt?"

"No, happens that I did not."

"Well, if you had studied chemistry, you would have known what learned circles in those days thought of the potential wealth of Palestine. Reschid Bey here took a doctor's degree in chemistry at a German university. He can tell you all about it."

"You embarrass me, Professor," said Reschid modestly, "when you ask me to show off my bits of learning in your presence. ...As a matter of fact, every young chemistry student twenty years ago knew that the Palestinian soil was potentially precious. The Jordan Valley and the Dead Sea region were used as textbook examples. At the end of the nineteenth century, a German chemist wrote concerning the Dead Sea: "This water-filled valley, which lies farther below sea-level than any other in the world, contains an almost wholly concentrated salt of a lye composition not found elsewhere, and it throws off asphaltic masses which nowhere else appear in this form." When you see our water-power apparatus, you will realize that we have taken full advantage of the difference in levels between the Dead Sea and the Mediterranean. But that is something else. You will see it later. I merely want to tell you

**189**

now that the Dead Sea water forms a saline lye whose like is to be found only at Stassfurt. You must have heard of the great Stassfurt potash works which dominated the world market. We have the same thing now at the Dead Sea, and on a much larger scale."

"Marvelous!" shouted Kingscourt.

"Not at all," smiled Reschild. "It's perfectly simple. What could be done in Stassfurt could be done just as well at the Dead Sea. Our water, in fact, was richer in chemical content than any other. It reminds me of the old legends about sunken treasures. Children imagine such treasures only in the form of golden bracelets, chains, and coins. But the Dead Sea salts, also, are golden. They are richer in brome than any other natural lye. And you know how expensive brome is.

"What was formerly the most barren, the most lifeless part of our country is now the most productive. In the Jordan Valley and-the Dead Sea there is bituminous lime from which we produce the best asphalt in the world. Eichner, a German chemist, said long ago that the geological character of the region indicated the presence of petroleum. Oil was in fact drilled for, and found. Sulphur and phosphate, too, exist there in inexhaustible quantities. You know as well as I how important phosphate is in the manufacture of artificial fertilizer. As a matter of fact, our phosphates compete successfully with those of Tunis and Algiers; and, at that, we produce more easily and cheaply than Florida. The artificial fertilizers which we have been able to produce in such great abundance have of course contributed immeasurably to the progress or our agriculture...But I fear I am boring Mrs. Gothland with all these dry details."

"Not at all," declared the lady amiably.

"There are connections of that sort between modern industry and agriculture," added the Professor. "Understand? Everything belongs with everything else. There must be only the knowledge and the business enterprise to make the contacts. I myself, as you see me, am only a learned ass; but I do my bit to foster industry and agriculture."

"Won't you explain that, most honored breeder of microbes?" begged Kingscourt.

"You shall have it," chuckled Steineck. "It is a familiar fact in bacteriology that various kinds of tobacco and cheese owe their aroma to some of the micro-organisms I'm always battling with. We have therefore tried to breed these for our tobacco planters and cheese manufacturers. And now our cheese competes with the best brands of France and Switzerland. In the Jordan Valley we grow weeds that are not inferior to Havana."

Steineck now led the way through his laboratories, which were patterned after those of the Pasteur Institute in Paris. His numerous assistants were not disturbed by the presence of visitors, and quietly went on with their work at test tubes, microscopes and crucibles after answering questions briefly and civilly. One, however, turned upon the Professor with rough good nature. "Leave us in peace, sir I have no time for all these catechisms. Else this fellow will escape me again!"

**191**

Steineck obediently marshaled the visitors out of the room. Outside, he remarked, "He was quite right. The fellow he referred to was his bacillus. Understand?"

"I work here," he added a moment later, showing them into his own laboratory, which was as simply equipped as those of his young assistants.

"At what, if I may ask?" inquired Friedrich.

"The scientist's eyes grew dreamy as he replied, "At the opening up of Africa."

The visitors mistrusted their ears. Was the seeker after scientific truth a bit mad?

"Did you say, 'at the opening up of Africa'?" asked Kingscourt, suspicion gleaming in his eye. "

Yes, Mr. Kingscourt. That is to say, I hope to find the lure for malaria. We have overcome it here in Palestine thanks to the drainage of the swamps, canalization, and the eucalyptus forests. But conditions are different in Africa. The same measures cannot be taken there because the prerequisite-mass immigration-is not present. The white colonist goes under in Africa. That country can be opened up to civilization only after malaria has been subdued. Only then will enormous areas become available for the surplus populations of Europe. And only then will the proletarian masses find a healthy outlet. Understand?"

Kingscourt laughed. "You want to cart off the whites to the black continent, you wonder-worker!"

"Not only the whites!" replied Steineck gravely. "The blacks as well. There is still one problem of racial misfortune unsolved. The depths of that problem, in all their horror, only a Jew can fathom. I mean the negro problem. Don't laugh, Mr. Kingscourt. Think of the hair-raising horrors of the slave trade. Human beings, because their skins are black, are stolen, carried off, and sold. Their descendants grow up in alien surroundings despised and hated because their skin is differently pigmented. I am not ashamed to say, though I be thought ridiculous, now that I have lived to see the restoration of the Jews, I should like to pave the way for the restoration of the Negroes.'"

"You misjudge me, Professor," replied Kingscourt. "I am not laughing. On the contrary. It's splendid of you, Devil take me! You show me horizons I hadn't even dreamt of."

"That is why I am working to open up Africa. All human beings ought to have a home. Then they will be kinder to one another. Then they will understand and love one another more. Understand?"

Mrs. Gothland murmured the thought in the minds of all the others. "Professor Steineck, God bless you!"

**Theodor Herzl**

# Chapter VI

The party had left the Steineck Institute in a solemn mood, but grew more light-hearted on the return journey to the town. As they were passing the bathing establishment, Reschid suggested that they get out for half an hour to listen to the music in the gardens. They rambled through the well-laid-out grounds, where they saw the usual Kurort crowd, sitting, strolling, listening to the orchestra. Gossiping, flirting, commenting on the passersby -as is their way in all the world- these people sat about in groups on wrought-iron benches beneath the palms.

"Ah, here they are at last!" jeered Kingscourt, grimly pleased. "The Jewesses with the diamonds, I mean! I really missed them. I had said to myself that this whole thing must be a hoax- that perhaps we were not really in Jewland at all. Now I see it's real. The ostrich feather hats, the gaudy silk dresses, the Israelitish women with their jewels...Don't mind what I say, Mrs. Gothland. You're different."

The lady assured him that she did not take offense. Steineck roared with laughter. "We don't mind at all, Mr. Kingscourt. There was a time when such remarks hurt our feelings. But not any more. Understand? Fops, upstarts, bejeweled women used to be regarded as representative Jews. Now people realize that there are other types of Jews also. Go ahead and criticize this riff-raff all you please, esteemed stranger! When night falls, I'll curse along with you!"

**195**

Their merry little group attracted attention. Many of the people in the gardens evidently knew the Professor, and there was much craning after his distinguished-looking companions. In trying to escape the stares of the curious, Steineck led his friends into a by-path, and there walked directly into the very thing he wished to avoid. In a circle of bushes sat a group of men and women engaged in lively chatter. One of the men jumped up boisterously and ran toward Friedrich. "Doctor Loewenberg! Doctor Loewenberg! Guess whom we've just been talking about? Yourself! I'm so happy!"

The happy gentleman was Schiffmann. He drew Friedrich into the circle, introduced him exuberantly, and pressed him into a chair. The whole thing happened so quickly that he had no chance to resist, even had he not been dumbfounded at suddenly seeing the love of his youth. Ernestine greeted him with a glance and a smile before she spoke. He himself found no words.

In the meantime, Schiffmann had hurried over to the Professor, whom he knew. He made the entire party to come forward, like a street barker forcing people to come into his shop. The Professor obviously did not care to accept the invitation, but Kingscourt pointed out that they could not leave Friedrich in the lurch. "Captured together, hang together!" he declared. Schiffmann, who was dragging chairs forward for the newcomers, laughed ingratiatingly at the ambiguous pleasantry. He introduced his friends: Mr., Mrs. and Miss Schlesinger, Dr. and Mrs. Walter, Mrs. Weinberger, Miss Weinberger, Messrs. Gruen and Blau, Mr. Weinberger.

Friedrich saw and heard everything as in a mist. Old times rose hazily to his mind. He saw himself again at the betrothal party at the Loefllers. Here were the same impossible people he had then fled from in desperation. All had aged, and yet all had remained the same. Only the presence of the two young girls indicated another generation. That dainty girl looking at him so blankly was the very image of the youthful Ernestine. He was so much enthralled by his old memories that only confused echoes of the talk reached his consciousness.

Gruen, the jester, was holding forth. "Well, Dr. Loewenberg, and how do you like it here? What! You find no words! Perhaps you think there are too many Jews here!"

Laughter. "I am frank to say," remarked Friedrich slowly, "that you are the first person to have made me think so."

"Ha! Ha! Ha! Very good!" neighed Schiffmann. The others joined in the merriment. Only then did Friedrich realize that his remark had been construed as one of the rude jests common in this set. Gruen, accustomed as he was to worse treatment, did not, take it amiss, But, the rival jester, grinningly followed up the persccution. "Gruen could make even the people here anti-Semitic."

"Your jokes are stale, Mr. Blau," interposed Dr. Walter. "Thank God, anti-Semitism has ceased to exist."

"If I could be sure of that," retorted Blau, "I should go into the business myself."

Kingscourt leaned over toward the Professor, and whispered, "Seems to me you couldn't tell these people anything about your project for the Negroes. They'd laugh at you."

**197**

"Proves nothing against it," rejoined Steineck in the same undertone. "They also ridiculed the Jewish nationalist idea in the old days. They are the last people to whom one could speak of something big."

Friedrich reverted to the remark of Dr. Walter. "Is it true," he asked, "that Jew-hatred has declined?"

"Declined, you say!" cried Schlesinger. "It's disappeared."

"No one," struck in Blau saucily, "can give you better information on that subject than Dr. Veiglstock. He behaved like a captain...the last to leave the ship."

The lawyer was vexed. "I shall have to pull you up by the ears, Mr. Blau, and tell you my name. It is Walter, once and for all. Just note that. Now, I've never been ashamed of my father's honest name. Everyone knows that. But formerly one had to make concessions to the prejudices of his environment in order to escape unpleasantness."

"And now it's no longer necessary?" probed Friedrich.

"No. But, for once, what Mr. Blau tried to say in his would-be humorous way is true. I came here to settle only recently. That, however, proves that I was not forced to do so by necessity, but obeyed my own impulses."

"Once a Jew, always a Jew!" bleated Gruen in support of the declaration. But Blau in an undertone inaudible to the lawyer muttered something about a dwindling clientele.

Dr. Walter assumed an air of importance, and launched on a description of the effects of the Jewish mass migration upon the Jews who had remained in Europe. He was bound to say for himself, it had always been clear to him that Zionism was bound to be as salutary for the Jews who remained in Europe as for those who emigrated. He had been among the first to recognize the significance of the movement. Though he had not then been able to give free rein to his ideas and impulses, he had done his modest bit for the national idea. As proof of this statement, he mentioned the fact that he had not dismissed a poor student then working in his law office, even though he knew the young man attended Zionist meetings. He had given his mite, also, to the National Fund, when it amounted t6 several million pounds sterling (that is to say, when its large capital was security for its success).

Blau sought a flippant revenge for his humiliation. "Mite? Pardon me, sir, if I ask, is that a new coin? Mite...mite...."

Dr. Walter refused to be upset by this fling. He merely shrugged contemptuously, looked past his interlocutor, and went on. Everyone today knows that Palestine is a happy domicile for all who have come here. And the condition of those who remained behind was improved. Ever since Jewish competition had either decreased or disappeared altogether, they were safe from attack. In the countries with too large a number of Jews-the Judaized countries, as the phrase went on those days-there was a remarkable amelioration socially.

The laboring classes and the poor had indeed been the first to migrate, but the effects of their going were soon felt by the middle and upper classes of Jews. The first to leave for the Old-New-Land were those who had nothing to lose and

**199**

everything to gain. Since emigration was entirely voluntary, only those went who were certain of improving their condition. The unemployed and the despairing rushed to a land which opened up such broad vistas of work and of hope. That was a natural phenomenon. All the world knew that numerous successful enterprises in Palestine provided immigrants with the opportunity to earn their bread from the first, and later to achieve a certain degree of prosperity.

To all this, continued Dr. Walter, add the lure of freedom. No discrimination because of race or creed. That in itself was alluring enough.

Then, all the great Jewish philanthropic associations pooled their resources. They had been burdened with the co-religionists forced to wander from one country to another under the pressure of persecution and poverty. When the destitute Jews of some East European Country could endure their lot no longer and set out on their pathetic journeys, their brethren in the remoter communities had to extend a helping hand. They gave and gave to the wandering beggars, but it was never enough. Vast sums were spent without opportunity to investigate the merits of individual cases. There was, therefore, no way to make certain that only the deserving would receive aid. The result was that misery was not alleviated even temporarily, while pauperism was fostered.

The Zionist idea provided a base on which all humanitarian Jewish effort could unite. Jewish communities everywhere colonized their own poor in Palestine, and thus relieved themselves of these dependents. This method was cheaper than the former planless sending of wanderers to some foreign land or other; and there was the certainty that only willing workers

**200**

and the deserving poor were receiving assistance. Anyone who wished to do honest work was certain of an opportunity in Palestine. If a man declared that he could not find work even there, he thereby stamped himself as a ne'er-do-well deserving of no sympathy.

In the early days there had been people who could not believe 'that colonization by the proletariat could be successful. But he, Dr. Walter, and others who, like himself, took a broad view of things, had always realized that this was an ignorant, stupid attitude. Had not new settlements always been founded by hungry people? The well-fed had no incentive to leave the confines of civilization.. They remained at home. The world therefore belonged to the hungry. The Puritans, persecuted for their religious beliefs, had colonized North America. South Africa and India had been settled by fortune-hunters. And where could a colony be found that had been established by worse elements than Australia, that great, proud, prosperous land? At the beginning of the nineteenth century, it was a despised penal colony. Yet only a few decades later, it had grown into a great, sound commonwealth; and, before the century was out, it was a jewel in the British crown.

As he had said, he and other educated men had ridiculed the objection that proletarians could not found a colony. Surely, if convicts had been able to do so much in Australia, how much more could be achieved by Jewish pioneers, whose labors for the freedom and honor of the nation would be upheld by the whole House of Israel? In all modesty, Dr. Walter wished to point out that the event had justified his prevision.

The vast works of colonization had required a large staff of trained engineers, jurists and administrators. Large

**201**

opportunities were suddenly opened to educated young men who in the anti-Semitic times had had no sphere for the exercise of their skill. Jewish university graduates, men trained in the technological institutes and commercial. colleges, used to flounder helplessly; but now there was ample room for them in the public and private undertakings so numerous in Palestine. The result was that Christian professional men no longer looked askance at their Jewish colleagues, for they were no longer annoying competitors. In such circumstances, commercial envy and hatred had gradually disappeared. Furthermore, the less Jewish abilities were offered in the marketplace, the more their value was appreciated. The value of services always increased with their scarcity. Everyone knew that. Why should not this rule have applied to Jews in commercial life?

And so the effects of the improved situation had made themselves felt on all sides. In countries where there was a tendency to restrict Jewish immigration, public opinion took a turn for the better. Jews were granted full citizenship rights not only on paper, but in everyday life. Compulsory measures could never have moved Jews to .Joyful participation in art, science, trade, commerce and every other sphere. But they had been won with kindness. Only after those Jews who were forced out of Europe had been settled in their own land, the well-meant measures of emancipation became effective everywhere.

Jews who wished to assimilate with other peoples now felt free to do so openly, without cowardice or deception. There were also some who wished to adopt the majority religion, and these could now do so without being suspected of snobbery or careerism, for it was no longer to one's advantage to abandon

Judaism. Those Jews who felt akin to their fellow-citizens in everything but religion enjoyed undiminished esteem as adherents of a minority faith. Toleration can and must always rest on reciprocity. Only when the Jews, forming the majority in Palestine, showed themselves tolerant, were they shown more toleration in all other countries.

Dr. Walter concluded his little lecture with an ingratiating, sidelong glance at Professor Steineck, "Therefore I have come forward as an adherent and advocate of the Littwak-Steineck party. I shall defend their idea unflinchingly, to my last drop of blood!"

"You mustn't forget to tell that to your brother, Professor," cut in Blau witheringly. "With Dr. Walter on your side, you have the majority."

"What do you mean by that?" exploded the lawyer, growing purple in the face. "You-you!"

"Nothing at all," replied the jester with assumed naivete. "I have never seen you anywhere but with the majority. Therefore people must be congratulated when you support them."

"If you mean to insinuate by your nasty witticisms that I am in the habit of changing my convictions, I can afford to laugh. Every reasonable man grows wiser with time. What counts is, that once I am convinced of an idea, I hold to it unswervingly."

"Yes, yes!" said Gruen, rubbing his "unseamed" ear between thumb and forefinger. "I, understand that when Dr. Walter has a conviction, he' holds to it steadfastly, unflinchingly. But when he no longer entertains it, or prefers another conviction, it would not be ethical for him to hold fast to what he no longer believes in."

Schlesinger, who still enjoyed a certain prestige as the representative of the Baron von Goldstein, threw himself into the breach with authority. "But what does this mean, gentlemen? Are we at a mass meeting now? What care we for convictions? I know only two: Business and Pleasure!"

"Bravo!" shouted Kingscourt. "And Business first!"

"You see, this gentleman agrees with me," inferred Schlesinger. "This is out of business, hours. Therefore, let us leave ourselves in peace!"

"You always hit the nail on the head, Mr. Schlesinger," remarked Schiffmann flatteringly, and continued, in an undertone that all could hear, addressing himself to Kingscourt and Friedrich. "It's not for nothing that he enjoys the confidence of the Baroness von Goldstein! He's the Jaffa representative of that important firm."

"You don't say so!" remarked Kingscourt with an admiring mien.

Schlesinger gazed modestly before him, like a celebrity being shown off to the public.

The ladies in the meantime had resumed their discussion of the latest thing in Parisian millinery. Mrs. Laschner took the lead. She always ordered her things, she said, directly from the Rue de la Paix. But Mrs. Weinberger signaled to Friedrich to bring his chair nearer, and chatted in an undertone. "Yes, this is my daughter. What do you think of her? Pretty? Ugly?"

"The image of her mother," he replied mechanically. "Ugly, then. You naughty man!" She widened her eyes coquettishly. Friedrich was heavy at heart as he looked at the faded, would-be arch coquette. After twenty years, then, the causes of our bitterest griefs looked like this! How could he have suffered so acutely for such a reason. Alas, the wasted years!

Without any notion of what was in Friedrich's mind, the lady frisked on. What did he intend to do now? Was he remaining here, or going on to Europe? If he did stay, wouldn't he be thinking of settling down, courting a wife?

"I?" he answered in surprise. "At my age? I have missed all that, as I have missed many other more important things in life."

"That's not honest. You are still of marriageable age. You look much younger than you really are. Your solitary island preserved you well. ...Let me ask a candid child to guess your age...Fifi, guess how old Dr. Loewenberg is.

Fifi, the candid child, looked at him for a moment, dropped her eyelids and lisped, "In the early thirties, mama!"

"Ah, no, my dear young lady. You have not looked at me closely."

"Indeed I have," she lisped again. "I saw you at the opera with Miriam Littwak."

**205**

"Apropos," said Ernestine, "how do you like Miriam Littwak? I don't mean as to outward appearance. She's quite good-looking. But her manner-her pose. She's putting it on a bit thick with duties and all- that sort of thing. She plays at teaching. That's the latest here."

Friedrich was annoyed. "My dear lady, as far as I know, Miss Littwak does not play but actually works at teaching. She takes her duties as seriously as they deserve."

"See, see, how he defends Miss Littwak!" scoffed Ernestine.

"My friend is signaling me.," 'said Friedrich rising. He made his farewells.

When he rejoined the party, Kingscourt grasped his arm, saying, "Fritze, guess what I was thinking all the while we were with that delightful crew."

"I've no idea."

"That it's time we're moving on. We're not robbers or murderers to be ending up with the agent of the Baron von Goldstein. Or do you want to anchor here?"

"Why ask me, Kingscourt? You know very well that I belong to you, and go with you wherever and whenever you choose."

The old man stopped short and squeezed Friedrich's hand.

# Book Four

# Passover

### Chapter I

It was evening when the guests returned to the Littwak villa, where the Passover celebration had been prepared. The Russian priest was the first to arrive from Sepphoris. Then David appeared with the Franciscan monk, Father Ignaz, a well-nourished, red-cheeked blond-bearded man, whose brown cowl made him seem even stouter than he was. He had come from Cologne a quarter of a century previously, but could still speak nothing except his native dialect. The Russian priest and the English clergyman made praiseworthy attempts to speak to him in his own language.

The Seder table was set in the dining room on the ground floor. Twenty covers were laid on the snowy cloth. David assigned the guests to their places, and himself sat at the foot of the table, since his father was conducting the ceremony. The place at the elder Littwak's right remained vacant. The invalid mother did not feel equal to sitting up. Mrs. Gothland sat on his left.

The ancient, melodramatic Seder service was begun with the filling of the First Cup with wine, and the host's recital of the Kiddush. He rendered thanks for the fruit of the vine and for all the mercies God had shown His people. ..."Eternal, our God, Who hath appointed unto us seasons of rejoicing, feasts and holy days for our happiness, as on this Festival of the unleavened bread, the season of our redemption at Thy holy proclamation, in memory of our exodus from Egypt. ..."

The First Cup was drunk. Kingscourt merely looked on. Mrs. Gothland leaned toward him and whispered in English, "You are expected to do like the others. That is the custom."

Kingscourt smothered several "Devils!" in his windpipe, but had enough savoir taire and humor to imitate the curious rites. The Christian clergymen did not hold aloof.

The host washed his hands in a silver basin brought by Miriam, took a bit of parsley from the platter before him, dipped it into salt water, pronounced a blessing and ate it. Sprigs of parsley were then handed around the table. Kingscourt ate his with a lively grimace at which Mrs. Gothland smiled gently. The egg and roast joint were removed from the platter, and the covered dish was held up with the solemn words, "Behold, this is the bread of affliction which our forefathers ate in the land of Egypt. ..."

Mrs. Gothland came to Kingscourt's aid once more by pointing to the German translation opposite the Hebrew text of the Haggadah.

The Second Cup was filled with wine; and David, as the youngest man in the company, rose to put the traditional Four Questions.

"Mah nishtanah ha-leilah ha-ze mikkol halleloth?" "Wherein doth this night differ from all other nights?" On all other nights we may eat bread, both leavened and unleavened, while on this night we may eat only unleavened bread. On all other nights we may eat every manner of herb, while on this night we may eat only bitter herbs. ...

The flat Passover cakes on the platter were uncovered, and all replied in unison to the Four Questions: "Slaves were we unto Pharaoh in Egypt. And the Eternal our God drew us forth with a mighty hand and an outstretched arm... "

And so they went through with the Seder ceremony half ritual, half family festival. This most Jewish of all the festivals dates back farther in history than any other civilized usage in modern times. For hundreds and hundreds of years it has been observed without change, while the whole world changed. Nations disappeared from history, others rose. The world grew larger. Undreamed of continents emerged from the seas. Unimagined natural forces were harnessed for the pleasure and comfort of man. But this one people still remained unchanged, retaining its ancient customs, true to itself, rehearsing the woes of its forbears. Israel, a people of slavery and freedom, still prayed in ancient words to the Eternal its God.

One guest at that Seder table pronounced the Hebrew words of the Haggadah with the zeal of a penitent. He was finding himself again, and his throat was often so tight with emotion that he had to master his longing to cry out aloud. It was almost thirty years since he himself had asked the Four Questions. ...Then had come "Enlightenment," the break with all that was Jewish, and the final logical leap into the void, when he had

**209**

had no further hold on life. At this Seder table he seemed to himself a prodigal son, returned to his own people.

The first part of the ceremony ended, dinner was served. Kingscourt called across the table. "Fritz! I'd no idea you were so perfect a Hebrew scholar."

"I confess I did not know it myself. It seems one forgets nothing learned in childhood."

The name of Joseph Levy, whom Kingscourt and Friedrich had not yet met, recurred continually in the table talk. The Steinecks spoke of him as "Tschoe."

"It's all wrong that Tschoe's not here," said the architect loudly.

"Yes," supplemecnted his brother, "it's unnatural for him to be missing. The party is incomplete without him. Understand?"

"Not at all," declared Kingscourt. "I've been wondering all this time what you want of this unknown Joe."

"He doesn't know Joe!" shouted the architect, holding his sides.

"That's a fault in your education, gentlemen," said the Professor. "Joe is a person one must know. Without him, many a man would not be where he is today. Joe has achieved wonders with practically nothing. He's a remarkable fellow. He has a quality that's rarer than gold or platinum or uranium or the rarest metal there is."

"The Devil! You make me curious, Professor! What is this wonderful quality?'

"Simple, sound common sense. Understand?"

"I begin to. ...But now I should like to see this remarkable Joe."

The architect formed a speaking tube with his hands, and shouted, "Tschoe! Tschoe!"

Mrs. Gothland motioned the bawler to be quiet. "My dear friend," said she, "not even you can speak loudly enough for him to hear you. Unless you were to telephone him to Marseilles. Then it would be easy, of course. He arrived there this afternoon, and sends his greetings to all of you. I spoke to him a little while ago."

"Wha-at!" shouted the architect. "So suddenly! And without saying a word to anyone!"

"He decided on the trip several days ago," reported Mrs. Gothland. "You know our Joe. He heard that a manufacturer in Lyons had some new kind of machine. I must have a look at that,' he said, and left for Europe the same day. Notice of his arrival was cabled to the newspapers over there. He is probably being besieged by manufacturers, machinery agents, and engineers. It's always like that when Joe goes to Europe."

"Representatives of all kinds of industries call on him," added Reschid. "He has contacts with England, Germany, France, and particularly with America. Tomorrow he may be on his way to America if he does not go on to London or return to Palestine. You never know what he will do next. But you do know that it will be the right thing. He closes a deal for $5,000,000 sooner

**211**

than another man buys himself a coat. He orders quickly, pays well, and never makes a mistake."

"Donnerwetter! I like that man!" roared Kingscourt. "What does he do here?"

"He is general director of the Department of Industry," replied David. "Though there is no position he could not fill in our society. He understands everything that reveals itself to sound observation and an iron will. His mind works like lightning, and he can explain the most complicated matter to you in a moment. And when Joe Levy undertakes a thing, you may take your oath upon it that he will see it through. I thought, gentlemen, that you would be interested in meeting this all-round man. You shall hear him speak after dinner, since I cannot otherwise show him to you except in a photograph."

"Then we shall have to go to the telephone," Suggested Kingscourt.

"No, that will not be necessary," smiled David. "You shall listen to him more comfortably than that. And not only yourselves, but posterity, will listen to this speech of Joe's. It occurred to me that it would be worth while preserving the voice of the man who carried through the new Jewish national project. I therefore asked Levy to tell the story of the colonization on the phonograph. You were familiar with that invention twenty years ago, gentlemen, of course. I have had many duplicates made of the Wax rolls on which Joe spoke, and have presented several hundred to the schools as a Passover gift. But you shall enjoy his premiere tonight."

"Capital!" shouted Kingscourt. "A brilliant idea, most estimable man of the future. All this while I have been asking myself about the transition period. The finished product is before us. But how did it come about? That's the gist of the matter! We ignorant Europeans knew all about railways, harbors, factories, automobiles, telephone, photo- and Lord knows what other graphs before We ever set foot in Palestine. But how did you transplant them all? I had been intending to ask you."

"Now that we have shown you the end, Joe will tell you about the beginning," replied David. "This Seder evening seemed the appropriate time. The old Haggadah, which we read at dinner, has a story about the sages who assembled at Bene Berak on a Seder evening, and discussed the Egyptian exodus the whole night through. We are the successors of Rabbi Eliezer, Rabbi Joshua, Rabbi Eleazer ben Azariah, Rabbi Akibah and Rabbi Tarphon. And this is our evening of Bene Berak. The old passes over into the new. First we shall finish our Seder after the manner of our forefathers, and then we shall let the new era tell you how it was born. Once more there was an Egypt, and again a happy exodus-under twentieth century conditions, of course, and with modern equipment. It could not have been otherwise. The age of machinery had to come first. The great nations had to grow mature enough for a colonial policy. There had to be great screw steamers, with a speed of 22 knots an hour, to supersede the sailing vessels. In brief, the whole stock-in-trade of the year 1900 was needed. We had to become new men, and yet remain loyal to our ancient race. And we also had to win the active sympathy of the other nations and their rulers. Otherwise, the whole enterprise would have been impossible."

"God has helped us," murmured the elder Littwak, and added a Hebrew phrase under his breath.

The Reverend Mr. Hopkins reminded his colleagues of the Easter riots in the old days, and rejoiced that those old quarrels had been resolved into new harmonies. Now they, though Christians, could participate in a Passover celebration at the home of a Jew, without being offended by other people's beliefs. A new springtide had risen for humanity.

"He has risen indeed!" assented the priest of Sepphoris.

# Chapter II

The grace after meals was recited, and the Seder service completed. The company then retired to the drawing room, where the phonograph with Joe's narrative stood ready on a little table. It was the same mechanism Kingscourt was familiar with, but it now had a simple automatic device whereby the rolls glided out smoothly one after the other so that there was no noticeable break in the narrative. If it was desired to repeat something, a slight pressure reversed the roll to the desired point. When they had made themselves comfortable on sofas and easy chairs, David sat down beside the machine, set the horn toward his audience, and announced, "Our friend, Mr. Joseph Levy, has the floor."

The machine rattled for a moment. Then a strong masculine voice spoke up clearly.

"Esteemed audience! I am to submit to you a report on the new Jewish migration. It was all very simple. Too much fuss has been made about it. I had nothing to do with the political preliminaries. Fortunately. I am not a politician. Never was one. Never shall be. I had my job, and did it.

"Our association was organized under the name of 'The New Society for the Colonization of Palestine.' It entered into a colonization treaty with the Turkish Government, the terms of which are known to all the world. When the charter 2 was about to be signed, I was asked whether we should be able to meet the large annual payments to the Turkish treasury which it called for. I replied with a decided affirmative. We had to pay the Turkish Government two million pounds sterling S in cash when the charter was signed. In addition, we were to make payments of fifty thousand pounds a year for thirty years, plus one fourth of the net annual profits of the New Society for the Colonization of Palestine, to the Turkish Treasury. And, as you know, we shall divide the net profits of the New Society with the Turkish Government at the expiration of the thirty-year period, unless they prefer a permanent annual tribute based on the average of our last ten annual payments. They are obligated to indicate their choice during the twenty-seventh year of the agreement. We may assume that they will prefer to take one-half of the net annual profits of the New Society, since this will bring them a much larger sum. In return for these payments, we received autonomous rights to the regions which we were to colonize, with the ultimate sovereignty reserved to the Sultan.

"Very large sums were, of course, required. It seemed doubtful at first whether the New Society could prosper to such an extent that it would be able to meet these commitments. The land was beggarly, our settlers were drawn from the proletariat of every country. There were, however, at that time several large foundations devoted to national Jewish purposes. In 1900 their combined assets amounted to twelve millions sterling. But, in addition to the money we were to pay to the Turkish Government, we had to find large sums for the purchase of land, for colonizing destitute people, for reclaiming and improving the neglected soil.

"How were all these needs to be met? In our small inner committee there were timid souls who foretold the collapse of the whole undertaking. My friends and I overcame their objections. We proved to them that we could reckon not only with existing values, but with those which-judging by all historic experience-must be created as a result of our work. The enterprise we were building up for the future would be strengthened by the future itself. In ten years the boys we brought here would have become men. And, having men, we should have everything. We would bring men, and train them as needed for their own good and for the good of the community. The logic was the simplest in the world. It was being done in the smallest countries, by the most insignificant peoples. The Jews alone had unlearned the ABC of nationhood.

"There was still another and more important factor which, strangely enough, the Jews did not reckon with, though they utilized it every day in other connections. I refer to their love of enterprise. I shall simply cite the example of the gold rush to the inhospitable Klondike at the end of the nineteenth century. Hordes of fortune hunters stampeded to Alaska. I am speaking now not of the gold-seekers, but of their camp followers. All sorts of things suddenly appeared in the Klondike-beds, tables, chairs, shirts, shoes, coats, tinned foods, wines; all sorts of people-doctors, teachers, singers. In a word, all sorts of things, necessary and unnecessary-found their way to the Klondike because a few people had found money there in its most concentrated form. Only some of those who followed them were gold-diggers. They did not go after the wealth hidden in the ground, but after that already in circulation in the form of money."

The Professor broke into the story with an irrepressible "Understand?" But his brother hissed at him so violently that he relapsed into a shamed silence.

Joe Levy continued. "I quote you this glaring example to prove that every undertaking conceived in a spirit of enterprise soon gives rise to other productive undertakings. Every practical person knows that almost instinctively. He does hot have to be told it by professors of political economy in obscure phrases. The Jews had, as a matter of fact, long been among the most ingenious entrepreneurs. It was only our own future that we had never built upon a business basis. Why? Because guarantees had been lacking. But once those guarantees were created, we could be no less enterprising in Palestine than elsewhere.

"I did not, therefore, worry about the required capital. If the land were prepared and the migration set going, we could get any reasonable amount of money. That is why I replied in the affirmative when I was asked whether we should be able to meet very large obligations to the Turkish Government without fear of running short of capital for investment. I did not feel that we were undertaking an experiment. We were merely utilizing world-old facts and experiences.

"The charter was signed. We made our first payment. Since the direction of the work was entrusted to me from then on, I asked that the signing of the charter be not made public for the moment. I wanted no rush of immigrants, since that would have led to serious disorders. The poorest and the greediest elements would have streamed in. The aged and the sick would have dragged themselves hither, and we should at once have been in the thrall of famine and epidemics. There is an old French play entitled 'The Fear of Joy.' I too feared the effects of joy upon our unfortunate Jews. I had to prepare them carefully. And I had to prepare my working group as well.

"When our New Society was founded, I was named general manager for five years, and allowed a preliminary credit of one million pounds by the board of directors. One of my engineers thought it too little. ..."

"Damned little!" shouted Kingscourt, with a violent gesture. "Stop the rattle trap, please!" David obediently halted the phonograph. "If you really want to explain all this to me, there's just one thing you'll tell an old sea dog. Otherwise, I'll never be able to understand what your Joe and his telephonograph are driving at....What's this New Society? Is it the one they talked about so much in Neudorf? And what sort of a board of directors was it? And where did they get the money, though it wasn't much?"

"I can see why you ask all these questions," nodded David. "Joe Levy did not think of telling about things that every child here understands. The former New Society and the present one are the same organization, and yet different. Originally, it was a stock corporation, and now it is a co-operative. The co-operative is the legal heir of the stock corporation."

"Understand?" queried the Professor.

"No. Did the stockholders give their money away? If that's the idea, it's all a fairy tale."

"It will be clear to you in a moment, Mr. Kingscourt." David assured him. "You need only distinguish between the various legal entities involved. We have here three judicial or abstract persons. Number one comprises the endowed foundations which had a combined capital of twelve millions sterling in 1900. Number two was a joint stock company organized with a

**219**

capital of ten millions by London financiers who became interested in our cause when the grant of the charter was assured. Number three was the co-operative association of the colonists. The latter were represented at the congresses by their chosemeaders. These leaders set the masses in motion only after an agreement had been reached with the joint stock company that it would later become a co-operative association."

"You astonish me, noble fairy prince!" laughed Kingscourt. "Do you mean to tell me that stockholders, syndicate hyenas, agreed to anything of that sort?"

"They were not syndicate hyenas, Mr. Kingscourt, but reputable business men who contented themselves with a fair profit. Capital and labor came to terms. Neither by itself could have surmounted all the difficulties. The money-people required guarantees. The labor people as well. Had they not agreed between themselves in advance, injustice would have been done one party or the other in the course of time. Either the people would have disregarded the rights of the stockholders, or become enslaved by them. Both eventualities were obviated by an agreement granting the colonists an option for taking over the stock ten years later. The shares were to be redeemable at the equivalent of the average income of the New Society during the previous five years, capitalized at five per cent. But the total of this redemption fund was not to be less than the actual paid-up value of the shares, plus interest..."

Friedrich hesitantly offered an objection. "But that condition seems to me impossible. Where were the impecunious colonists to find the sums required to buy the shares of the stock corporation?"

"Ah, there, my son!" said Kingscourt. "Now I see it all as clearly as a hole in a doughnut. If the enterprise prospered, it would not be difficult for the colonists to find the money. As a prosperous co-operative society, they could get it on tick."

"That's correct," assented David. "When the co-operative decided to redeem the shares, it secured the required capital in the form of a loan at four per cent. And it came off very well on the transaction. The net profits of the settlement from the fifth to the tenth years averaged one million pounds annually. The settlers therefore needed twenty millions to redeem the shares. But, if they undertook an annual interest obligation equal to their net annual profits up to that time, they could borrow twenty five millions through their co-operative society. They did so, and had a balance of five million pounds on hand after taking over the shares...."

"Damn the fellows!" cried Kingscourt. "How did the joint stock company get so rich?"

"Primarily through the increase in the value of its land. However, since the increased values were due to the efforts of the workers, it was only just and proper that they should derive the benefits. You see now how we were able to transfer the land to the commonwealth. The stock corporation came into the possession of the co-operative which, from then on, was officially called the 'New Society.'"

"It may not seem right to our friends," remarked the architect, "that we should have availed ourselves of disreputable means like shares and that sort of thing. But we had no other way of helping ourselves."

"If you think me such a donkey," retorted Kingscourt, "you're very much in error. I have lived in America. I know a spade when I see one. A stock company is a vessel, into which one may put either good things or bad. We might as well object to a bottle, because it can be filled with poison or bad whiskey. Moreover, there are plenty of examples in history of such stock companies for colonization. The East India Company was not at all bad. I even see a kind of moral principle in your New Society...that part where it was turned into a co-operative. ...Now I'd like to hear how it was after that open the rattle trap!"

# Chapter III

Joe Levy resumed his narrative, repeating the last words. ..."I was named general manager for five years by the board of directors, and allowed a preliminary credit of 1,000,000 pounds. One of my engineers thought it too little. But it was enough to begin with. I made my plans. It was autumn. I wanted to arrange a systematic immigration immediately after the winter rains. That left me only four months to work in. There was not an hour to lose.

"I established general headquarters in London at once, and appointed as department heads men whom either I knew personally, or who came highly recommended. There was Smith for passenger traffic, Steineck for construction, Rubenz for freight, Warszawski for purchasing machinery, Alladino for land purchase, Kohn and Brownstone for the commissariat, Harburger for seeds and saplings, Leonkin for the accounting department. Wellner was my general secretary. I name them as they occur to me. Fischer was my first assistant and chief engineer until his premature death. He was a splendid fellow, earnest and enthusiastic. We shall always miss him.

"The first thing I did was to send Alladino to Palestine to buy up all the available land. He was a Sephardic Jew who traced his pedigree from a family whose ancestors had been among those expelled from Spain. He knew Arabic and Greek, and was a reliable, clever man. Before the signing of the charter was made public, the price of land was still moderate. I knew that the inscrutable Alladino could not be outwitted even by the

**223**

shrewdest of real estate agents. The cost of the land was of course charged by the New Society to another account than my grant of 1,000,000 pounds. A sum of 2,000,000 pounds was set aside for land. Fifty million francs, in the Palestine of those days, was a large sum for real estate.

"Having asked the Turkish Government to keep the immigration restrictions in force temporarily, I was secured against a precipitate rush of immigrants.

"I divided a map of Palestine into small squares, which I numbered. It was kept in my office, and an exact copy given to Alladino. He was simply to wire me the numbers of the parcels he had bought, and so I knew from hour to hour just how much land we already owned, and what kind of land it was.

"At the same time, I sent Harburger, our botanist, to buy eucalyptus saplings in Australia. He had carte blanche to buy all the Mediterranean plants he wanted for use or decoration. He and Alladino traveled together to Marseilles, and there separated. Alladino took the next boat for Alexandria, while Harburger traveled slowly down the Riviera, placing his orders with horticultural firms for delivery in the spring. A week later he shipped at Naples for Port Said, and I had no further word from him till he reached Melbourne.

"Then, I sent Warszawski, who was a mechanical engineer, to America to buy the most up-to-date agricultural machinery and implements, all kinds of transportable motors, steam rollers, etc. Like all my department chiefs, he understood that my instructions were not to be taken too literally, and that he was always to follow his own judgment on the spot. I wanted no long reports. All important data were cabled to me promptly, with facts and figures. Any of my chiefs who saw something new or practical that we could use-whether it came under his department or not-was to inform me of it, preferably by cable. Some brilliant suggestions came to me in this way. We succeeded because we always kept our methods up to the minute. Before he left, I said to Warszawski, 'Buy me no old scrap iron!' He understood me.

"Warszawski also had an incidental task, namely, to arrange for the re-migration of the East European Jews in America to Palestine. I considered these people very important. They had already shown their mettle by wrenching themselves free from their wretched environment in Eastern Europe, and I had learned to make their way in the good American school of experience. New York was the largest Jewish city in the world, though the vast numbers of East European refugees could not maintain themselves comfortably there, but crowded each other like sardines in a box. They found that they had jumped from the frying pan into the fire. Drawing off the surplus numbers from America would therefore be as great an act of redemption as for the East European Jews themselves. The two migrations to Palestine-from America and from Eastern Europe-were to be prepared for in exactly the same way.

"I instructed Warszawski to have a private conference with the leaders of the local Zionist groups. In order to prevent a premature airing of the plan, he was to tell them merely that a company had been formed with a large amount of capital, which had obtained concessions in Palestine for agricultural and industrial enterprises. Capable workmen, skilled and unskilled, would be needed in February. They were to prepare lists of reliable persons in their groups, showing each person's age, place of birth, present occupation, family circumstances, and economic status. Unmarried men would be preferred for the unskilled labor; married men for the skilled. Each district would be held morally responsible for its nominees. Any district whose nominees refused to serve or showed themselves incompetent would not be permitted to make further nominations. They must make it a point of honor to name only really suitable persons. The manner of choice would be left to the districts. They might designate nominees either at general meetings of their membership, or leave the choice to the executive committees of the district groups. It would be easy to determine the character of the nominees from the reports of their fellow-members in the districts.

"These instructions were also sent to the Zionist district groups in Russia, Roumania, Galicia, and Algiers. Leorikin went to Russia for tQis purpose, Brownstone (who knew Jassy well) to Roumania, Kohn to Galicia, and Smith to Algiers. Leonkin returned to London in three weeks, the others in a fortnight. They had set the machinery going in all those countries.

"Our work had to be closely centralized. I had it announced in the various countries that our office would communicate only with the respective headquarters The leaders of the local groups chose central district committees, and the heads of the district committees in turn appointed national committees. With the offices of these national committees alone did we have any contacts. Otherwise, we would have been deluged with scrawls. All we needed was a record of the local Zionist groups arranged by districts and countries.

"In order to visualize the situation as it developed from day to day, I used a little technical device. I had glass headed pins made in many different colors-dark blue, light blue, red, black, green. Maps of various countries were stretched on boards, and I used the pins to indicate the situation in the various local groups. For example, a white-headed pin meant merely that a local group was compiling lists of workingmen; green signified agricultural workers; red, artisans; yellow, master-workmen. Light blue, again, betokened vocational co-operative societies with capital of their own, which asked only for a tract of land on lease. Districts whose nominees had not made good were stigmatized by black pins. Some of the pins were partly-colored-red-green, blue, pale-yellow, etc. These are trivial details, I admit; but my work was enormously simplified by means of such devices. Thanks to my reports and maps, I was able to keep in daily touch with the most detailed phases of the undertaking through many years. These maps and telegrams followed me everywhere. Later we used numbered pins to denote ships and railways. I knew at any moment the number and whereabouts of all transports under way. When I was traveling, Wellner, my secretary, forwarded me a brief summary of the incoming cables twice a day from London.

"Many people thought in those days that the prospect of emigration would demoralize our people, meaning that they would not care to work or perform their duties because they were so soon to leave. The contrary turned out to be the case. Since the Zionist districts, in their own interest, named only the most industrious and respected men, there was widespread competition for the honor of inclusion in their lists, which, by the way, became rolls of honor. If a man wanted to be thought worthy of being sent to the Promised Land, he must make an honest exertion to qualify. I admit this was a by-product I had not dreamed of. Yet it could quite easily have been foreseen. Many a despairing, negligent man was aroused, and improved his conduct. Many a half-demoralized family pulled itself

together. The effects of the systematic migration were thus
beneficial for those who still had to remain behind. And, as
they strove to improve themselves, they fulfilled their duties all
the more conscientiously. The districts were instructed that we
would accept only such persons as could show proper
emigration certificates from their governments. We had no use
for vagabonds. The various governments were kept fully
informed of our work, and assisted us as much as they could.
But I am anticipating.

"During the first few weeks after sending Alladino,
Warszawski and the others on their respective missions, I
remained in London with Fischer, Steineck, and Wellner. It
was then that we outlined our great technical plans. Many of
them were carried into effect; some we had to abandon; while
still others were executed far better than we had dared to hope.
I do not claim that we created anything new. American,
English, French, and German engineers had done the same
things before us. But we were the first heralds of technical
civilization in the Orient.

"I had Steineck prepare plans for station buildings and for
workmen's houses. A few cheap models had to suffice at the
beginning. The chief thing was to get them up quickly. We
could not stop to consider beauty of construction in those days.
Steineck's systematic and at times magnificent work in town-
planning came later. When we began, his task was merely to
provide bare shelter. At his suggestion, I ordered five hundred
barracks from France -a new kind that could be taken apart like
a tent and put together in an hour. They were to be delivered at
Marseilles by the middle of February, when Rubenz would take
charge of them. After the plans for the buildings had been
prepared, I gave Steineck general instructions for finding his

building materials and workingmen as quickly and cheaply as possible. Wishing to give him an absolutely free hand, since he had to organize his department with the utmost speed, I said, 'Go on to Palestine at once.' His reply startled me. He said, 'I am going to Finland and Sweden first!' ..."

Here the architect's hearty roar drowned out the narrative. His brother called him sternly to order. "Be quiet! You're disturbing everyone!" David set the roller back, repeating the last words... "startled me. He said, 'I'm going to Finland and Sweden first!'...That was hardly the route to Palestine? But I judged too hastily. He went to Sweden to buy lumber. From Sweden he went to Switzerland, Austria and Germany, where he asked the technological institutes for their latest graduates.

"Six weeks later his construction bureau was operating full blast in Jaffa. He had a staff of about the hundred construction engineers and draughtsmen, some of whom soon displayed fine talents. The news of an un-hoped for demand for Jewish technicians was quickly spread through all the institutes by the students' societies. The experience we had had in the Zionist districts repeated itself in a smaller way. The prospects of work, and even perhaps of brilliant careers in Palestine, stimulated the young men in their studies. They took their examinations earlier, and wasted no more time on political tomfoolery or card playing. Their one thought was to make themselves fit for work as soon as possible.

"Steineck reported to Rubenz day by day as he placed orders for lumber in Sweden and Finland, for iron in Germany and Austria. Rubenz made his arrangements with railways, steamship companies, and port authorities. He was an expert traffic manager, and carried out his task very efficiently during those months. His services are quite forgotten nowadays because our facilities for transportation by water between Europe and Palestine are so good. But during the first three or four years, it required much wit to find cheap means of transporting freight. Rubenz used to avail himself of the most curious opportunities on Spanish, Greek, and North African ships. I often suspected him of looking upon freight traffic as a kind of sport. He would send his goods on the oddest journeys and detours, but it was always on hand on the day it was wanted. Often we realized that he had chosen slow transport in order to save storage charges. To him a ship was a floating dock. He, too, had numerous maps in his office, on which colored pins indicated shipments of grain, flour, sugar, coal, wood, iron, etc. I needed only a few moments with his maps to have a complete view of the supply department. Rubenz was thrifty with the pence, too, and she saved us large sums.

"It was he who thought of negotiating with large firms in England, France and Germany before the beginning of our immigration. They would be only too pleased to find a market for the large quantities of shopworn goods they I had on hand; and for us it was a distinct relief because; we had to provide for all the needs of the immigrants. How could we have prepared all the beds, tables, cupboards, mattresses, pillows, blankets, bowls, plates, pots, underwear, boots and clothing they would need? That would have been a large undertaking in itself. We preferred to leave it to the competing firms which eagerly sought a market in Palestine. True, in our poor immigrants, the merchants had a public of very small cash purchasing power. Payment for purchases was, however, guaranteed because the New Society deducted the agreed-upon installments from the earnings of its officials and laborers, and sent the money directly to the department stores. In this way we had the opportunity of influencing the prices charged to the settlers. Our accounting department entered into agreement with the firms only after fixed price lists had been submitted. The settlers were thus secured against overcharges, while the department stores sold large quantities of goods for which payment was guaranteed. Rarely in the history of commerce have purveyors of goods been able to estimate so closely the amount of stock required for a given period. There was something military about the procedure, and yet competition was entirely free and open to all. The formation of a department store trust was easily hindered, because our accounting department would serve no firm that was a party to a price-fixing agreement. It might whistle for customers.

"We thus arranged a market for the first two or three months. While the local Zionist groups were selecting their best human material for Palestine, English, French, and German firms established branches in Haifa, Jaffa, Jericho, and before the gates of Jerusalem. The natives were astonished at the sudden appearance of Occidental goods in the country, and at first could find no explanation for the marvel. We had an amusing letter from Steineck at the time, in which he described the solemn puzzlement of the Orientals. 'Grave camels stopped stock still,' he wrote, 'and shook their heads.' But the natives began to buy at once, and word of the new bazaars spread quickly to Damascus and Aleppo, to Bagdad and the Persian Gulf. The customers streamed in on all sides. Our enterprise, casting its shadow before, brought on a commercial revival. The business of the first few months was so good that some of the firms began to manufacture the articles most in demand within the country, so as to save freight charges. There was the beginning of our present flourishing industries.

"I was reproached with having enriched the business men. The newspapers, also, attacked me on that score. I did not mind. I had no choice, and one can't please everybody. It was my duty to see to it that no official of the New Society received more than his proper salary. And I did see to it. I was ruthless in such matters. Everyone will bear me out. That I did not enrich myself is also known. But if independent firms made large profits, I was well content. Our own cause was served in that way. People will rush to a place where gold grows out of the earth. How it grows does not matter. I do not underestimate ideal and sentimental motives. But material incentives have their value as well.

"Again I am anticipating a later development. Once Steineck was gone, I found leisure to study Fischer's plans. His sketches for streets, water and power supply, railways, canals and harbors were classic. It was at that time that he submitted to me his plans for his greatest work: the canal from the Mediterranean to the Dead Sea in which he utilized the difference in levels very cleverly. In drawing up the canal plans he was helped by a Christian Swiss engineer, who was so enthusiastic a Zionist that he became a Jew and took the name of Abraham. Fischer, who was very modest, always put him forward as the real author of the plan.

"The excellent maps of the English General Army staff, and especially the relief maps prepared by Armstrong for the Palestine Exploration Fund, were of the highest value to us in those days.

"I was urging at this time the formation of the first railway companies. The wretched little Jaffa-Jerusalem line would of course be wholly inadequate for the coming needs. First of all,

we made sure of a coast-line railway southward from Jaffa to
Port Said and northward to Beirut, via Caesarea, Haifa, Tyre
and Sidon, with a junction at Damascus.s After that came the
new line to Jerusalem; the Jordan Valley trunk line with spurs
to the east and one to the west to Lake Kinneret; the Lebanon
lines. The capital for the railways was raised by Leonkin in
Russia and by Warszawski in America. I had my troubles with
the board of directors over the interest guarantees. They
thought me- insanely bold to be willing to guarantee profits
from such railways. But I forced my ideas through, and the
event justified me. .It took me five years to secure approval for
one line after the other. All that is an old story now, and the
railways have been taken over by the New Society.

"After transportation problems, I occupied myself chiefly with
the question of draught animals-one of my tasks being to found
a very large agricultural settlement. We not only had to find
our cattle, but to transport them to Palestine and to feed them. I
had many conferences about it with Brownstone, within whose
department the matter came. I was not altogether satisfied with
his proposals. The idea of buying thousands of heads of cattle
in the Danubian countries and transporting them slowly over
land and sea gave me much anxiety. Brownstone was urging
that it was high time to act, but I could not make up my mind. I
should have preferred to bring in the cattle from Egypt. But
there were objections to that scheme as well.

"It was impossible for me, during those first weeks, to leave
London. Once, though, I did manage to run over to Germany to
look at a new electric plow. It was just what we needed. The
electric plow is one of the greatest inventions of the nineteenth
century. In its present form, it is much more practical to be
sure; but I thought it excellent even then. I bought up the

factory's entire stock at once, and ordered all they could promise to deliver by February.. I also telegraphed Warszawski in New York: 'Buy as many electric plows as possible by February.' He replied: 'Shall see.' Returning to London, I found a second telegram: 'Three hundred electric plows middle February Jaffa.

"These electric plows relieved me of various cares. My first meeting with Brownstone after I came back from Germany was funny. As I spied him, I shouted exuberantly, 'My dear fellow! You've become superfluous! We don't need any more oxen!' I can still see his dumbfounded, insulted expression. And I didn't even realize how droll it sounded until the bystanders laughed. I begged his pardon and explained. He cheered. So did everyone else. But our friend Brownstone had by no means become superfluous. Even though he was expected to provide fewer draught oxen, there was plenty of work left for him to do. We still had to find large numbers of horses, milch cows, sheep, poultry, and feed for the whole menagerie. This happened soon after Brownstone returned from Roumania. I sent him also to Holland, Switzerland and Hungary to buy cattle.

"Instead of fodder for oxen, we had to buy coal for our plows. That was Rubenz's affair. Asiatic coal was not so easily obtainable in those days as now. He wired an order for coal to England, and the matter was arranged within twenty-four hours. It was one of those happy moments in which one sees civilization making strides forward....We did not yet have water power from the Dead Sea Canal. Nowadays we do not need English coal for plowing the soil of Palestine. We have wires which carry electric power from the Jordan falls, the Dead Sea Canal, and the brooks of the Hermon and the

Lebanon to plows in all parts of the country. Instead of coal, we have water.

"Such, in outline, were my first measu..."

The Professor noisily asked permission to speak. David halted the machine.

"There's something I want to say at this point," he said. "It's rather in the nature of a literary remark, so don't take it amiss. Do you know what that invisible Joe of ours is describing? I'll tell you. The new Had Gadyal Understand?"

Kingscourt naturally did not understand. They told him that "Had Gadyal Had Gadyal" ("One Kidl One Kidl") was a serio-comic legend in the book of the Seder service. The cat ate the kid, the dog mangled the cat, the stick beat the dog, the fire consumed the stick, the water extinguished the fire, the ox drank the water, the slaughterer killed the ox, the Angel of Death carried off the slaughterer, while above all was God, Who reigns all the way from the Angel of Death to "One Kid! One Kid!"

"That's how," added the Professor, "the story of the New Society runs. The ox is replaced by the coal, and the coal by the water. ..."

Whereupon the elder Littwak said, "And above all is God!"

Theodor Herzl

## Chapter IV

It had grown late, and the listeners were weary. The end of the phonograph narrative was postponed, and the party broke up.

The walk from the villa along the lake shore in the full moonlight was very pleasant. Kingscourt walked ahead with Professor Steineck, asking one question after another. He had gradually warmed up to this "Jewish affair," but insisted that for him the most attractive element in it (attractive more or less, that is to say) was its "big business" aspect. In the destiny of human beings, Jews or non-Jews, he was not the least interested. He was and would remain a hater of mankind. Sheer nonsense to trouble about your neighbor. You'd get nothing in return but black ingratitude. But he rather liked the idea of this Jewish migration as a curious sort of mass undertaking. He would even be ready tomorrow to listen to the rest of Joe's story.

The others followed in twos and threes, Sarah and Friedrich bringing up the rear. The latter was so deep in reverie that he had no word for his charming companion. When they had almost reached the hotel, she teased him about his silence.

"What a night'" he sighed, coming to life. "That moon over Lake Kinneret, and all the remarkable things that have been done here. I too should like to ask the Seder question. 'Wherein doth this night differ from all other nights?' I can guess the answer. The difference is in the freedom through which we

**237**

have at last become human beings. Ah, Mrs. Littwak, if a man might only enjoy it here...."

"And may you not?"

"No, Kingscourt wants to go on immediately."

"Oh," she laughed, "we'll arrange all that. You both belong to us-you as the savior of our family, and he as your friend. You'll see, I'll soon have you settled here. You're not to contradict me, please! I've a word to say in this too. As for that old growler-bear, I'll chain him with bonds of love."

"Do you mean to marry him off?" cried Friedrich, highly amused.

"I could if I cared to," she declared. "To Mrs. Gothland, for instance, or to my sister-in-law Miriam."

"The joke bears a bit hardly on the old man."

"A man is never too old to marry," replied Sarah seriously. "You still have that advantage over us, in spite of our equal rights. But I was thinking of other bonds of affection for Mr. Kingscourt. He's enchanted with my Fritzchen...I've noticed that. I'm not a bit surprised. Anyone can see that there was never a child like him." Friedrich smiled indulgently at the maternal naivete. "So lovely'" he assented.

"He is cleverer than he is beautiful, and his good nature exceeds even his cleverness," continued the mother ardently. "Do you think that my Fritzchen won't twine himself around Mr. Kingscourt's heart if I leave him, often with the old man?

**238**

He'll never be able to tear himself away, and so he'll have to remain here and you with him."

Friedrich, though he smiled, was touched by the maternal foolishness of the clever woman. He did not disturb her faith that no one could tear himself away from her baby. Fritzchen really was a sweet, merry little fellow; and it even seemed that Sarah had not in fact overestimated her son's hold on the old gentleman.

For, the very next morning Friedrich surprised Kingscourt in a shameful situation. The old man was crawling about the nursery on all fours with Fritzchen riding on his back. "That fellow will certainly become a cavalryman," he said in confusion, as Friedrich helped him to his feet. "And now go to your nurse, or I'll spank you until your hide cracks!"

Since the threat was accompanied by Kingscourt's friendliest grin, Fritzchen showed no fear, not knowing that he was having commerce with a most ferocious enemy of the human race. The little boy was about to be sent on a visit to his grandparents; but, because Kingscourt was remaining behind, he howled so frightfully that the desperate mother asked him to help her out. What was Kingscourt to do? He offered with a show of resignation to sacrifice himself, but smiled broadly when Fritzchen showed a sunny face again. Let the others follow later if they liked; he'd give in this once to the naughty young villain. A few moments later, Sarah, David and Friedrich followed them along the lake shore. Kingscourt was walking a step or two behind the nurse, who carried the child on her arm. Ignoring the passersby, he played the clown all along the road for the baby's amusement. Kingscourt had grown old without having known the tyrannical witchery of a little child, and had

had no idea that a rosy baby could so endanger a man's peace of mind. Therefore he fell unsuspectingly and defensively into a very amusing serfdom. Fritzchenhad named him "Otto." The philologists of their circle derived the name from the "Huh! Hottoh.!" which had marked the beginning of friendly relations between Adalbert von Koenigshoff and Fritzchen Littwak. Be that as it may have been, old Kingscourt was "Otto!" to Fritzchen.

When Fritzchen was awake, "Otto" was not allowed to .concern himself with anything or anyone else. It was therefore not until the rosy cheeked despot had fallen asleep after his lunch that Kingscourt was free to ask for the continuation of Joe Levy's tale. Not all of last night's company were present. Mrs. Gothland, who was head of a nursing society, had gone to visit the sick. The Russian priest had returned to Sepphoris. Father Ignaz, too, was occupied. The Steinecks were to come later in the day. But, as the story could be repeated at any time, there was no need to wait for anyone's return.

David had the machine brought up to the first floor salon adjoining his mother's room. They wheeled in the invalid, who was feeling slightly better. She sat and listened with a wistful smile playing over her waxen features. Miriam squatted on a stool beside her, occasionally feeling her pulse. The older Littwak and Kingscourt made themselves comfortable in great easy chairs. Reschid helped David to adjust the machine, and then slid quietly into a chair. The Reverend Mr. Hopkins took a seat beside Friedrich. The latter, from where he sat, had a view of the lake and the mountains on the farther shore. In a line with the view was Miriam's figure outlined in light.

Joe Levy took up the thread of his story. "...my first measures. Alladino sent favorable reports about his land purchases. Steineck promised that by March he would have a new kind of brick kiln and cement factory going in Haifa. Leonkin and Warszawski reported a splendid spirit in the Zionist districts. Brownstone and Kohn had already arranged to have grain and cattle delivered by the spring.

"We had to think not only of the penniless masses, but of the more well-to-do elements whom we wanted to attract to Palestine. Offers of employment or of direct assistance would not tempt them, of course. Some other inducement had to be found. I followed in the steps of the Khedive Ismail of Egypt, who had offered a free building site to anyone pledging himself to erect a home costing no less than 30,000 francs. I did the same thing, but made the proviso that the land was to revert to the New Society after fifty years (since we had reinstituted the old jubilee year). As everyone knows, it was through the Khedive's clever device that the delightful city of Cairo sprang up. It worked equally well in our case.

"Hardly had our representatives abroad announced the offer than we were deluged with applications from all parts of the world. Wellner worked out a set of model plans for homes in consultation with Fischer. The town plans for Haifa, Jaffa, Tiberias and other places had been prepared by Steineck before he left London. Steineck had also made several model plans for pretty middle-class homes. Simultaneously with the announcement of the free building sites, we had large numbers of copies made of his plans and sent them to prospective home-builders. The latter were not obliged to follow these plans. It was only intended to show them what kind of homes could be put up in Palestine and at what cost.

**241**

The allotment of the sites was to take place on the twenty-first of March, the first day of spring. The application lists were closed on the first of March. Whoever was given a site was required to join the general co-operative association of our settlers, and to deposit one-third of the building costs in cash or securities with the New Society. Applicants were required, also, to appear in person or by proxy when the allocations were made. The deposits might be withdrawn as soon as building was actually begun.

"I had Wellner work out the method of allocating the plots. Officials of the New Society were to come to all places where would-be builders were reported, and to arrange for the formation of committees of three, five, or seven persons according to the length of the respective lists. Precedence was given to those willing to build immediately. When there was no difference in time, groups were given the preference over individuals. If all other conditions were equal, lots were cast.

"Our preference for groups was due to our desire everywhere to found strong colonizing nuclei, which would be expected to assume local communal responsibilities themselves. As it worked out, individuals attached themselves to groups even before the allotments were made; and the smaller groups attached themselves to the larger ones. In this way, controversies were avoided, while all due freedom of action was observed.

"There were also rules for the allotment of sites to individuals within the groups. Anyone who was willing to assume a larger share of the local responsibilities, such as laying of streets and roads, sewerage, lighting, water supply and so on, received a

correspondingly better or larger site. These just, simple rules
were easily observed. The New Society officials recorded the
assignments, and their record was countersigned by each local
committee.

"That same day the lists of allotments were forwarded to our
legal department at Haifa." If the rules had been followed and
no protest was lodged by any responsible person, the
allotments were held to be legally binding and title was
registered after one week. If, however, a protest was received,
the case was investigated immediately and on the spot.

"For this purpose I organized a staff of traveling investigators,
who were attached to the legal department in Haifa. This staff
consisted of two officials with legal training and a secretary.
They were provided with a list of the places from which the
complaints had been received, and instructed to go from place
to place; as speedily as possible. The costs for investigating the
complaints were defrayed by the party against whom judgment
was rendered. There was no further court of appeal.

"For such and similar tasks, I had Wellner, who was in charge
of the Haifa bureau, engage fifty young graduate lawyers and
doctors; of law from various countries. We needed these
multilingual legal forces for our correspondence as well, which
had to be carried on in many languages.

"Most of our letters were sent in reply to requests for data
received from independent business men. Here Wellner's legal
bureau worked hand in glove with Fischer's engineering
department. We had announced in the press of many countries
that business men with some capital who were interested in
establishing industries in a Mediterranean country could secure

reliable data and advice on labor and market conditions, and even credits for the purchase of machinery. Every mail brought sheaves of inquiries from the offices of the newspapers in which we had advertised. They were easy to answer, as most of them merely asked which country was meant. I had six or seven forms worked out in reply to such inquiries, and the office merely had to fill in the names and addresses. However, some hundreds of serious business men did emerge from among the thousands of inquirers. They were by no means all Jews. At first, indeed, the English and the German Protestants predominated, since those nations are the most enterprising and boldest of colonizers. In replying to questions, we were not in any way swayed by considerations of race or creed. Everyone who wanted to work the soil of Israel was welcome. Our technical bureau and our secretariat conscientiously furnished whatever information was desired. Of course, before we entered into close relations with anyone, we investigated his references carefully. Business men who came to us bought their experience more cheaply than elsewhere, because we told them where competition was keen or likely to become so. In its own interest, the New Society was obligated to foster all enterprises which attached themselves to it. We therefore regarded independent business men as persons who were furthering our own plans.

"Out of all these questions and answers there was gradually evolved a department of labor and industrial statistics to which were greatly indebted for our prosperity. Working on the information with which it provided us, we were able to establish ourselves in commercial freedom without either hectic over-production or interference in the affairs of the individual manufacturer....

"When all of these projects were under way, I permitted myself a jolly diversion...."

The invalid beckoned to her son. He halted the machine, and hurried over to her. She was tired and wanted to be put back to bed. David and Miriam shoved the wheel chair back into the sick room. The poor invalid made her farewell to the guests with a gentle glance. The elder Littwak sighed, and the whole company felt under a cloud.

Theodor Herzl

# Chapter V

When David returned to the room, he asked whether they desired to listen further to Joe's narrative. There was ready assent, and Joe resumed his story.

"Permitted myself a jolly diversion. At first, it was looked upon as a sort of game or entertainment, and I was very much criticized for it. I am referring to my Ship of the Wise. I wanted this ship to visit 'Old-New-Land' prior to the Return of the Jews. Its very appearance in Mediterranean waters was to herald the new era.

"It was not difficult to arrange. I explained my idea to the manager of a large English tourist bureau. Two weeks later he handed me estimates, contract forms, and plans.. At his suggestion, I chartered a fine modern steamer, the 'Futuro,' from an Italian line plying between Naples and Alexandria. She was to be ready for us at Genoa on the fifteenth of March, and would remain at our disposal for six weeks. In the meantime, the tourist manager reserved accommodations for five hundred guests at first-class hotels in Italy, Egypt, Asia Minor and Greece, and provided them with tickets on the Italian railways (they were to embark either at Naples or at Genoa, as they chose). Outwardly, the expedition resembled the pleasure tours of the Near East already common in those days. But it was really much more.

"The ladies and gentlemen whom we invited for that six weeks' spring Lour of the eastern Mediterranean belonged to the

**247**

intellectual aristocracy of the whole civilized world. The choicest spirits were called, without distinction of race or creed; and they came. They came not only because we offered them a delightful excursion, but because they knew this to be a unique occasion for meeting with their peers. On board the 'Futuro' were gathered poets and philosophers, inventors, explorers, investigators and artists of every type, political economists, statesmen, publicists, journalists.

"Ample physical and intellectual recreation was provided. All the comforts known to tourist agencies were to be found on board, for our guests were to enjoy six weeks without a cloud. Nothing that could give them pleasure was overlooked from the ship's orchestra that played at mealtime to the ship's paper published every morning. With such a passenger list, you may imagine that that sheet did not lack fascinating content. The trip was taken along many coasts; and, at every port, the 'Futuro' picked up news telegrams from the whole world, which promptly appeared in the next morning's paper. But, of course, by far the most valuable section was the literary page, where the events and experiences of each day were described by master pens. For example, the celebrated 'Table Talks,' which were later referred to as the New Platonic Dialogues, appeared there from day to day. Questions of the highest import were discussed -on an exalted level, you may be sure. The noblest minds of the period were expressing themselves, giving and receiving memorable stimulation.

"I shall mention only a few of the topics they discussed, such as the establishment of a truly modern commonwealth, education through art, land reform, charity organization, social welfare for workingmen, the role of women in civilized society, the progress of applied science, and many other topics.

The 'Futuro Table Talks' have long been a gem of world literature. I myself know them only from the printed page, for it was not given me to hear them with my own ears.

"I had not the time then to make a pleasure trip, since I had to keep closely at my work. When the 'Futuro' anchored at Genoa, I had already been in Palestine for some time. But I read the ship's bulletin with a close attention and appreciation I have never given a newspaper before or since. I am not a philosopher, and in those days certainly was too busy to occupy myself with abstractions. But I searched in those 'Table Talks' for whatever seemed practical, and then tried to apply the ideas.

"It was as if the spirit of the times were speaking to the Jewish people from the 'Futuro' at the very moment when we were about to re-establish ourselves as a nation. The words that came from the ship were treasured and taken to heart by us. But it was when our honored guests actually trod upon the soil of Palestine that their comments were particularly fruitful and stimulating.

"The Ship of the Wise sailed along our coast. The passengers traveled about the country in large groups or small as they preferred. Their comfort was well looked after in every case.

"Not all of them were interested in the same things or in equal degree. The geologists wanted to see this, the electrical engineers that. Botanists, architects, painters, political economists-all sought out their own fields. The groups formed themselves naturally for the expeditions on shore; but so delightful was the spirit on the 'Futuro' that some of the passengers rarely left the ship at all. There were among them

**249**

some who saw nothing of Palestine but the railway between Jerusalem and Haifa. There is a story, which I do not vouch for, that one accomplished writer never left the ship for a moment, declaring, 'This ship is Zion!' Later, however, he described Palestine and its people very fully.

"I must admit that this writer had excellent sources of information. When his fellow-passengers returned to the boat, they brought back an abundance of material which they had observed with expert eyes, and described it in masterly fashion. Each time after an excursion there were new themes for the table talk, which gave rise to the marvelous dialogues concerning what could be done in Palestine. I read and re-read those dialogues until I knew them by heart, as I do to this day. The comments of the artists impressed me most deeply-perhaps because I am myself no artist. On its practical side, our enterprise required only enough common sense to adapt the available facilities to Palestinian conditions. But it is to the artists. of the- 'Futuro' that I owe the valuable lesson that our land had much natural beauty; and that it must be made beautiful everywhere, always more beautiful. For beauty gladdens the heart of man.

"It is one of my most curious experiences that I never properly saw the 'Futuro.' I arranged the cruise, followed its developments, took to heart the words of wisdom that came from the ship, but-saw nothing of it. This is how it happened:

"When the 'Futuro' appeared off our coast, I was busy inland. Fischer, Steineck and Alladino presented the compliments of the New Society when she anchored at Jaffa. I intended to present myself when I should have completed an urgent piece of business. But it was a time when I was traveling day and night from one labor camp to another. Very often I slept in my touring car. And in those days there were no such comforts as we now have. When I knew in advance where I was going to spend the night, a barrack was knocked together for me. However, it was not always possible to foresee this. Besides, it was just as well for me to appear here and there unannounced in order to inspect the laying of the roads, the distribution of land, and the agricultural work. Though detailed plans and instructions had been prepared for everything, I preferred to convince myself in person that all was going according to schedule. I was in constant touch with my Haifa headquarters. Thence came messages which sent me scurrying from one end of the country to the other. Despite all our planning, it was not possible always to prevent occasional hitches with the workmen or in the commissariat. These things required rapid action and revised arrangements. At times there would be Gordian knots in connection with assigning land that no one but myself could cut.

"We were doing the spring planting on the lands of the New Society. Though we had organized agricultural producers co-operatives on the Rahaline model, our people were still new at it, needing guidance, and also at times someone in authority to make decisions. Our tasks were by no means extraordinary, but they did require close attention. There's no art in planting summer wheat, barley, oats, maize or turnips. And yet all sorts of difficulties arose. We had to battle with the neglected soil, which resisted our efforts. However, we had the newest agricultural equipment and cast-iron determination so that in the end, we mastered the soil, and it became our friend. Organization is the chief thing; and we had organized everything down to the last detail before our mobilization.

**251**

"The men in the employ of the New Society worked only several hours a day, but they concentrated all their strength into those seven hours. They laid roads, dug canals, built houses, cleared stones from the fields that were to be plowed with electric plows, planted trees. Each man knew that he was working for all his comrades, and that all were working for him. They went out singing to their work in the morning, and returned singing at night. Our work was like a sudden burst of spring, when bare trees turn green over night. And every day increased our momentum.

"I installed a telephone and telegraph system immediately. Though these services could not be made available to the public in the beginning, we made use of them at once in our administrative work. The wires ran out from Haifa. In the convoy car behind mine, .I carried a telegrapher who connected me quickly with my Haifa office and with the London headquarters. Only in this way could I have supervised the distribution of labor and materials.

"Every day five hundred, a thousand or two thousand immigrants arrived at the various ports between Beirut and Jaffa. They were set to work the day after they landed. No delays! We needed tens of thousands of men for railway construction alone, and still more to erect the public buildings of the New Society-the administration offices, schools, hospitals, etc. No great skill was required once the plans had been adopted, and all that had been arranged well in advance. For their work on the roads, railways and other public utilities, our laborers received not only wages (minus deductions for goods they might have purchased from the department stores), but they were also entitled .to be settled on the land. An immigrant whom we assigned to various jobs that spring, was to have a house built for him by the autumn in which to receive his family.

"As I have said, carrying out the work was a simple matter once the plans were there. The military staffs of the great European powers had far more difficult tasks in the nineteenth century. It is really immodest to compare our tasks with achievements like theirs. We had only to settle half a million people by the autumn, and could count upon a harvest in the meantime, while the old military staffs had to feed millions of men, often in enemy territory, and usually in times of a general dislocation of commerce and traffic. We, however, were in a friendly country, on our ancestral soil, in fact. And we not only did not frighten business off, but attracted it strongly. The people for whom we had to provide began at once to produce the means for their own maintenance and also for the later comers.

"All over the country independent manufacturers were erecting factories that were to be roofed over by the autumn. As a matter of fact, any sensible person could see what splendid industrial prospects were opening up in this country: the local market for goods created by the large immigration; the low freight rates on the outbound ships, which still carried little return cargo; the long coast line; the central situation of the country between Europe and Asia. All these factors tempted people hither.

"After our first harvest, which was not especially good, but only fair, I reviewed the situation and decided that it was not necessary to interrupt the immigration in the autumn as we had planned originally. When I cabled the local Zionist federations that it was not necessary to halt the stream of immigrants, there

**253**

was great enthusiasm everywhere. I date the triumph of our New Society from that first harvest. We were to have more abundant harvests in later years; the old gold of the wheat was to grow more plentifully out of our soil; but we never again harvested so much as in that year, for we then reaped the confidence of our brethren allover the world. Barely a twelve-month after I had established our headquarters in London, I was able to say to my staff in Haifa that it had been a good year.

"Our administration building in Haifa was roofed over by the autumn, but still unfinished within. We were to occupy it only in the spring. But I could say to my valiant assistants, 'Now we have a roof over our heads.' I referred to the whole structure of the New Society. We had merely to keep on as we were going, to overlook no detail, and to keep a watchful eye on our work. Our tasks grew more extensive, but they were easier to carry out as time went on.

"The larger engineering enterprises-the water works had been finished. We linked ourselves with a very ancient Jewish heritage-the Pools of Solomon's which still bear witness to the skill of our ancestors. We had, indeed, to do more than furnish water for Jerusalem and the other cities; electric light and power also had to be produced. The Dead Sea Canal and our other engineering works prove that our engineers did not spare themselves-Fischer, their splendid chief, less than anyone else.

"There also poured into our land a stream of capital and credit. Our purposeful work and immediate successes had won for us the confidence of the public. Just as we had organized agricultural producers' co-operatives with our new peasants, so we had brought modern agricultural credits into the country. At first some people thought that we should soon exhaust our credits if we gave our settlers dwelling houses, farm buildings, machinery, horses, cows, sheep, poultry, wagons, implements, seed, and fodder. The cost of settling one family on the land was about 600 pounds. Our clever opponents therefore calculated that the cost of settling one thousand families would be 600,000 pounds, ten thousand families 6,000,000 pounds, etc., etc., and so ascertained the exact date when our funds would give out altogether. These expert calculators overlooked one trifle, namely, that settlers represent an appreciable economic value, and that money can always be borrowed on good collateral. The New Society could if it chose, have increased its cash resources very largely by well-covered, amortizable loans. In a word, the more settlers we brought into the country, the more money flowed in. So it is allover the world with good management. Why should it not have worked out equally well in our case?

"But I see that I have digressed from the subject in hand. As I have said, the 'Futuro' visited us at a time when I was busy in the interior. I was forced to postpone my trip to Jaffa from one day to the next all the while the Ship of the Wise lay anchored there.

"Once it happened that a party from the boat was driving in several cars along a new road bordering some fields where I was riding about on horseback. They glanced at the great steam roller being used there, and observed some of our men working in the fields. The bright silk veils fluttering from the ladies' hats was a pretty sight. I did not ride up to them, because I was all dusty and perspiring and looked like a highwayman. I still thought then that I should be able to present myself to their distinguished company while the 'Futuro' lay at Jaffa. But it turned out otherwise. The next day I received a telegram which obliged me to hurry off to Constantinople. There was a very important matter to be arranged with the Turkish Government. I ordered my yacht put under steam at once, and called my department chiefs together. I appointed Fischer (who knew all my views) acting director, and sailed for Constantinople the next day with my secretary.

"It was impossible for me to visit the 'Futuro' then, but I counted upon her remaining along the coast of Palestine until I returned. I did everything in my power to hurry things in Constantinople, but everything dragged as it occasionally does in that charming but sleepy city and my impatience helped me not at all. In spirit I was in Palestine all the while. I was in hourly touch with Fischer and my London office. Only with those delightful people on the 'Futuro' I could have no communication. My regrets grew the greater as the ship sailed northward. Fischer kept me informed as to her movements. Now she was in Tyre, then in Sidon. She was to stay over a bit in Beirut, so as to allow time for an excursion to Damascus. I hoped that she would still be at Beirut when I finally got away from Constantinople. My presence was urgently required in Palestine, but I did want to allow myself half a day at Beirut in order to board the 'Futuro.' My good yacht flew over the waves, for I had asked my captain to make his best speed. And at that we were too late. Passing Cyprus one morning I noticed a ship in the distance bound in the opposite direction. It flashed upon me that she might be the 'Futuro.' I rushed to the bridge, but was not a good enough seaman to identify a ship at that distance. The captain unfortunately was downstairs in his cabin. By the time he had been called to the bridge, the ship was out of sight. To race after her on a chance was inadvisable. For one thing, it was doubtful whether we could overtake her;

for another, the 'Futuro' might still be lying at Beirut, and then I would probably miss her. When we reached Beirut, I learned that my surmise had been correct: the ship I had seen in the morning sunlight off Cyprus had indeed been the 'Futuro.'

"I felt a certain pang. Ever since then I have cherished the wish that it might be granted me to see the return of the 'Futuro' after twenty five years. I don't mean the same boat, of course-she would be obsolete, and we shall have a splendid new one; nor the identical group of guests: Some of .them will have died, and there many new stars will have arisen on the horizon of civilization in the meantime. But we intend that every twenty-five years a ship named the 'Futuro' shall bring us such an Aeropagus, before whose judgment we shall bow. We shall set up no make-believe villages as at a world's fair, but shall place our whole country on exhibit before the 'Futuro' as an honored jury.

"When they come again and it is given me not to miss them...should they find that Joe Levy has performed his simple but onerous task with some degree of skill, why then-I shall go on the retired list. And when I die, lay me beside my dear friend Fischer, up there in the Carmel cemetery, overlooking our beloved land and sea."

# Theodor Herzl

## Chapter VI

Joe's story was finished. His last words had deeply touched his listeners.

Kingscourt cleared his throat noisily. "Seems to be a charming fellow, this .Joe. Very charming fellow. Too bad he's not here. Should like to shake his hand. Hope to see him before we move on. There's one thing he's got me excited about-that Dead Sea Canal. Seems to be a kind of world's wonder. When do we get a peep at this myth?"

David promised to take them immediately after Passover. Meanwhile, life was pleasant in Tiberias. Kingscourt ate the unleavened bread valiantly, and swore that he, a Christian German nobleman, was becoming thoroughly "judaized." His most violent oaths were aimed at Fritzchen, whose tyranny grew more exacting from day to day. The little rascal thought, did he that Kingscourt had nothing better to do in his old age than to play hobby horse for him? However, he permitted himself rebellious remarks only when his tyrant was asleep. When the baby woke and called for "Otto," the growling bear became his obedient slave immediately.

When they made plans for the trip through the Jordan Valley to Jericho, David thought of leaving the baby with his grandparents; but Kingscourt interposed all sorts of objections. The boy ought to learn something about the country, just like other people. David would be an unnatural rather if he left him behind. In the worst event, if Fritzchen did not come along, he

would forego the whole .Dead Sea Canal and stay with the
baby. He was so determined that the parents finally yielded;
then he pretended utter indifference. He wasn't at all concerned
personally. He had merely taken the part of a helpless child!

In the meantime, Reschid Bey returned to his family,
promising to meet his friends in Jerusalem. Steineck (the
architect) also went on to Haifa, being much concerned with
the elections to the forthcoming congress. Judging both from
private and newspaper reports, the Geyer party seemed to be
exerting itself mightily. Steineck therefore had to be at his post
at the Haifa campaign headquarters, which was in hourly touch
with the local committees.

David, however, had some private business to transact in the
Jaulan district before he would be free to make the Jordan
Valley trip. He invited Kingscourt and Friedrich to accompany
him. The latter assented readily, since Miriam and Professor
Steineck were also to be of the party. Kingscourt, however,
remained in Tiberias because-so he said-he did not wish to let
Sarah and Mrs. Gothland travel alone in the motor car to
Beisan. His weakness for Fritzchen being already pretty well
taken for granted, he was not teased overmuch for this
decision. It was arranged that all of them meet at a Beisan hotel
(in the Jordan Valley) two days later.

A handsome electric launch was waiting to take the four
travelers across Lake Kinneret. Those who were remaining in
Tiberias came to the pier to see them off. When Friedrich
shook hands with Kingscourt, the latter said, "Do you know,
Fritze, that this is the first day we have spent apart in twenty
years? Don't get lost on a byroad in the place with the crazy
Arab name-or may a thousand salted Donnerwetters overtake

you! And you, Miss Miriam, please don't take advantage of the
opportunity to turn this boy's head. He's forty-three years old.
The most dangerous age! And now God bless you! We'll meet
you at Beisan!"

Miriam and Friedrich both blushed at the old man's crude joke,
and showed their embarrassment as they entered the launch.
Kingscourt winked significantly at Mrs. Gothland, much
pleased at his success in discomfiting them.

It was a mild spring day. The yacht skimmed over the waves,
which were slightly rippled by a playful breeze. The lovely
mansions and villas of Tiberias receded as the steep shores of
the eastern side of the lake loomed up before them. They had a
magnificent view of Mount Hermon to the north, and enjoyed
watching the craft of all shapes and sizes that dotted the lake.
The crossing was as fleet as a dream, and the launch soon
docked in a little bay. It was only a few yards walk to the
electric railway station, where they soon caught a train. Their
destination was EI-Kunetra, where David had his
appointments. From their seats in the drawing-room car they
observed the gradual ascent of the roadbed to the town, which
lay a thousand feet above sea-level. EI-Kunetra, as a railway
junction between Safed and Damascus, was a town of some
commercial importance in Transjordania.

When they alighted from their train, they noticed a train on the
next track marked for Beirut. Boyish voices were singing in
one of the cars-they guessed the youngsters to be from fourteen
to sixteen years old. "Are they off on a little trip?" asked
Friedrich. "Yes," smiled Professor Steineck, "around the
world!"

**261**

Miriam explained the character of this school excursion. It was modeled after the trips which the French Benedictine monks used to arrange a quarter of a century previously for pupils under the escort of their teachers. The young men learned foreign languages and customs on their travels, so that study and seeing the world were systematically interwoven. They were much more mature for their years than the youth of the previous generation. Their education was not only more sound, but less expensive, since they were ready to assume adult duties earlier. The money invested by the New Society in these school caravans soon bore interest.

Only the best pupils were given this opportunity. No public moneys were wasted on lazy or incompetent boys, while the honor was eagerly sought by those who were diligent and ambitious. The love of adventure which boys had in the trying adolescent age was not only curbed by this means but stimulated into wholesome channels, just as an automobile was propelled forward by a series of little explosions.

These school caravans were systematically planned by the Education Department of the New Society, which had equipped school buildings in the various countries visited, where every provision was made for the care as well as for the instruction of the boys. These buildings were always situated in small towns near the great capitals. In France, for example, the educational building of the New Society was at Versailles. It was better for the physical and spiritual welfare of the pupils that they should live away from the dangerous capital cities. Each of the institutions was in charge of a resident principal, and the caravans were conducted by class teachers who spent three months abroad with their pupils. The itineraries were arranged at the educational headquarters in Jerusalem. Thus the boys saw something of the world without interruption of their studies.

"What about the girls?" quizzed Friedrich.

"Girls don't go on such tours," replied Miriam. "We believe that the place of a growing girl is beside her mother, even when she has been well trained for her duties in the New Society and fulfills them."

While David was engaged with his affairs, Miriam, Friedrich, and Professor Steineck sauntered through the busy town. They saw very little Oriental merchandise in the shops, most of which were agencies for European firms.

They had very good accommodations at an English hotel. Friedrich no longer marveled at the comforts found in Palestine. It was natural enough that a center of international traffic should provide for the comfort of travelers.

That evening they had an early dinner, intending to make an early start the next morning for the so called "granary" of Palestine.

The morning sky was glowing with delicate color as they boarded the electric train that was to carry them through a bewitching spring landscape. Friedrich felt stirring of the springtides of his boyhood in his blood. And, though he dared hardly admit it to himself, the proximity of the lovely Miriam was not without its influence upon his mood. How capably she explained the things that attracted his attention. Sometimes, when she was not fully enough informed, David and Steineck helped her out.

Friedrich, having been trained only in the law and never having studied the applied sciences, really had little notion of modem technical progress and in this he was like most of the educated men of his day. He therefore thought Steineck must be teasing him with some scientific joke when he said that the waters which flowed up from the north and the south met at the watershed here. Steineck did, as it happened, want his little joke with the unscientific Friedrich, but did not long withhold the explanation. Of course, the waters did not flow uphill of themselves, but were forced up by hydraulic pressure. Even in "Old-New-Land" it had been no more possible to change the laws of Nature than the nature of man. But, with the progress of civilization, men had come to understand natural forces better, and had learned how to utilize them. It was no longer necessary to set a mill wheel directly under a waterfall, as in the simple old days. Nowadays the mill wheel was driven by a brook flowing fifteen or twenty miles away, whose power was carried in the form of electric current over cables. By the end of the nineteenth century, this problem had been fully solved; in America, especially, they had gone far in this respect. Electric power from Niagara Falls had been transmitted over a distance of one hundred and sixty-two kilometers and current had also been carried, with a very slight loss of power, for one hundred and thirty-three kilometers from the San Bernardino mountains in Southern California to the city of Los Angeles. These things were easily copied in Palestine. The water power of the Dead Sea Canal in the south and of the springs of the Hermon and the Lebanon in the north was also transmitted in the same way.

"The real founders of 'Old-New-Land,'" said David, "were the hydraulic engineers. There was everything in having the swamps drained, the arid tracts irrigated, and a system of power supply installed."

After traveling for an hour and a half, they reached a model farm established by a millionaire benevolent association and supervised by the New Society. The manager showed them over the whole magnificent estate. Friedrich was especially taken with the central electric station near the administration building. Its walls were covered with buttons, numbers, and little tablets. Two simply dressed young girls were working there under the instructions of an official who sat at a desk and continually put up the telephone receiver to his ear. It reminded Friedrich of a visit he had once paid to a telephone exchange. The manager explained that the electric current was transmitted from this station to all parts of the estate as needed, and shut off the moment it was not needed. The station served not only the farm, but also several allied industrial enterprises-a sugar factory, a brewery, a spirit refinery, a mill, etc.

The farm buildings which they saw, like the .factories, roads, and fields, had the last word in technical appliances. The place was painfully clean, and all work was performed so quietly that one could not help noting it. The great wheels of the estate turned with a minimum of noise. A group of workers in uniform passed by, tools slung over their shoulders, and eyes averted. Some of them seemed sullen, others shy. They gave the manager the military salute.

"May I be allowed a criticism?" asked Friedrich. "We have admired so many fine things in 'Old-New-Land' that perhaps I may venture a misgiving."

"Certainly!" replied David. "What is it?"

**265**

"These laborers seem peculiarly depressed, as if the splendid machine they serve had somehow crushed something in them. Of what good are all the clever mechanical devices if people are none the happier for using them? These men remind me of the factory workers of my day. I admit, they look less sad, and seem to be healthier. Nevertheless, there is a resemblance. That is what troubles me. Knowing that this farm belongs to a benevolent association, I expected to see happier-looking people. I confess, I am a bit disappointed."

The manager gave him a surprised glance, and turned questioningly to the others. "Doesn't Dr. Loewenberg know where he is?" he asked.

"No," replied David. "We purposely did not tell him, as we wanted him to gain an unbiased impression. It Was to be a surprise for him that this is a penal colony."

"Impossible!" cried Friedrich. "A penal colony! That alters the case, of course! Will you please tell me," he asked the manager, "if you get effective educational results?"

"Our people are restored to physical and moral health. Most of them come to love life on the land, and don't want to leave it. After serving their terms, they are often glad to remain here as hired laborers. Sometimes we settle them as independent farmers in remote districts. The profits of the estate are used to finance such settlements, which begin to repay the loans after a few years. We restore the dregs of society to manhood."

When, the next day at Beisan, Friedrich reported what he had seen to Kingscourt, the old man exploded, "Of course! All the

266

marvels happen when I'm not there. Water flows uphill, and prisons are free!"

The Noah's ark carried them southward along the Jordan Valley on a well-paved road, which often followed the river bed and as often diverged from it. The Jordan was at its spring rise, the landscape on both shores softly green. Lovely villages, towns, and residential suburbs peeped out from wooded slopes on the eastern and western heights. Every now and then the Jordan Valley train rushed by on the right bank. There was also lively traffic on the high road. It was the season when most of the tourists forsook Jericho now a famous winter resort. The Jordan Valley was already too warm for the spoiled darlings of fashion who had run away from the European winter. There were many large touring cars on the road which resembled David's ark, with parties of smartly dressed men and women traveling northward, the Lebanon season being now at its height. The tourists would take ship for Europe at the end of April from Beirut, unless they preferred the quicker land route to Constantinople by the Asia Minor express.

But, though the pleasure-seekers left the Jordan Valley when the hot weather set in, the sturdiest elements - the workers- remained at home there. The plains on both sides of the river, famed since ancient times for their fertility, were more luxuriantly planted than ever before. Now that the Jordan Valley was worked with the newest and best agricultural machinery available, it yielded abundant crops of rice, sugar cane, tobacco and cotton, which brought rich profits.

The hydraulic engineers had achieved remarkable things in this region. Regulation of the Jordan had been only one of their tasks. By means of magnificent dams in the valleys between the mountains on the eastern side, the abundant water supply of the land had been utilized to the full. In the ages when the land had lain neglected, the rain had been allowed to run off into the ground. Now, by the simple system of dams so well known throughout the civilized world, every drop of water that fell from the heavens was exploited for the public, good. Milk and honey once more flowed in the ancient home of the Jews. Palestine was again the Promised Land.

All these useful works were placed in a setting of beauty. White structures gleamed out of green gardens upon the terraced slopes on both sides of the river. Marble villas towered above the level of the travelers' vision. The marble was brought from quarries not far away-near the Dead Sea. One pleasant surprise after another revealed itself to Kingscourt and Friedrich as they drove along. When they approached the beautiful town of Jericho, even the critical Kingscourt became speechless at sight of the many beautiful hotels, mansions and villas nestling within tropical plantations and clumps of palm trees. He had never imagined it to be so enchanting a health resort. Now he asked that they drive down directly to the Dead Sea before stopping at their hotel. Fortunately for him Fritzchen had fallen asleep, or "Otto" would not have been allowed such separatist notions. The ladies alighted at the hotel with the child, and the others drove down the short distance to the valley where the Dead Sea was spread out like a deep blue mirror. Their ears were assailed by a roaring-the thunder of the Canal waters, led hither through tunnels from the Mediterranean, rushing down to the depths.

David briefly explained the plan of the works. The Dead Sea, as everyone knew, was the lowest point on the earth's surface, lying three hundred and ninety-four meters below the level of the Mediterranean. To convert this tremendous difference in levels into a source of power was the simplest idea in the world. There was a loss of only eighty-odd meters in the course of the Canal from the coast to the Dead Sea. There still remained, therefore, a net difference of over three hundred feet. The Canal, which was ten meters wide and three deep, provided about 50,000 horsepower.

Kingscourt would by no means admit surprise. "Even in my time," said he, "the power station at Niagara Falls provided 40,000 horse-power."

"But," retorted David, "the Dead Sea Canal cannot be compared with the Niagara Falls. Even though the Falls are only fifty meters high, there are millions of horsepower there because of the enormous amount of water. But we are quite satisfied with the total of 500,000 horsepower that we produce at the various power stations in the Jordan Valley and the Dead Sea Canal."

"Quite right, highly esteemed water-power artist," admitted the old man. "But there's one thing I don't understand. Much more water now flows into the Dead Sea basin than before, but it still has no outlet. Is the evaporation greater now?"

"Not a bad question," remarked the Professor. "Only you must realize, gentlemen, that we draw as much water out of the Dead Sea as we pour into it. We take great quantities of fresh water from it, which are pumped into reservoirs and used for irrigation in areas where water is as necessary as it is superfluous here. Understand?"

"Of course I understand!" shouted Kingscourt, and this once his shouting was pardonable because they stood by the roaring waterfall. "You're damned sly fellows, I must admit!"

And now they were in front of the power station. While driving down from Jericho, they had not been able to get a full view of the Dead Sea. Now they saw it lying broad and blue in the sun" no smaller than the Lake of Geneva. On the northern shore, near where they stood, was a narrow, pointed strip of land extending behind the rocks over which the waters of the Canal came thundering down. Below were the turbine sheds; above, extensive factory buildings. There were, in fact, as far as the eye could reach around the shore, numerous large manufacturing plants. The water power at source had attracted many industries; the Canal had stirred the Dead Sea to life. The iron tubes through which the waters of the Canal beat down upon the turbine wheels reminded Kingscourt of the apparatus at Niagara. There were some twenty of these mighty iron tubes at the Dead Sea, jutting out from the rocks at equal distances. They were set vertically upon the turbine sheds, resembling fantastic chimneys. The roaring from the tubes and the white foam on the outflowing waters bore witness to a mighty work.

They stepped into one of the turbine sheds. Friedrich was overwhelmed by the immensity of the power development shown him, but Kingscourt seemed quite at his ease in the tumult of this industrial apparatus. With all his might he screamed comments no one could possibly hear; but they could see from his face that for once he was wholly satisfied. It really was a magnificent, Cyclopean sight as the waters crashed down upon the huge bronze spokes of the turbine wheels and drove them to furious turnings.

From here the tamed natural forces were conducted into electric generators, and the current sent along wires throughout all parts of the country. The "Old-New-Land" had been fructified into a garden and a home for people who had once been poor, weak, hopeless, and homeless.

"I feel myself crushed by all this greatness," sighed Friedrich, when at last he could speak.

"Not we," responded David earnestly. "We have not been crushed by the greatness of these forces-it has lifted us up!"

# Theodor Herzl

# Book Five

# Jerusalem

## Chapter I

Twenty years before, Kingscourt and Friedrich had entered Jerusalem by night and from the west. Now they came by day, approaching from the east. Then she had been a gloomy, dilapidated city; now she was risen in splendor, youthful, alert, risen from death to life.

They came directly from Jericho up to the top of the Mount of Olives with its wide views. Jerusalem and her hills were still sacred to all mankind, still bore the tokens of reverence bestowed upon her through the ages. But something had been added; new, vigorous, joyous life. The Old City within the walls, as far as they could see from the mountain top, had altered least. The Holy Sepulcher, the Mosque of Omar, and other domes and towers had remained the same; but many splendid new structures had been added. That magnificent new edifice was the Peace Palace. A vast calm brooded over the Old City.

Outside the walls the picture was altogether different. Modern sections intersected by electric street railways; wide, tree-bordered streets; homes, gardens, boulevards, parks; schools,

**273**

hospitals, government buildings, pleasure resorts. David pointed out and named the important buildings. Jerusalem was now a twentieth century metropolis. Fascinating indeed....but the Old City drew their eyes back ever and again. There she lay in the afternoon sunlight, on the farther side of the Kidron Valley....Kingscourt had put all sorts of questions, and David had answered them all. Now he asked, what was that wonderful structure of white and gold, whose roof rested on a whole forest of marble columns with gilt capitals? Friedrich's heart stirred within him as David replied, "That is the Temple!"

Friedrich's first visit to the Temple was on a Friday evening. David had engaged rooms for the party at one of the best hotels near the Jaffa Gate, and at sundown invited his guests to go with him to the Temple. Friedrich walked ahead with Miriam, David and Sarah following. The streets which at noon had been alive with traffic were now suddenly stilled. Very few motor cars were to be seen; all the shops were closed. Slowly and peacefully the Sabbath fell upon the bustling city. Throngs of worshipers wended their way to the Temple and to the many synagogues in the Old City and the New, there to pray to the God whose banner Israel had borne throughout the world for thousands of years.

The spell of the Sabbath was over the Holy City, now freed from the filth, noise and vile odors that had so often revolted devout pilgrims of all creeds when, after long and trying journeys, they reached their goal. In the old days they had had to endure many disgusting sights before they could reach their shrines. All was different now. There were no longer private dwellings in the Old City; the lanes and the streets were beautifully paved and cared for. All the buildings were devoted to religious and benevolent purposes-hospices for pilgrims of all denominations. Moslem, Jewish, and Christian welfare institutions, hospitals, clinics stood side by side. In the middle of a great square as the splendid Peace Palace, where international congresses of peace-lovers and scientists were held, for Jerusalem was now a home for all the best strivings of the human spirit: for Faith, Love, Knowledge.

Whatever a man's attitude toward religion, he could not escape a reverent mood in the streets of Jerusalem when he saw the quiet throngs exchange the Sabbath greetings as they passed.

Miriam and Friedrich met an old gentleman leaning heavily on his cane, and greeted him respectfully. He stopped to wait for Sarah and David, who then slowed their pace to his. "This old man, too, has found peace here," whispered Miriam to her escort. "You must get my brother to tell you how he found and converted him. David had gone to Paris on business, and met this M. Armand Ephraim by accident. You know our David - people always like him. M. Ephraim was very much attracted to him, more than to his own relatives, who were merely waiting for his death to enjoy his fortune. All his life M. Ephraim had done nothing but earn money and spend it on his pleasures; and then, when he became too old for pleasures, he did not know what to do with his money. But he did know one thing, that he did not want to leave it to his frivolous heirs. David persuaded him to come to Jerusalem. He took him to the Peace Palace, which is an international center for great undertakings. Its activities are by no means limited to Palestine and the Jews, but include all countries and all peoples.

"In the New Society," she continued, "we have found the answers to many of the troublesome old problems. Unfortunately, though, there is still much misery in the world,

**275**

which can be alleviated only through concerted effort. When a disaster occurs anywhere in the world-fire, blood, famine, epidemic-it is reported here at once. Large sums of cash are always available here for emergency relief, because contributions continually flow into a central fund. A large permanent international council sees to the just distribution of the funds.

"Inventors, artists, and scholars also turn to the Peace Palace for encouragement. They are attracted by the motto over its portals: 'Nil humani a me alienum puto'-'Let nothing human be alien to me.' When such men are found worthy, they are aided as much as possible. M. Ephraim enjoys attending the committee meetings at which appeals for relief are considered, and he always leaves them lighter in heart and in pocket. He is gradually giving away his whole fortune except what he needs for the rest of his life. Whatever is left will go to good works."

"If he carries out that intention," smiled Friedrich, "his heirs will mourn him indeed."

They stopped to wait for the others. M. Ephraim was coughing out the end of a story. "And today I gave five hundred pounds sterling to a seaside home for neglected London children. A hundred thousand francs today "all told. Not a bad day, hoho!-not a bad day! If I were gone, my nephews would have lost as much at the races. As it is, I have enjoyed my money. And they...my heirs...shall not laugh...hohoho ...I am the one to laugh. ..hohoho! And those London tots will laugh, too, when they get out into the fresh air. ...Poor little things!"

They reached the Temple. The times had fulfilled themselves, and it was rebuilt. Once more it had been erected with great quadrangular blocks of stone hewn from nearby quarries and hardened by the action of the atmosphere. Once more the pillars of bronze stood before the Holy Place of Israel. "The left pillar was called Boaz, but the name of the right was Jachin." In the forecourt was a mighty bronze altar, with an enormous basin called the brazen sea as in the olden days, when Solomon was king in Israel.

Sarah and Miriam went up to the women's gallery. Friedrich sat beside David in the last row downstairs. "When the places were assigned," said David, "I chose the very last row. I wanted nothing else."

The great hall resounded with singing and the playing of lutes. The music recalled to Friedrich far-off things in his own life, and turned his thoughts to other days in Israel. The worshipers were crooning and murmuring the words of the ritual, but Friedrich thought of Heine's "Hebrew Melodies." The Princess Sabbath, she that is called the "serene princess," was at home here. The choristers chanted a hymn that had stirred yearnings for their own land in the hearts of a homeless people for hundreds of years. The words of the noble poet Solomon ha-Levy, "Lecha Dodi, likrath kallah!"... ("Come, Beloved, to meet the bride!") How beautifully Heine had put it:

> "'Komm, Geliebter, deiner harret
>
> Schon die Braut, die dir entschleiert
>
> Ihr verschaemtes Angesicht."

Yes, Heine was a true poet, who sensed the romance of the national destiny. He had sung German songs ardently, but the beauty of the Hebrew melodies had not escaped him.

What a degraded era, that was, thought Friedrich, when the Jews had been ashamed of everything Jewish, when they thought they made a better showing when they concealed their Jewishness. Yet in that very concealment they had revealed the temper of the slave, at best, of the liberated slave. They need not have been surprised at the contempt shown them, for they had shown no respect for themselves. They crawled after the others, and were rejected in swift punishment. Curious that they had not drawn the obvious moral! Quite the contrary. Those who succeeded in business or in some other field often openly forsook the faith of their fathers. They were at pains to hide their origin as though it were a taint. Those who forsook Judaism denied their own fathers and mothers in order to be quit of it: they must have thought it something low, reprehensible, evil. To be sure, renegades had not got off scot-free, for they were treated like refugees from plague-stricken countries. After baptism, they were still suspect, and remained, as it were, in quarantine. Marranos, the baptized Jews of medieval Spain had been called. Marranoism, then, was the quarantine for refugee Jews.

And all that time Judaism had sunk lower and lower. It was an "elend" in the full sense of the old German word that had meant "out-land,"-the limbo of the banished. Whoever was "elend" was unfortunate; and whoever was an unfortunate sought for himself a nook in "elend." The Jews had thus fallen always lower, as much by their own fault as by the fault of others. Elend... Golus...Ghetto. Words in different languages for the same thing. Being despised, and finally despising yourself.

And out of those depths they had raised themselves. Jews looked different now simply because they were no longer ashamed of being Jews. It was not only beggars and derelicts and relief applicants who professed Judaism in a suspiciously one-sided solidarity. No! The strong, the free, the successful Jews had returned home, and received more than they gave. Other nations were still grateful to them when they produced some great thing; but the Jewish people asked nothing of its sons except not to be denied. The world is grateful to every great man when he brings it something; only the paternal home thanks the son who brings nothing but himself.

Suddenly, as Friedrich listened to the music and meditated on the thoughts it inspired, the significance of the Temple flashed upon him. In the days of King Soloman, it had been a gorgeous symbol, adorned with gold and precious stones, attesting to the might and the pride of Israel. In the taste of those days, it had been decorated with costly bronze, and paneled with olive, cedar, and cypress,-a joy to the eye of the beholder. Yet, however splendid it might have been, the Jew could not have grieved for it eighteen centuries long. They could not have mourned merely for ruined masonry; that would have been too silly. No, they sighed for an invisible something of which the stones had been a symbol. It had come back to rest in the rebuilt Temple, where stood the home returning sons of Israel who lifted up their souls to the invisible God as their fathers had done upon Mount Moriah.

The words of Solomon glowed with a new vitality:

> "The Lord hath said that he would dwell in
>
> the thick darkness. I have surely built
>
> Thee a house of habitation,
>
> A place for Thee to dwell in forever."

Jews had prayed in many temples, splendid and simple, in all the languages of the Diaspora. The invisible God, the Omnipresent, must have been equally near to them everywhere. Yet only here was the true Temple. Why?

Because only here had the Jews built up a free commonwealth in which they could strive for the loftiest human aims. They had had their own communities in the Ghettoes, to be sure; but there they lived under oppression. In the Judengasse, they had been without honor and without rights; and when they left it, they ceased to be Jews. Freedom and a sense of solidarity were both needed. Only then could the Jews erect a House to the Almighty God Whom children envision thus and wise men so, but who is everywhere present as the Will-to-Good.

Friedrich watched the dignified, clear-eyed people exchanging Sabbath greetings as they left the great house of worship. He turned to David. "You were right-up there on the Mount of Olives-when you told me the name of this place. It is the Temple indeed!"

## Chapter II

The following Sunday general elections were to be held allover the country. That Saturday evening David went up to Haifa in order to take charge at campaign headquarters. The Geyer party was extremely active. Special editions of its papers appeared all day long with confident forecasts of its own success, mingled with vague aspersions against its opponents. One of the yellow sheets made Joe Levy its special target, referring to his all-too unlimited powers over the millions of .the New Society. The writer protested repeatedly that he was not accusing Mr. Levy of anything; his only concern was for the public welfare, the hard-earned pennies of the poor, the security of the beloved commonwealth. The whole article was written in a sweetish vein, piously interlarded with Biblical quotations.

Professor Steineck received this .paper in Kingscourt's presence. He glanced at it and broke into smothered cries of rage. "You carrion...swine...you...you...you Geyer....The scoundrel knows very well that our Joe is integrity itself He knows how Joe sweated to bring the New Society up to its present level. Every child knows it ...the whole world knows. ...And this dog dares to take Joe's name upon his wicked, lying tongue! It's all electioneering. Understand? To influence the people in favor of our opponents. Understand?"

He tore up the paper in a fury, balled the shreds into a lump, and threw it out of the window with an exclamation of disgust.

Kingscourt merely laughed. "Do I understand? Beloved begetter of microbes, I too have lived in the world. I know what low beasts men are. I admit frankly, I have been incredulous about many things in your New Society, despite the evidence of my own eyes. The whole thing was too rose-colored, too Potemkin-like. But now that I see all sorts of rascals in your camp, I begin to believe that the thing is real after all. Now I, old desert-wanderer that I am, must own that it's true."

On the whole, the elections were little discussed in. the Littwak circle, difficult as it was to ignore the current topic, which seeped in through every cranny. David's friends were sorry to see him so deeply involved in political strife, but he would soon have done with it. He declared that, as soon as the voting was over, he would go back to his own affairs. He did want to have a delegate's mandate and to exercise it; but the congress sat only a few weeks in the year.

On election day, in order to keep aloof from the political tumult, Miriam took Friedrich and Professor Steineck to the studio of Isaacs the painter, whose home was in a quiet neighborhood in the eastern section of the New City of Jerusalem. The studio contained many treasures of art, she told Friedrich. And, as he was fond of society, he gave frequent parties at his studio which were famed for their elegance and good taste.

The wall which sheltered the artist's home on the street side gave no hint of the beauty within, and the visitors were the more surprised when they entered the forecourt. The entrance hall, whose glass roof rested upon marble columns, was draped with antique Gobelins, and contained fine copies of antique

sculptures. A servant led them to an inner court which was
really a roofless salon. Only the blue sky covered it. This court,
which was paved with stone, was surrounded on three sides
with colonnades, and on the fourth was separated from the
garden by a movable gilt trellis that was standing wide-open.
The garden, which lay several steps below the court, was not
large, but seemed to have a considerable depth owing to a
skillful arrangement of bushes. Noble marble statues gleamed
here and there among the green palms. Gently murmuring
water flowed through the wide basin of the fountain in the
court. Comfortable easy chairs of all sorts were grouped cozily
in the corners. The broad arcade could be easily transformed
into a closed room by raising its glass doors from their grooves
along the sides. At the moment, it stood open in the mild spring
air. Carved doors opening off the court into various rooms
were partly open, and allowed glimpses of magnificent
furnishings. It was obviously the palace of a prince of art.

The door of the atelier opened, and Isaacs came out to greet his
visitors. With him was a distinguished-looking couple.
Steineck introduced Friedrich to the host, who in turn
introduced him to Lord and Lady Sudbury. They were staying
in Jerusalem while Isaacs painted the portrait of the beautiful
Lady Lillian.

The artist was a dignified man of forty or so, who carried
himself with charming distinction, and obviously accustomed
to meeting great folk on a level of equality, though he had been
a poor Jewboy whose present position in the world was won
through sheer grace of talent.

Isaacs soon set his guests at their ease. Servants brought in
refreshments. The gentlemen lighted cigars. The fragrant

**283**

weeds, remarked Isaacs smilingly, were Palestinian a fact in which he took obvious pride. This brand was called the "Flower of the Jordan," because it was made from tobacco grown in the Jordan Valley.

While the gentlemen talked over their cigars, Lady Lillian approached Miriam, whom she had previously met at the studio, and whispered some request into her ear. Friedrich noticed that Miriam refused, though with a smile. It seemed to him that she glanced his way as she shook her head. Lady Lillian also sent a fleeting glance in his direction. The two were standing beside the trellis, their slender figures a pleasing sight. Miriam, dark-haired and somewhat the shorter cut no poor figure in her simple gown beside the tall, blonde Englishwoman whose costume bespoke a Parisian tailor. Friedrich felt a vague pride as he observed .the daughter of the Jewish peddler carrying herself so modestly and yet with such dignity beside the great English lady. In the manner of his absent friend he said .to himself, "All the Devils! We've even achieved a modest entree into Society!"

Lady Lillian and Miriam walked slowly out into the garden. Friedrich, who would gladly have followed them, was obliged to remain because the conversation was directed chiefly at himself. They were speaking of things still not known to him,- of the place of art and philosophy in the New Society. Only now, as he was listening to Isaac's mellow tones, did he realize that he had as yet heard nothing on these questions. He had seen the Temple and the electric machinery, the ancient people and its new social order in the Old-New-Land. But how did sensitive souls, the artists and the scientists, come off in all this? The so-called moderns of his day had objected to Zionism, to the idea of the national rebirth of the Jewish people, on the ground that it would be a stupid reaction, a kind of millennial terrorism. And here was Isaacs declaring it to be nothing of the sort. There was anything but intellectual deterioration in the New Society, even though everyone was allowed to find salvation in his own way. Religion had been excluded from public affairs once and for all. The New Society did not care whether a man sought the eternal verities in a temple, a church or a mosque, in an art museum or at a philharmonic concert.

Art and philosophy had their independent places in the Jewish Academy. This institution was no brand-new creation, but had been patterned after the centuries-old model of the French Academy. It was endowed by a rich American who had been among the guests of the "Futuro," and the statutes of the Society provided that, as far as possible, the spirit of the "Futuro" was to pervade it The membership was limited to forty, as in the Palais Mazarin. When a vacancy occurred through the death of a member, the survivors chose the most meritorious successor that could be found. The members received ample salaries, which relieved .them of the cares of livelihood so that they could devote themselves to art, philosophy or scholarship without an eye to any man's favor. It was natural that the forty Jews of the Academy should be free from chauvinism. When the Academy was established, the original members came from various countries whose cultures had been developed in their respective languages; and they united on the basis of their common humanity. Their fellowship thus created a spirit that could not be overthrown, since they chose their own successors. The founder's first condition was: "It shall be the duty of the Jewish Academy to seek out meritorious persons who work for the good of

**285**

humanity." This duty was obviously not limited by the boundaries of Palestine.

The forty members of the Academy also formed a Jewish Legion of Honor like the French Legion of Honor. The emblem was a knot of yellow ribbon worn in the button hole. Friedrich had seen several persons wearing the ribbon, but had thought it a mere survival of the old foolish honors system. He was the more impressed when he heard Isaacs says that he himself, like Professor Steineck, had the knot of yellow ribbon. "You must not believe, Dr. Loewenberg," he added, "that we were either stupid or vain when we founded our Legion of Honor. Statesmen in the old days recognized that honor needs a currency of its own. Why should we have despised a means whereby so much can be achieved for the common good? We have setup a very high standard, so that the decoration is difficult to obtain. The higher grades are very rare. The grand master of the Legion is the president of the Academy. The" Legion consists of men without private interests of any kind, who, above all, hold themselves entirely aloof from politics. No one, therefore, can win the yellow ribbon for financial or partisan services. That was what made orders so ridiculous in the old society. The erstwhile silly emblem is a token of high achievement among us. The color recalls evil times in our national history, and reminds us to be humble in the midst of our prosperity. We have taken the yellow badge of shame that our unhappy, revered ancestors were compelled to wear, and made of it a badge of honor."

"Understand?" cried Steineck.

Friedrich nodded reflectively.

Dr. Marcus was announced. Isaacs rose quickly to receive the white-bearded visitor. "You come like the wolf in the fable, sir," he remarked, and introduced Dr. Marcus as the president of the Jewish Academy. "I have just been speaking of the Academy. Lord Sudbury already knew a good deal about it, but it was all new to this gentleman though he is a Jew."

"How is that possible?"

Friedrich briefly sketched the circumstances of his life. The old man shook his head gently. "Twenty years ago? Yes, yes! I understand your surprise. Yet everything already existed at that time. You remember the words of Ecclesiastes: 'That which hath been is that which shall be and that which hath been done is that which shall be done. And there is nothing new under the sun.'"

"Pardon me, Mr. President!" shouted Steineck. "That must be taken with a grain of salt. All that now is did not always exist, and all that is to be does not lie behind us... I recall not Ecclesiastes, but Stockton-Darlington. Understand?"

"What about Stockton-Darlington?" asked Lord Sudbury. "Do you refer to the first railway, built by George Stephenson a hundred years ago?"

"Quite so, my lord!" cried the Professor. "A few days ago the Academy decided to suggest a worthy world-wide tribute to Stephenson in 1925. Our suggestion is that at the exact moment when the hundred years are fulfilled locomotives in every part of the world, wherever they may happen to be, shall stop and whistle slowly three times. That is the Stockton-Darlington ceremony which we propose. Passengers in trains all over the

**287**

world will be obliged to remember Stephenson, the harbinger of a new era. You will admit, dear Mr. President, that between Stockton and Darlington the wisdom of Ecclesiastes goes off the rails, will you not?"

"I admit it the more readily," responded Dr. Marcus pleasantly, "since I did not contradict it. I was thinking only of the co-existence of things, a favorite theme of mine. I meditate on it when I relax, and it calms my spirit. I welcome the years, the months or the days that still remain to me for its sake. It is my comfort that all things which once existed still continue to exist. The future too is already here, and I recognize it: it is the good. Thus, while I start from the same premises as the Preacher, son of David, who ruled over Israel in Jerusalem, I reach a conclusion different from his. Still, Solomon may have meant the same thing, though he said that all is vanity, and inquired what reward had a man for all his toil under the sun. All is indeed vanity if we look at things from the transitory viewpoint of our own personalities. But once we can think beyond ourselves, all is not vanity. Even my dreams are eternal, for others will dream them when I am gone. Though the creators of beauty and wisdom pass away, Beauty and Wisdom are themselves immortal. Just as the conservation of energy is self-evident, so must we infer that there is conservation of Beauty and Wisdom. Has the joyous art of the Greeks, for instance, ever been lost? No, it is always reborn in later ages. Are the sayings of our sages extinguished? No, they still burn, though perhaps less brightly in the daylight of happiness than in the dark night of misery. In that they are like all flames. What follows? That we are in duty bound to increase beauty and Wisdom upon the earth unto our last breath. For the earth is we ourselves. Out of her we come, unto her we return. Ecclesiastes said it, and we today have nothing to add to his words: 'But the earth shall endure forever.'"

After Dr. Marcus had finished, each man gave himself silently up to his own thoughts. Suddenly, the voice of a woman singing, though muffled by the intervening doors and walls, penetrated into the quiet room. All were hushed as they listened.

"Who is that?" whispered Friedrich.

"Don't you know?" Isaacs whispered back. "It's Miss Miriam." He rose and walked down the arcade to the door of the music room, which he noiselessly set ajar. Now the glorious tones were heard in their full strength. Miriam, unconscious of her audience, sang Schumann, Rubinstein, Wagner, Verdi, Gounod, the music of all the nations, for Lady Lillian. The melodies flowed in a ceaseless stream. Friedrich listened blissfully, happy to be among these choice spirits who realized life in Beauty and Wisdom, when Miriam began the wistful song from "Mignon" that he had always loved, "Knowest thou the land," he whispered to himself, "This is the Land!"

Theodor Herzl

# Chapter III

The hours at the artist's studio passed like a dream. Toward evening Professor Steineck was called to the telephone. Kingscourt speaking. The Professor must return to the hotel at once.

"Miss Miriam," said Friedrich as they drove back with the Professor, "I want to thank you for revealing yourself to me through your music. Now I feel that I know you."

She blushed and was silent.

At the hotel, where the whole party was staying, an unwelcome surprise awaited them. Kingscourt stood bare-headed at the gate and shouted at the Professor. "Zum Wetter! You might have hurried!"

"What's the matter?" asked the Professor calmly.

"Matter! ...The baby...little Fritz. ..he's sick. Now don't fuss around, but come upstairs at once, please!"

They hurried to the nursery. Fritzchen lay in bed, his cheeks hot and his eyes burning with fever.

"Otto!" he called to old Kingscourt. "Otto" quickly obeyed his small despot. He sat down beside the head of the crib, a post that he was rarely to leave during the next few days. If

Fritzchen well had ruled over Kingscourt with a strict hand, Fritzchen sick had unbounded sway over him.

Professor Steineck examined the child and shook his head. He quieted Sarah, who was beside herself with anxiety; but he did not conceal his concern from Kingscourt. The child was very ill. A serious inflammation of the throat. Kingscourt was more frightened than he cared to show. He dragged Friedrich off to a remade room and swore blasphemously. The child's illness would upset all their plans. One couldn't do as one pleased any more. Other plans must be made in the circumstances.

"I understand, Kingscourt," replied Friedrich, who was worried. "You want to leave. Very well, then. I am ready to go."

"Who wants to leave?" shouted Kingscourt, red in the face. "You don't understand me any more. That woman's society seems to have affected your wits. That's the Schlim-mazel of it, as you Jews say. We can't decently leave now. You must think me a fine sort! First accept hospitality, entertainment-like parasites-and once there's a shadow over the house, we run away. No, my dear chap. You may go on to Europe if you feel you can't do without it any longer. I stay here until Fritzchen recovers,-out of sheer decency. There's simply no other way."

The old man was trying to give the usual amusing twist to his vulgarity, but it rang hollow. He did not want to show how worried he was about the little fellow. He watched all night in the nursery with the mother and the nurse. Fritzchen, as if sensing the old misanthrope's remarkable change of heart, clung to him as to no one else. Steineck tried to rationalize the phenomenon. Kingscourt's handsome, long, white beard had

captivated the child; or perhaps his jokes and grimaces.
Whatever the reason, Fritzchen clung to his irascible friend. As
the fever mounted, his little hand held fast to Kingscourt's
index finger. From no one else would he take his medicine. No
one else was allowed to croon him to sleep. Kingscourt's
musical repertory was not large. His Piece de resistance ran
like this:

"Wer reit't mit zwanzig Knappen ein

Zu Heidelberg im Hirschen?

Das ist der Herr von Rhodenstein,

Auf Rheinwein will er pi-a-ia-irschen!"

Fritzchen had once approved of the song, and now the
Rhodensteiner had to ride unceasingly to the Stag at
Heidelberg. Kingscourt's other song was very much to the
point:

"Der Gott, der Eisen wachs en liess

Der wollte keine Knechte."

With these two musical masterpieces he lulled his little friend
to sleep.

David had not been notified of the baby's illness. They did not
want to worry him, since in any case he was returning to
Jerusalem the following day. He came out a victor in the
elections. The Geyer party had been beaten in almost all the
districts where it had presumed to set up candidates. Dr. Geyer

himself had achieved a relative majority in only one district, and even there would have to submit to a recount the following Sunday. David, however, had been elected by thirty-one districts. He decided that he would accept only one mandate,- that from Neudorf.

His elation vanished as he entered the nursery. His wife threw herself weeping on his shoulder. "We were too happy, David! Now God is punishing us. Perhaps we were too presumptuous...took our prosperity too much for granted."

"We shall humble ourselves before Him," he replied gravely. "And then we shall fight the disease to the utmost."

And they fought. Specialists met in consultation every morning and every evening. All the arts of healing were employed to save the little life. But the disease seemed to sneer at the efforts of the skilled physicians. The child's condition grew worse rapidly. One evening the physicians left the hotel in a very pessimistic mood. Only the Professo remained, watching in the sick room with Kingscourt and the nurse. Sarah had collapsed from fatigue and anxiety. Miriam and Mrs. Gothland were looking after her. David established himself in a salon between the two sick rooms, and moved from one to the other. Friedrich and Reschid, who stayed with him, admired the calmness I with which he gave his orders, and answered the inquiries of friends. Finally, however, the strain grew too great, and he asked that one of his companions receive visitors in the lobby. Reschid volunteered. The news of Fritzchen's serious condition had spread rapidly in David's circle, and people came in large numbers to inquire after him. The president of the New Society asked for hourly bulletins. The affection and esteem which his fellow-citizens felt for David showed itself at this opportunity.

People stood in groups in front of the hotel. Few of them had ever seen Fritzchen; but it was enough for them that he was Littwak's son. Many prayed that the little boy's life be spared for it might well be a blessing for the land in days to come. Upstairs, David was speaking calmly to Friedrich. "See, Dr. Loewenberg, we cannot change the order of things. As they were twenty years ago or two thousand years ago, so they are today. When Job's hour strikes, he must compose himself and say, 'The Lord hath given, the Lord hath taken away...!'"

Steineck appeared in the doorway of the babies room, and whispered, "Not yet!" But his tone betrayed the slightness of his hopes. "If only the child could fall asleep," he said. "A good nap would be a boon-it might even save him."

"Doesn't Kingscourt's humming disturb him?" asked Friedrich.

"Oh, no! He has to sing whether he wants to or not. Whenever Fritzchen comes out of his doze, the old man has to sing. It's touching to watch him."

David began to weep. From the nursery they heard Kingscourt's hoarse voice:

"Der Gott, der Eisen wachsen liess, Der wollte keine Knechte."

Then on to the Rhodensteiner, who wanted to "pi-a-iairschen" on Rhine wine. But ever more wistfully the lord of Rhodenstein rode to the Stag at Heidelberg. The two men in the salon listened with inheld breath lest the song give out for good and all.

A pause. Silence. Kingscourt appeared in the doorway with his finger on his lips. His eyes were bloodshot. "Hush! He's asleep....Not a sound in the whole house! I'll knock down anyone who makes a noise in the corridor! I'm going to sit out there. ...When Fritzchen wakes, call me!"

The old man seated himself in the corridor before the child's door, and kept guard. He frightened away guests and servants with his fierce glances, growling that there was a patient here, let them go elsewhere!

An hour passed, two hours. Friedrich came out to Kingscourt. The old man jumped up. "Has he called me?"

"No," whispered Friedrich. "He's still asleep." The next instant Kingscourt seized his friend's head between his hands, and whispered in his ear. "Fritze, if that worm recovers, I'll stay here forever. That's a solemn promise. I offer this sacrifice for his recovery, as truly as my name is Adalbert von Koenigshoff...."

Hour after hour passed. Fritzchen slept on until he had slept himself into health. Night gave way to morning. With the sunrise, hope awakened. When Kingscourt was called to the nursery, Fritzchen's eyes were bright again as he cried, "Ottoh! Ottoh!"

"What a rascal!" growled Kingscourt, trying to look cross. He was ashamed of his weakness before Friedrich.

"Now, Kingscourt, go to sleep!" commanded Friedrich. "You need rest. As for what you said in the corridor last night, I heard nothing."

"No, my dear fellow," retorted Kingscourt proudly. "You still know me only by halves. I have sworn an oath, and it stands. ...But I must sleep around the clock. After that we'll see about having ourselves admitted to the New Society. That we shall."

Friedrich still did not know whether the old man was in earnest. To remain was his own most ardent wish. To become a member of the New Society, to participate in its high enterprises, to join hands with its valiant men. There was something else, besides, but he dared not admit it to himself.

Kingscourt, however, kept his word. The very next day, Fritzchen being well and cheerful again, and Sarah recovered from the fright that had been all her illness, Kingscourt himself referred to his plan. Did he guess how much joy he was giving to his comrade of twenty years? It may be assumed that he did,-he, the alleged misanthrope, who had succumbed so wholly to a child's fascinations. When his love for Fritzchen could no longer be denied, he tried to rationalize it. He admitted that he could stand the little boy well enough, just as one is fond of any innocent creature. Fritzchen was not yet a man, and a hater of mankind sacrificed nothing of his principles when he took a fancy to such a little fellow.

"I make you a present of your motivation, Kingscourt," laughed Friedrich. "The fact suffices me. When shall we apply for admission to the New Society?"

Theodor Herzl

# Chapter IV

Kingscourt and Friedrich decided to join the New Society
immediately. They therefore went to call on President
Eichenstamm to ask his advice as to how they could best
become useful members of the New Society. The presidential
mansion reminded them of the palazzi of the Genoese
patricians. Just ahead of them was another car, from which
Professor Steineck alighted with two elderly gentlemen. The
Professor was already on the doorstep when he saw his two
friends parleying with the gate-keeper. He waved to them, and
the gesture immediately solved their difficulties with the
functionary... But the next moment the Professor had vanished.

They asked for Dr. Werkin, secretary to the President. A
servant led them to his office, and asked them to wait. After
they had spent a few moments in the beautiful, high-ceilinged
room, Kingscourt grew impatient.

"I won't stand this another minute. I shall not wait seven years
in the ante-room. Talk to one of the minions, Fritze! I don't
believe we've been announced."

"There don't seem to be any minions," smiled Friedrich. "But
I'll ask that typist there."

The typist informed them that Dr. Werkin had been with the
President for the last two hours. Dr. Eichenstamm had fallen ill
very suddenly.

**299**

"Ah-hah. Now I see. That's why Steineck disappeared so quickly. Can you tell me, honored Mr. Typist, who were the two gentlemen with Professor Steineck?"

"Yes, sir. Two medical professors from the Zion University."

"Kingscourt," said Friedrich, "we'll not stay now. We'll leave our cards for Dr. Werkin, and come another time when the President is feeling better."

The two friends had learned their way about the streets of Jerusalem. They now left the boulevards and turned into a large park laid out in the English fashion. Near the entrance was a large building marked "Health Department of the New Society."

"Look!" laughed Kingscourt. "Here's another copy of a good thing. This is evidently modeled after the Imperial German Health Department. I don't have to ask the natives about it. I know Old-New-Land quite well. It's a mosaic. A Mosaic mosaic. Good joke, what?"

"As good as the rest of your jokes, Kingscourt. And no better...But it seems to me that we don't get at the essential character of Old-New-Land merely by noting that all its institutions already existed elsewhere twenty years ago. It's true enough that all these things did exist then. Natural forces were well understood in those days-well, enough, at least, for their needs here. The technical appliances, also, were available. No educated person of the year 1900 would be surprised by anything we've seen here. Even the degree of social progress achieved here is not surprising. The average decent man of our day realized that the raw egotism of the individual had to be

**300**

curbed by society. The restrictions are not, indeed, oppressive here, because the New Society compensates the individual in one form for what it takes from him in another. Producers' and consumers co-operatives were well known in our day. Old-New-Land is something more-it must be something more than a fusion of the elements of social and technical progress."

"What makes you say so?" questioned Kingscourt. "I find even this very fine."

"As a jurist and fin de siecle European," continued Friedrich, "I ask myself what it is that keeps this community in equilibrium. I see order in freedom, and yet nowhere do I glimpse governmental authority."

"Ah, Fritze, there's the rub. Legalism and Europeanism obscure your vision. One can get along with very little govemmental authority. If you had lived and loved, as I did, in America, you would know better. No, that doesn't surprise me. But what I do not know how to account for is-these trees. The trees in this park cannot be less than forty or fifty years old. Where did the fellows get them?"

He had spoken so loudly that a passerby overheard him, smiled, and stopped short. Kingscourt naturally spoke to him at once. "Honored passerby, I see that I amuse you. Perhaps you can answer my question?"

"Certainly, sir. I am on the staff of the Health Department, and know something about these things. It has long been known that it is possible to transplant grown trees safely. In Cologne, for example, where I formerly lived, forty-year-old trees were planted in one of the parks. It is very expensive, of course, but

**301**

we spend a great deal on the public health. We think nothing too costly for our parks, because they benefit the growing generation. However, we did not plant old and expensive trees like these everywhere. For instance, we brought eucalyptus trees from Australia which grew very rapidly. Our first funds for this purpose came from a national tree-planting Society which collected money in all parts of the world. People in the Diaspora contributed money for trees whose shade they were afterwards to enjoy in Palestine."

"Thank you, sir," said Kingscourt. "I understand now. And will you please complete your favor by telling me where all these children come from?" (They were walking past playgrounds where half-grown youngsters were playing English games. The girls were busy with tennis, the boys with cricket and football.)

"They come from the schools near this park. The classes are led out here by turns for athletic games. Physical exercise is considered quite as important as mental development."

"They seem to belong only to well-to-do families," commented Friedrich. "All of them are clean and neatly dressed."

"Not at all, sir. They come from all kinds of homes; we do not permit distinctions of any kind in our schools, either in clothing or in anything else. The only differences are those created by the pupils themselves through effort or natural talent. Our New Society is thoroughly opposed, .however, to any leveling process. To each according to his deserts!

"We have not abolished competition. Conditions are alike for all, as in a race or prize competition. All must be equal at the beginning, but not at the end. Under the old order, it would

happen that a man could make his children and grandchildren
independent for life through one fortunate business deal, and
ensure for them all the advantages of the higher education.
Conversely, a man's descendants were punished not only for
his sins, but for his business reverses. Once a family became
impoverished, it was reduced to the proletariat, from which
superhuman effort was needed to escape.

"We neither reward nor punish our children for their fathers'
business transactions. Each generation is given a new start.
Therefore, all our educational institutions are free from the
elementary schools to the Zion University. All the pupils must
wear the same kind of simple clothing until they matriculate
into the secondary schools. We think it unethical to single out
children according to their parents' wealth or social rank. That
would be bad for all of them. The children from the well-to-do
families would become lazy and arrogant, the others
embittered. But you will pardon me. I must go back to my
work."

He left them with a courteous bow.

Kingscourt and Friedrich remained for a while to watch the
merry, agile youngsters. Kingscourt who, in his youth, had
been an excellent cricketer and football player, felt his old
passion for games stirring within him, and shouted
encouragement to the children. He would have liked best to
take a hand himself in their play, but Friedrich drew him away.
"Come, you old Ottoh crow! Let's go and see how Fritzchen is
getting along. There may be some word about Dr.
Eichenstamm at the hotel, too."

Fritzchen was well and cheerful, and greeted his friend with a song in which Kingscourt thought he detected his own "ia-i-a-i-a" of Rhodensteiner fame. The old man and the baby were soon engaged in an intimate conversation understood by no one but themselves.

The reports from the presidential mansion were not good. Steineck had sent a brief bulletin to David: "Hopeless!" When the Professor returned to the hotel in the evening, they read the news in his face.

"He died greatly," he told them. "I was with him to the end. He spoke of death. It was painless, he said, if one contemplated it long in advance. 'I feel,' said he, 'my consciousness gradually growing dimmer. I still hear myself speak, but always more feebly. Probably I shall still have blurred thoughts when I can no longer speak. I have already made my farewells to myself. Too bad that I cannot say a last word to all who were so kind to me.' Then he was silent for a while, staring into space. r had friends,' he began again, looking toward me, 'many friends. Friends are life's best treasures....Where are they now? I had many, many friends. Where are they?'...The end was coming. He murmured something with a wistful glance that seemed to say, 'You see, I cannot speak, but I can still think.' At the last he pulled himself together, and spoke the thought he had repeated so often: 'Let the stranger be at home among us!' His eyes glazed, and I closed them."

So died Eichenstamm, president of the New Society.

# Chapter V

On the eighth day after President Eichenstamm's impressive funeral, the Congress was called into session to elect a new president.

Almost all of the four hundred men and women delegates had arrived in Jerusalem by the evening before the first session. Heated discussion was going on in numerous clubs and hotels. As far as could be guessed, the choice lay between Dr. Marcus, President of the Academy, and Joseph Levy, managing director of the New Society, whose chances were about equal. Assuming that minor candidates would divert a few votes on the first ballot-so that neither would receive an absolute majority-a second ballot would have to be taken.

Levy had not yet returned from Europe, but was expected hourly. Some said that he would refuse the nomination for the presidency. Others resented this as a prejudicial rumor spread by the partisans of Dr. Marcus. The usual election excitement was in full swing. And there was the usual partisan noise, quarrels, jests, tricks, etc.

On the morning of the opening of the Congress, David came into Friedrich's room much distressed. "You must go to the session without me," he said. "I have received a telegram calling me to Tiberias. My mother..." His eyes grew somber, and his voice caught, "Miriam and I are off at once. My wife and the baby will come later."

"Shall we go with you?" asked Friedrich, all sympathy.

"Ah, there's no help you can give. I fear no one can. Stay for the Congress. It will be an interesting experience for you. As for me, nothing matters now. Let them elect whom they please."

"We shall come up to Tiberias with your wife and Fritzchen," Kingscourt assured him.

"Thank you. Please do not mention my leaving town now to anyone. There are times when even one's friends are superfluous. I should be deluged with inquiries"

"I hope your mother will soon feel better," said Friedrich.

"I know what that 'better' will be," David shrugged hopelessly. "Good-by!"

After Miriam and David had left, they went to the Congress. A large crowd stood in front of the great building, which was decorated with blue and white flags draped in mourning for the late President.

The auditorium was a lofty marble room with overhead lighting from an opaque glass ceiling. The delegates were in the committee rooms and lobbies, so that their seats were still vacant. The galleries, however, were already crowded, and every now and again some delegate would come up to tell his friends of developments behind the scenes. Most of the women in the galleries wore subdued costumes, since the thirty days' period of mourning for President Eichenstamm was not yet completed.

However, in the box next to Friedrich's, there sat several women in very light costumes and striking hats. The party consisted of Mrs. and Miss Weinberger, Mrs. and Miss Laschner, Mr., Mrs. and Miss Schlesinger, Doctor Walter, and Mr. Schiffmann. The humorists Gruen and Blau were also among those present. Friedrich would have preferred to leave his box, but there was no more room anywhere in the galleries. Besides, Kingscourt was so much amused by his neighbors that he refused to budge. They could hear everything that went on in the next box, where Mr. Schlesinger sat in front with the ladies. The witty Mr. Gruen was making puns about the Congress, the point being that he wouldn't want to be in the shoes of the defeated candidate.

"I hear that Marcus will lose," declared Schiffmann.

"How do you know that?" asked the representative of the Baroness von Goldstein. "Entre nous, it's all one to me."

Schiffmann smiled mysteriously." I have my sources of information. Know everything, need nothing."

"Schiffmann has good tips that he plays on the stock exchange," said Blau enviously."

"I should like to know," said Dr. Walter, "what this election will mean in terms of bulls and bears.'"

"That's very simple," thought Schiffmann. "Levy is an enterprising man. If he comes in, there will be more business in the country. Therefore, the bulls win. Marcus, however, is more of the academic type. No business. Hence, bears on top."

"That's brilliant," sneered Blau. "Mr. Schiffmann, if I had as little sense as you, even for twenty-four hours, I should stop worrying for the rest of my life."

"It's well you have more sense than I. Otherwise, you couldn't crack jokes at weddings for a fee."

"Who are those people in Isaac's box?" Ernestine asked Friedrich across the partition. "I saw you bow to them."

"Lord and Lady Sudbury."

"'Pon honor, she looks like the wife of a baronet at the least," broke in Mrs. Laschner. "She certainly had that hat made in Paris."

"The presence of such people proves that the higher classes, also, find our institutions interesting," proclaimed Dr. Walter sententiously.

"When I listen to these fellows," whispered Friedrich to his friend, "I want to go back to our island with you."

"Hoho! You're backsliding. But I've got beyond all that. I know there must be one good monkey cage in every well equipped zoo."

Things were becoming lively in the hall below. The delegates were drifting into their seats. Groups formed on the steps between the semi-circular rows of benches. In one group to the right Mrs. Gothland was talking to some women, evidently electioneering in favor of her candidate. (She was known to support Dr. Marcus.) And whoever watched Steineck, the architect, making violent motions at the foot of the speakers' platform could be in no doubt that he was advocating joseph Levy for the presidency. "Tschoe! Tschoe!" he was shouting above the increasing tumult.

Reschid Bey came up to the gallery to report the latest news from the lobbies. Joe's election was almost certain. He would come through on the first ballot. He was very popular throughout the country, because it was realized that the general prosperity was due to his energy and ability. Marcus, on the other hand, was known only in cultured circles. Joe had already returned from Europe, and would of course come to the Congress.

"Most beloved Pasha," said Kingscourt. "You must point that man out to me as soon as he comes. Must be a very keen fellow. I'm curious to see how he will direct his cohorts."

The "monkey cage," as Kingscourt jestingly dubbed the adjoining box, was indulging in flippant comments. The more impressive the scene below, the worse some of its occupants felt. It was as if this gathering of free, self-respecting men and women were a personal affront to them.

Mr. Schlesinger held forth. "Now then! I see the game. One wanted this post, the other that. Now they have their jobs, and the Jewish problem is solved."

Dr. Walter had been greedily watching the assemblage below, where there was, alas, no room for him. He replied to the distinguished representative of the banking house. "Pardon me, Mr. Schlesinger, if I venture to disagree somewhat. I can see nothing unworthy in a man's seeking the suffrages of his equals. Of course, in individual cases there may be ulterior motives. You are certainly right about that. And I can also understand that a man like yourself, connected with the house of Goldstein for thirty years, would expect a great deal from people. But, after all, why shouldn't a man try for a post in the New Society?"

"If it brings a salary," supplemented Blau. Seeing Schlesinger's smile of encouragement, he went on. "But I believe, Dr. Walter, that you should have rise earlier in the day if you wanted one."

"It's a long time, Mr. Blau," growled Dr. Walter, flushing angrily, "since you had your ears boxed!"

Schiffmann restored peace, summing up rather wistfully what was in all their minds. "It seems to me that we have all been too late. Here we are again, standing behind bars and looking out at free people. That's how it has been with me since my youth. Wherever I went, I met only Schlesinger and Laschner, Gruen and Blau. It is like pitch.."

A bell rang, the signal for the entrance of the presiding officers. The galleries were suddenly hushed. Even the "monkey cage" held its peace.

Delegates crowded in through all the doors. "There's Joe Levy now," said Reschid, pointing downward. "That man with the bushy gray mustache and the bald spot, shaking hands with Steineck."

Joe was a lanky man of medium height, tanned up to the line of his hat, very quick and energetic in his movements. He shook hands with the numerous delegates who came up to welcome him home. To others further away he nodded smilingly, and occasionally waved a salute. He seemed very much at his ease, and not at all stiff or formal.

A prolonged ringing of the bell. All the delegates took their seats. Behind the raised platform both wings of the gilt doors were opened, and the chairman of the congress entered with his whole staff. He opened the proceedings with a tribute to the late President, which was listened to standing. This was followed by the announcement: "We have come here today to elect a new president."

To everyone's surprise, Joe, who was sitting in the center of the third row, rose and asked for the privilege of the floor. "Mr. Joseph Levy has the floor!" responded the chairman.

A murmur ran through the hall as Levy lightly ascended the steps to the platform. What would he say?

"Esteemed congress delegates," he began." I wish to make only a very short statement to you. While I was abroad, some of my friends kindly announced me as a candidate without asking me whether I would accept."

Slight stirrings in the Marcus ranks. "Hear! Hear!"

"Let him talk!" shouted Steineck.

Levy began over again. "I have only a very short statement to make to you. I am highly honored by this nomination. But I do

**311**

not wish to put the congress to the trouble of voting on a roll call. According to our rules for the presidential elections, each delegate must step up to the platform in person and deposit his ballot when his name is called. This procession consumes four hours. Then comes the count. Two hours more for that. Then, perhaps, a second ballot has to be taken. I cannot take such a loss of time on my conscience. Pity to waste it. Because I am determined, even if I am elected, not to serve."

"Why? Why?" cried his adherents.

"My reasons, ladies and gentlemen, are simple. I feel that I still have much energy to devote to my work. If you are satisfied with what I am doing, let me go on as I am. Electing me to the presidency would mean sending me into retirement. And, despite my gray hairs, I believe myself still too young for that. For the rest, Dr. Marcus will express my views. I called on him this morning immediately after my arrival, having heard that he was the opposition candidate. We came to an understanding. We're not so divided as our respective friends. ..(Laughter)... Dr. Marcus will state his own views and mine to you. As for me, I stick to my resolve. Dear friends, many thanks for your good intentions, but please don't elect me!"

There was a stir of uneasiness throughout the hall. From all sides rose cries of displeasure, surprise, and disappointment. As he left the platform, Levy was mobbed with questions by his followers. He smiled and shrugged.

"I like that man," announced Kingscourt. "Talk he cannot, but he seems a fine fellow."

The "monkey cage" interpreted the incident otherwise. Blau suggested that the grapes were too sour.

"His nation is resignation," suggested Gruen wittily.

But Schiffmann said, "Well, now, Mr. Schlesinger! Here is a man that doesn't want to snap up office. What do you say to this?"

"Eh? What I say? Do I know what his present post brings him? He seems able to get along on it. He is a practical man. Who knows what understanding he and Marcus came to? We ought to know that, too, before we can judge."

Friedrich was thoroughly irritated by these comments, though he had met Dr. Marcus only once arid was seeing Levy for the first time. His one wish was that Reschid and Kingscourt had not heard the nasty criticisms. Luckily, they were intent on the proceedings downstairs.

The chairman rang loudly for order. Dr. Marcus had asked for the floor. He ascended the platform a bit heavily, and waited for quiet, so that his feeble voice might carry. There was dead silence as he began.

"Honored Congress! My friend Levy in his efficient way, has spoken of saving your time. I believe it worth while to use some of the valuable time of the New Society in an attempt to understand each other. First let us understand, then decide.

"We have come here not to choose the head of a state; since we are not a state.

**313**

"We are a commonwealth. In form it is new, but in purpose very ancient. Our aim is mentioned in the First Book of Kings: 'Judah and Israel shall dwell securely, each man under his own vine and fig tree, from Dan to Beersheba.'

"We are simply a large co-operative association composed of affiliated co-operatives. And this, our congress, is really nothing more than the general assembly of the co-operative association which is called the New Society. Yet all of us feel that more is involved than the purely material interests of an industrial and economic co-operative association. For we establish schools and layout parks; we concern ourselves not only with utilitarian things, but with Beauty and Wisdom as well. For Beauty and Wisdom, too, benefit our commonwealth. We understand that a community must have an ideal in its own interest: let us say at once-an ideal is indispensable. For it is that which draws us on. We were not the first to discover the value of ideals: the discovery is as old as the world. The ideal is for the community what bread and water are for the individual. And our Zionism, which led us hither and will lead us still further to yet unknown heights, is but an ideal, an infinite, endless ideal.

"Do I seem to you to digress? No, my friends, lam keeping to the subject in hand, the elections. He whom we elect as the head of the New Society just be one who will concern himself with the ideal and keep aloof from material things. All his thought must be for the Ideal. He must be a quiet man, just and modest, above the strife of current opinion. We elect him for seven years.

"My friend Levy has refused the office because he feels he can serve us better during those seven years by continuing in his present post. I agree with him. But I too refuse. I am too old. I do not believe I shall live seven years longer. Too frequent elections are unwholesome. They incite too much personal ambition, lead to personal partisanships. Don't elect me. I am too old. My body is no longer flexible; perhaps my mind, too, has lost its elasticity. It may be that I can no longer understand the ideals of younger men. For ideals are always being reborn, and there may be rebirths which a man like myself can no longer comprehend.

"But Levy and I have not come before you merely in order to refuse office. We have a suggestion to make to you. It was Levy's idea, and he is a good judge of men. That. speaks in its favor. And I agree with all my heart.

"The man whose name we shall propose to you is still young,- younger than Levy, very much younger than myself. He is one of the new men who have made this old soil of ours fertile and beautiful again. He walked behind the plow with his father as a boy, but he has also sat behind books. He has a wholesome capacity for public affairs, but. does not let thcm swamp him. I do not see him here just now. But if he is present, he will be the last to apply my words to himself, so genuine is his humility. He is very capable in his personal affairs, and made his way up from very modest beginnings. If we elect him, we shall not only be honoring a man of high merit, but shall also give our youth an incentive to aim high. Every son of Venice could become a Doge. Every member of the New Society must. be eligible for its highest office."

Enthusiastic applause rewarded these words. "Name! Name! Who is he?" shouted delegates from all parts of the hall. Dr. Marcus raised his hand for silence. "I do not wish to name our candidate for the presidency from this platform," he added, "since it is not our habit to use the election Congress as a campaign meeting. I ask therefore, that the chairman declare a recess."

A recess was declared. The delegates swarmed tumultuously about Marcus and Levy. They named their man. The name was relayed from group to group, and in a few moments winged its way to the galleries: "David Littwak!"

"Thunder and glory!" cried the delighted Kingscourt. Friedrich pressed his hand. "And he is sitting by his mother's death bed. Shall we telegraph?"

"No, my boy, we'll do better than that. The poor fellow is excited enough now as it is. Why plague him with these elections? Suppose he doesn't get in after all? Let's take the next train to Tiberias. We can be there by the time the vote is counted. Then we shall simply come in and ask whether Mr. David Littwak, President of the New Society, lives at that address."

They took Reschid into their confidence, and asked him to wire the results to Tiberias. In the meantime, he was to keep David's whereabouts dark.

In the "monkey cage," David's name was greeted with mixed emotions. Gruen made silly puns on his name, while Blau announced that in his next incarnation he would choose to be nothing but a peddler's son. Mr. Schlesinger asked despairingly, "I ask you now, how can a man join this association? And they call it the New Society!"

Schiffmann, however, was remorseful. "Do you know what we are?" he cried out. "We-are a fine crew a fine crew!"

**Theodor Herzl**

# Chapter VI

Returning to the hotel, Kingscourt and Friedrich found that
Sarah had hurried after her husband by the next train. They
soon caught an express for Tiberias. Watching the landscape
fly past the windows of the electric train, they once more
reviewed all they had seen in Old-New-Land.

Kingscourt was taken aback when Friedrich suddenly remarked
that he would like to run over to Europe.

"How's that, you moody fellow? Are you already fed up with
the land of your Hebrew ancestors?"

"No, indeed, my dear Kingscourt. Your wish to remain here
makes me only too happy. I can at least try to become a useful
member of society. Perhaps I can make some good use of my
legal training in the New Society, or fill some administrative
post. Nevertheless, I want to run over to Europe for a bit to
observe the conditions there. It is impossible that no radical
changes should have taken place in Europe in these twenty
years. Realizing as I do that all we have found here is merely a
new arrangement of things that existed in our day, I am
inclined to think that something similar has happened in
Europe. Dr. Marcus put the thought into my head when he said
that the New Society was not a state, but a large co-operative
association..."

"The co-operative association with the infinite ideal," chuckled
Kingscourt.

**319**

"I ask myself, therefore," continued Friedrich earnestly, "if we are not on the threshold of the solutions to many of the problems of our day. There used to be a good deal of talk about the state of the future. Some spoke of it vaguely, some scornfully, some angrily. To portray what conditions might be like in the future was considered ridiculous by so-called practical people. They forgot that we are always living in future conditions, since today is only yesterday's future.

"They imagined an impossible future state on the improbable ruins of existing society, that is to say, a decline of civilization that only a coward would envisage. First they saw Chaos, and then something which would be a doubtful improvement on the old order.

"Something Dr. Marcus said lately about the coexistence of things has been running through my mind. Old institutions need not go under at one blow in order that new ones may be born. Not every son is posthumous. Parents usually live along with their children for many years. It follows that an old social order need not break up because a new one is on the way. Having seen here a new order composed of none but old institutions, I have come to believe neither in the complete destruction nor the complete renewal of a social order. I believe-how shall I put it? In a gradual reconstruction of society. And I also believe that such a reconstruction never comes about through systemic planning, but as the need arises. Necessity is the builder. We decide to alter a floor, a staircase, a wall, a roof, to install electricity or water supply only as the need arises, or when some new invention wins its way. The house as a whole remains what it was. So I can imagine the continued existence of the old state even if new features have been added. That is what I should like to seek in Europe.

"When we left the civilized world twenty years ago, new forms of life were sprouting everywhere. I understand the Stockton-Darlington jubilee. Everything began with that -it is to celebrate the birth of a new era. It had existed coincidently with the old order for a long time; pervaded it; was influenced by it. But the clever, practical people saw nothing. Though the old boundaries remained, men and goods were moving across the world. Whither had not machinery and railways penetrated? And they created hew conditions wherever they came.

"The co-operatives of the little fellows and the trusts of the big fish,-we knew all that. They existed side by side. Why, in the end, should the co-operatives not have organized themselves into syndicates when the individual manufacturers did so?

"Some sensible employers used to provide of their own accord for the welfare of their workers and the workers' families. Large factories had their own social welfare departments. The larger the factory, the more it was possible to expand such activities. The syndicates, again, could do more-when they chose-to improve the lot of their workers because they were richer than individual factory owners, more firmly established. That I know, Kingscourt, from your own descriptions of the American trusts."

"Quite so. And what do you infer from that?"

"I infer that it was inevitable that the producers' cooperatives should have organized to challenge individual enterprise. Their weakness lay in their lack of working capital. But, on the other hand, they were strong in that they were able also to organize the consumers co-operatively. The co-operative movement was bound to grow with the general spread of education. Finally, it seems to me that the trusts were beneficial because they paved the way for the organization of labor. And the producers' cooperatives modeled themselves on the methods of organization used by the trusts. I see in the New Society nothing but a syndicate of co-operative societies, a large syndicate which comprises all industry and commerce within itself, keeps the welfare of the workers in mind, and fosters the ideal for practical reasons. I should like to see whether the same sort of thing has been developed in Europe."

"So you think a New Society possible in other countries also?"

"Yes, I do. The New Society can exist anywhere,-in any country. Several such co-operative syndicates might even exist in one country. Where ever there are syndicates and cooperative associations, I can conceive transition to the New Society form. Then the old state is not forced out of the New Society which, in its turn, serves, strengthens and supports it. That is the coexistence of things in which I believe."

The train pulled in at the Tiberias station, and the friends hastened to the Littwak villa. When they asked the servant at the door about the patient, he shook his head gravely, and then handed them a telegram which had just been received. It was marked "Urgent."

Kingscourt glanced significantly at Friedrich as he tore open the envelope. There it was: "David Littwak elected president of New Society by 363 votes out of 395. Reschid."

They went upstairs to the salon adjoining the sickroom, where they found Sarah and the elder Littwak. Through the open door they could see the invalid lying against her pillows, her face white as the linen. But she was still alive. With infinite affection she gazed at her children as they spoke to her softly from the foot of the bed. The physician watched her closely.

Without speaking, Kingscourt handed the telegram to the elder Littwak, who took it listlessly and stared at it. The reading gave him a shock. He drew his hand across his eyes, and read again. Then he handed it to his daughter-in-law. "Read it to me, Sarah!" he asked, his voice in a quiver.

Sarah glanced over the telegram, and flushed deeply. Tears streamed from her eyes as she read it aloud to the old man. Then she jumped up and waved the paper as a signal to her husband.

David came out of the sickroom on tiptoe, and nodded gravely to the visitors, who were standing a little apart. Turning to Sarah, he asked with a slight show of displeasure, "What's the matter?"

The old father had risen, and was approaching David with faltering steps. "David, my child! David, my child!"

Sarah handed him the telegram. He read it calmly, and puckered his forehead. "I shouldn't have believed Reschid could play such pranks. I'm hardly in the mood for them."

"It's no prank," Friedrich assured him, and related the events at the congress to which he had been witness.

**323**

"No! No! That's not for me. Quite impossible. I was not even a candidate."

"That's just why they elected you," affirmed Kingscourt.

"I'm not fit for it. There are a hundred men better suited than I. I shall not accept. Please write Marcus at once that I decline.

"His father spoke up firmly. "You will accept, David. You must. ..for your mother's sake. It is the last pleasure you can give her."

David covered his eyes.

Miriam came out of the sickroom. "What's the matter?" she asked. "Mother is uneasy. She wants to know what is happening."

They returned to the sickroom and stood beside the bed of the dying roman.

"Mother!" cried the elder Littwak. "Dr. Loewenberg has brought us good news."

"Yes?" she breathed. Her face brightened. "Where is he? I want to see him. Please sit me up."

The physician called Friedrich. Miriam and David supported her slender back with pillows. She looked at Friedrich affectionately. "I thought-so-at once. Then when you-on the balcony outside here... children!..." She groped blindly. "Miriam-has told-me. ..nothing. But a mother...sees!

Children!...Give...each other ...your hands. My blessing-my blessing!"

Miriam and Friedrich had to reach out their hands to each other, but they were so hesitant that she took notice. She looked anxiously from one to the other, and whispered," "Or... or....

"Yes, indeed," said Friedrich fervently, and pressed the girl's hand. "Yes," repeated Miriam softly.

Thus a mother, even when weak and helpless, can always create happiness for her child. She leaned back exhausted, her eyes closed, barely breathing. The old man feared she might fall into the last slumber before she could be told of her son's elevation to the presidency.

"Mother!" he called loudly. Once more she raised her lids, languidly. There was regret in her glance at having been disturbed in the beautiful dream she was weaving toward. ..toward the Beyond. "Mother!" called the old man, still more loudly. "We must tell you something very important! Do you know whom they've elected president of the New Society? Our David is president, Mother! Our David!"

The son was kneeling by her bedside, weeping like a child over the bloodless, clay-cold hand. She withdrew it from his grasp and stroked his hair gently, as if to comfort him for the sorrow of her passing.

"Mother!" cried the old man fearfully. "Did you hear what I said?"

"Yes!" she breathed. "My-my David!"

And her eyes closed.

They chanted the ancient Hebrew prayers when they buried her. The venerable Rabbi Samuel of Neudorf conducted the funeral service. There was to be no sermon. David wished none.

But after they had returned from the cemetery, and sat in the seats of the mourners, David himself paid a tribute to his dead.

"She was my mother. To me she meant Love and Pain.

"In her Love and Pain were incarnate. My eyes brimmed over when I looked at her.

"She was my mother; but I shall not see her again.

"She was house and home for us when we had neither house nor home.

"She sustained us in affliction, for she was Love.

"In better days, she taught us humility, for she was Pain.

"In good days and evil, she was the pride, the ornament of our house.

"When we were so poor that we lay on straw, we still were rich: for we had her.

"She thought always of us; never of herself.

"Our house was a wretched hovel, and yet it held a treasure. Many a palace has no such treasure. That was she...my mother.

"She was an invalid. But Pain did not degrade her. It exalted her.

"Often she seemed to me the symbol of the Jewish people in the days of its suffering.

"She was my mother; and I shall not see her again.

"Never again, my friends. Never again. ...And I must bear it!"

His friends listened as he poured out his heartache, and were silent.

The room filled up with visitors. All came who had known David and his family.

To divert his thoughts, Dr. Marcus turned his conversation into other channels. The discussion was high and serious.

At last Friedrich put a question, and every man answered it after his fashion. "We see a new and happy form of human society here," he said. "What created it?"

"Necessity!" said Littwak the elder.

"The reunited people!" said Steineck the architect.

"The new means of transportation!" said Kingscourt.

"Knowledge!" said Dr. Marcus.

"Will Power!" said Joe Levy.

"The Forces of Nature!" said Professor Steineck.

"Mutual Toleration!" said the Reverend Mr. Hopkins.

"Self-Confidence!" said Reschid Bey.

"Love and Pain!" said David Littwak.

But the venerable Rabbi Samuel arose and proclaimed: "God!"

# Epilogue

...But, if you do not wish it, all this that I have related to you is and will remain a fable.

I had meant to compose an instructive poem. Some will say it contains more poetry than instruction. That it has more instruction than poetry will be the verdict of others.

Now, dear Book, after three years of labor, we must part. And your sufferings will begin. You will have to make your way through enmity and misrepresentation as through a dark forest.

When, however, you come among friendly folk, give them greetings from your father. Tell them that he believes Dreams also are a fulfillment of the days of our sojourn on Earth. Dreams are not so different from Deeds as some may think. All the Deeds of men are only Dreams at first. And in the end, their Deeds dissolve into Dreams.

Printed in the United States
94005LV00002B/22/A

9 781599 868301